FOXHUNT

FOXHUNT

Luke Francis Beirne

Baraka Books

Montréal

ISBN 978-1-77186-271-4 pbk; 978-1-77186-282-0 epub; 978-1-77186-283-7 pdf

Cover by Maison 1608
Book Design by Folio Infographie
Editing and proofreading: Robin Philpot, Blossom Thom

Legal Deposit, 2nd quarter 2022
Bibliothèque et Archives nationales du Québec
Library and Archives Canada

Published by Baraka Books of Montreal

Printed and bound in Quebec

Trade Distribution & Returns
Canada – UTP Distribution: UTPdistribution.com

United States
Independent Publishers Group: IPGbook.com

We acknowledge the support from the Société de développement des entreprises culturelles (SODEC) and the Government of Quebec tax credit for book publishing administered by SODEC.

For gravediggers, gamblers, and fishermen; for my dad.

Contents

I

Les Déracinés

I

Paris, 1949: Traffic Lights trembled. When the rain picked up, the windshield became a blurry screen for the city lights to melt upon. The city sounds—that ebbing, breathing blend—carried through the open window with the mist of shattered droplets from the roof.

"It's a shame about all of this," the driver said, gesturing broadly at the sky. "It's been gorgeous all week. The city will be glad for it, though. After such heat you need a little rain to flush the stink from the streets."

Milne nodded and watched the grid of cobblestones, glimmering in the rain and streetlights, pass by through the window beside him.

"Have you been to Paris before?"

"No," said Milne. "It's my first time."

"And what a time for it," the driver said. "The city's alive tonight. You can feel it in the air."

The car moved through the streets of Paris with ease. The streets were empty, save for the occasional person hurrying through the rain and fog with a dripping umbrella. Milne was headed for the opening function of a conference, The International Day of Resistance to Dictatorship and War, which spread itself over the whole weekend. After ten or fifteen minutes, the car stopped moving. Milne thanked the driver and stepped out onto the curb. The building in front of him stretched upwards, seemingly endlessly. He felt claustrophobic standing in front of it.

As the car pulled away, two men approached him with a wide umbrella. Water cascaded from its edges. The taller of the two extended his hand to Milne. "Welcome, welcome," he said with a faded Russian accent.

"Mr. Babichev," Milne said, accepting the handshake. Even in the shadow of the umbrella, he recognized the man. Nicolas Babichev was a well-known composer—the cousin of an even more famous novelist. His eyes were shielded by a pair of small, round glasses. He was older than Milne and looked distinguished, with a silver mane and sharp features.

"Yes," Nicolas said. "I almost forgot that we haven't really met. I feel like we already know one another from our correspondence."

Milne had received a letter from Nicolas a few months earlier inviting him to present at this conference—a festival of culture, Nicolas had called it, dedicated to freedom in the arts. It had been organized as a response, of sorts, to a recent debacle at the Waldorf Astoria, where an international peace conference revealed itself to be little more than a mouthpiece for Soviet propaganda. This conference would demonstrate the necessity of freedom from such ideological interference, Nicolas wrote.

The man standing next to Nicolas extended his hand as well. "Clifford Bernstein," he said. He was shorter than Milne but his shoulders were broad and his grip was firm. He was balding and his features were not distinctive. Milne wasn't sure that he'd be able to pick him out of a crowd.

"I'll be around, if you need me," Clifford said, "but, for the most part, stick close to Nicolas. He'll have you all fixed up."

Milne couldn't place his accent. "Pleasure to meet you," he said.

"Nicolas swears that you're a hell of a writer. Unfortunately, I haven't had the chance to find out for myself. Busy as all hell these days," he said. He paused and stared through Milne. "In any case," he continued, "I'd better get back to it. Nicolas told me that you were on the way and I wanted to greet you in person." As soon as he finished speaking, he turned, without pause, and walked back to the building.

Nicolas motioned for Milne to follow and they stepped through the door after Clifford. Nicolas fumbled with his umbrella for a moment and then handed it off to somebody else when he couldn't get it to close. The lobby was decorated with red and gold curtains and furniture. By the time Milne was inside, Clifford was already out of sight. Nicolas motioned again—Milne followed him towards the ballroom.

"We're glad to have you," the composer said as he walked. "We pulled in so many Americans and Brits that we nearly forgot about everyone else. You're the only Canadian here tonight, I believe. There are the French, of course, and some Italians too. Cliff's Estonian, originally. I served with him in the war. He's good stuff. Very dedicated."

The two men stepped into the room and Milne was immediately overwhelmed by the throb and pulse of the crowd. The crowd itself was divvied into small pockets which shifted, broke apart, and merged together in an irregular pattern. There must have been hundreds of people in the room.

"It's a big one this time," Nicolas told him. "After Stalin's charade at the Waldorf we needed to make a statement. It's hard to believe that in 1949 cultural freedom is still under threa—" His voice was drowning beneath the crowd. Around them, people moved and talked and ate and drank. Argument and laughter meshed. Milne thought he saw a friend through the crowd but couldn't be very sure. "Eleanor Roosevelt sent a letter

15

of support this morning," Nicolas said behind the drone. "Dos Passos got in last night."

Milne realized that a band was playing on the other side of the room but could barely make out the music above the crowd. "Ah! There's Eric," Nicolas said, looking into the shroud of faces. Milne tried to follow his line of vision but lost it in the low light and the perpetual flow of identically dressed bodies.

A European man, a painter or artist of some kind, appeared in front of him. He was already midsentence when Milne took notice: "…filthy bureaucrats. Small matter there, anyway. Have you met everybody yet?"

"I can't imagine that I have," Milne replied. "There are hundreds of faces here."

"Hundreds, maybe," the little man said, "but only a few that really matter."

Milne nodded and looked around for another face to engage. Nothing emerged. The artist was already carrying on: "Have you met Bernstein yet?"

"Briefly on the way in," Milne said. "I understand that he's an organizer of some sort."

"An organizer! No, no! Not simply an organizer! Bernstein … well, yes, I suppose that he is in one sense. In the real sense though, in essence, Bernstein is one of the *déracinés*."

"The *déracinés*?"

"One of those broken by the weight of this century." The man's arm snapped out to seize a martini from a passing tray. "His entire family was murdered by the Bolsheviks," he continued offhandedly. "He had nothing left to go home to after the war. He's been drifting around Europe ever since. Very involved in the de-Nazification process, from what I understand." The artist sucked an olive from his cocktail.

Milne turned his head—Nicolas was tugging at his shoulder. An American writer, an old friend from university, stood next to him. Milne was glad to see a familiar face. "Eric! Great to see you."

"They told me you were buzzing around here somewhere," Eric said. His voice was deep and clear, and carried New England with it.

"I hear that you had something to do with my invitation."

"Your work had everything to do with it. I simply mentioned your name."

Milne began to reply but Eric broke in: "Oh, hold on there, Milne. This is Ava, my wife. Ava, this is Milne Lowell, who you've heard so much about."

A tall, thin American woman lifted her veiled arm to Milne. "Pleasure to finally meet you," she said. "Eric's always talking up the boys from Montreal. Frankly, I was beginning to think that he'd made you all up."

Nicolas was already deep in conversation with another guest. "This European love of communism is a passing fad," he said, "most of them simply haven't been exposed to the realities of it yet."

Ava rolled her eyes. "Communists," she said, "it's all they talk about these days."

Eric spotted someone walking past. "Ignazio!" he called out. The man turned. Upon seeing Eric his face broke into a crooked smile. "Milne," Eric continued, "here's someone I'd like you to meet."

Ignazio was a short, stocky Italian in a perfectly tailored suit. "Ignazio," Eric said, "this is Milne Lowell, a Canadian writer. One of my oldest friends."

Ignazio clasped his hands together and grinned broadly. "Mr. Lowell, of course! I have read some of your commentary— not the novels yet, unfortunately."

Milne shook his hand. "It's a pleasure to meet you, Mr.... ?"

"Brown," Ignazio said. "I know, not very Italian," he laughed. "My father was, I must confess, an American." Ignazio glanced at Eric. "No offence," he added.

"None taken. My grandfather was an Italian and a crook."

"Milne," Ignazio continued. "I was very impressed by your statements in *The Times* about the future of American literature. Very impressed." He waved his hand for emphasis as he spoke. "It's precisely that kind of mindset that is needed in this decade. Although, I must confess, I took you to be American until now."

"Many do, Mr. Brown. And yesterday they thought I was a Brit."

"Are you presenting this weekend?"

"Yes, tomorrow afternoon."

"Excellent, excellent," Ignazio said. "I look forward to hearing it." He smiled. "Bernstein is hidden away somewhere, of course. A man like him isn't a great face for a conference like this, I suppose." He paused and looked around. "I must, unfortunately, excuse myself, gentlemen. I will try to root him out of whatever backroom he has burrowed away in!"

As Ignazio hurried into the crowd, Eric leaned in to Milne. "Ignazio's being escorted by the *Sûreté* this weekend," he said. "The communists put threats out on his life. One of the French rags published his address last week."

"Jesus," Milne said. "What did he do?"

"Spoke too loudly and too clearly would be my guess. He's never been one for shyness." Eric's attention broke. "Excuse me for a minute, Milne," he said. "I'd better go rescue Ava from that passionless French playwright." He turned away from Milne and headed towards a small group where Ava stood with a bearded man wearing a greatcoat, despite the heat.

Milne looked around the room. It was an incredible turn-out. A young man with a cane limped past—he waved at a

18

couple and grinned. During the war, Milne had been friends with many conscripted men in Quebec who refused to serve overseas. The press called them Zombies, derisively, because they were caught in some stage of limbo. When hordes of men began to pour back into the streets from train cars, lurching as they walked with wounds of war and hollow sunken faces, the life in their eyes not absent but dulled, the naivety of the name was lost on few.

The echo of the cane's click penetrated the wall of sound. Milne turned and wandered through the crowd, searching for another familiar face. He began to feel out of place in the group. He overheard conversations in Italian, Spanish, and a French which he could hardly understand. He took a drink from a passing tray and then found himself standing next to an extraordinarily tall, extraordinarily thin, blonde woman.

"Käthe," she said, and held out her hand.

"Milne," he replied. She stared blankly so he tried to keep the conversation alive. "Where are you from? Germany?"

"Yes," she said. "I suppose that makes you uncomfortable."

"No," he said. "I know a lot of people who have spent time there. A lot of people here speak warmly of Berlin after the war—the culture."

Käthe smiled. Her lips curled up over her teeth. "Yes, they do," she said. "And so do the Soviets, for that matter, but that's because they are not Germans."

"What do you mean?"

"Look," Käthe said slowly. "You have to understand that the Berlin that these friends of yours lived in after the war was not the same one I did. They sat in opera houses and smoking lounges with caviar and champagne," she sipped her drink. "At the same time, my young sister froze to death in a heatless, bombed out apartment."

Milne watched the way her thin wrist limply held the cigarette, as if her entire being might drift away with the smoke at any moment, and found little sympathy in his heart for the woman.

"Maybe there was little worth rewarding," he said.

Käthe's face remained stolid and unphased. "It is true," she said, pausing to draw life from her cigarette, "and yet, the Russians killed my father. The Nazis killed my brother. We had no love for them." She stubbed the cigarette into an ashtray on the table beside her. "But we had no men left for you Americans to use."

"I'm not American," Milne said and shifted uncomfortably, looking around for some way to disengage.

"It doesn't matter," she said.

Just as he felt entirely lost, Milne saw Ava's hand reaching through the crowd for his own. "Milne, come on now. We're getting out of here." He nodded gladly and tried to form some reply. He could barely hear his own voice above the crowd and his words were swiftly lost to the sea of sound around them. He clung to her hand and followed her from the room.

When Ava and Milne reached the front door, Eric was already speaking with the driver of a car parked at the curb. He waved them over. The three got into the little Citroën and it pulled out onto the street.

"So, what are you going to talk about this weekend, Milne?" Ava asked. "Communists or Nazis? Or, how there is no difference between the two?"

"She's only teasing," Eric said. "Beneath that act, she's as American as they come."

"I'm just going to talk about writing," Milne said.

"It's never really just writing though," she said. "Is it?"

"Just writing," he repeated. "And the kind of society you need for it to be done well."

"There it is," Ava said. "And the Russians don't do it well?"

"They're running on fumes," Eric broke in. "On the memory of the Russian greats. A society like that, conformity like that, there is no originality. No creativity. No artistry," he said.

"Eric has been practicing this speech for weeks," Ava laughed. Though she joked, silence sat heavy in the car as the passengers listened to the rainfall clatter on the roof and watched the lights in apartments and homes sweep past slowly, like lighthouses in a storm. They all agreed, more or less, that he was right. That what they were here for was important—that there was still a spark of light left burning in the broken heart of Europe, after the worst century that it had ever seen, and that it couldn't afford to be extinguished.

The car stopped along the curb and Eric pointed up the street at the hotel. It was tall and thin and seemed to stand alone among the buildings. *Novak Hotel & Suites* ran across the front in curling white letters. Eric paid the driver and the passengers got out of the car. They ran from the curb to the building. As they approached, the doorman pulled on the handle and opened the front door of the Novak. Dim golden light danced in the lobby, a hole in the dark stone wall.

Inside, the group approached the front desk. The lobby was a wide room with a white marble floor and deep red furnishings. The walls were wooden panel for the bottom third and wallpaper for the remainder. A brass chandelier hung in the center of the room, dangling crystal ornaments.

The attendant handed Eric his key. *"Madame et monsieur, vous êtes dans la chambre 720,"* he said.

Milne told the attendant his own name. The man looked in his ledger and then lifted a key from a hook beneath the counter. *"Vous, vous êtes dans la chambre 1312,"* he said. *"Il faut monter l'escalier."* He placed the key on the counter in front of Milne as he spoke.

"L'escalier?" he asked. "The stairs?"

"Oui, Monsieur. Votre chambre est au treizième étage. L'ascenseur n'y va pas. Donc, vous devez monter l'escalier derrière la vieille salle de bal."

Milne looked at the key sitting on the counter. He was tired and frustrated. "What do you mean the elevator doesn't go to that floor?" he asked. "Are there no rooms available on the other floors?"

Ava broke in before the attendant was able to respond. "How romantic! An entire floor that most people don't even know exists! Just think about it, Milne! It might give you something to write about, anyway."

The attendant shook his head. *"Vos valises sont déjà dans la chambre, mais si vous le souhaitez, je peux vérifier si nous avons une autre chambre. A mon avis, il vaut mieux que l'on ferme cet escalier—ou bien tout l'étage. Malheureusement il semble que le propriétaire y soit attaché sentimentalement. Alors, il reste ouvert."*

Milne thought for a moment. "No, that will be ok," he said. "Ava's right, it might do some good."

"We'll take the stairs with you," Ava said.

Eric looked baffled by the idea. "W-"

The attendant cleared his throat and cut him off. He spoke slowly in English. "I'm sorry, *Madame*, but only the thirteenth floor is unlocked in that staircase. If you'd like, you can use our main stairs just across the lobby," he said, pointing across the room.

"Oh," Ava said. "Ok. Thank you."

Milne picked up his key and they crossed the lobby to the elevator together. Ava paused and leaned against the wall when they reached it. "Why don't we just settle in for a moment and then all meet back in the parlour for a nightcap."

"Great idea," Eric said. "What do you say, Milne?"

Though Milne was tired and wanted to rest up so that he could focus on his preparations, he reluctantly agreed. He left Eric and Ava at the elevator and made for the stairs behind the old ballroom. The ballroom was closed and a sign on the door was all that let him know that it was even there. *A darkness looms over this century,* he rehearsed in his head. *Historically, literature has thrived in times of darkness …*

He passed the ballroom and turned down a little corridor. At first, he thought that he must have taken a wrong turn: there were two narrow wooden doors that appeared to be storage closets. When he turned back, however, there were no other doors to try. He opened the first door: it was a storage closet. The second door looked identical to the first but opened into a hallway with a narrow staircase winding up to the next floor.

He began to climb. The stairs creaked with every step. Moonlight cut in through the narrow windows, which ran along the side of the building. He seemed to be walking for far too long on every flight. By the time he reached the second floor, he felt displaced—isolated from the rest of the world. On the third floor, he tried the door handle: it was locked. From there on, at every level he tried the handle and found the same to be true for all. He spiralled further up into the body of the hotel.

On the thirteenth floor, the door opened when he tried the handle. He stepped out into a narrow hallway that ran along the back of the building. He was exhausted. He breathed the air deeply. From the little windows, he saw shingled roofs and clouded sky. The first door was 1301, so he walked down the hall, which turned off and twisted across the top floor in an irregular layout. When he reached room 1312, he slid his key into the lock and opened the door.

The room was small. Due to the slope of the ceiling, half of it descended into unusable empty space. Three windows, two

23

wide and tall and one small and round, fitted one side of the room. The glass was foggy. In the corner, there was a little desk with a brass lamp. A dark brown coffee table and faded pink armchair sat beside it. His suitcase was next to the door. He tried to remember the last time that he had stayed in a hotel but could not.

One of the windows was open and the air flowing into the room was cold and hard. Milne crossed the room to it. He looked out into the night: rooftops stretched out; narrow alleyways cut between them. He thought of Eric and the friendship they had once had—life had moved on. Eric's more than his own.

He stepped away from the window and sat on the edge of the bed. It was soft and comfortable, despite the outdated décor. His eyes were sore, aching in the back from strain. He looked around the room and exhaled slowly, feeling the pressure in his chest release. It had been a long journey. All that he wanted now was sleep. But, it was his first time in Paris, he thought, and he might as well make the most of it. He couldn't remember the last time he'd seen Eric. He closed his eyes and lay back on the bed. There was a lot he couldn't remember.

After a few moments, he stood, ran a comb through his hair, stepped into the hallway, and closed the door of the room behind him. The floor wasn't straight. It rolled and guided him through the crooked walls and past the skewed angles of the windows overlooking the quiet Paris streets. A faint glow carried through the panes of glass and spread across the floor. At the end of the hall, he took the stairs that led behind the old ballroom, the only stairs that led to this floor, and started down to the lobby. The carpet was faded red and gold. The stairs creaked with every step. At the bottom, he went through the lobby to the parlour.

Wind rose in the chimney and howled, aching for release. Rain battered the windowpanes along the far wall. Ava sank into the leather sofa with a drink in her hand. Eric sat next to her. The parlour was a long room with double doors paned with glass. The ceilings were high, at least twelve feet, he guessed. Along one wall ran photographs and paintings, along the other ran bookshelves, three small tables, and a little oak desk. Beside the fireplace were the chairs and sofa, and a thick Turkish rug, worn by generations of feet. The wallpaper was printed with luxurious patterns but peeled at the corners and seams. A water stain ran down the paper from a corner near the largest window.

Milne took the drink that Eric offered him and sat across from him on the sofa. "How have you been?" Eric asked. "We haven't really had a proper chance to talk."

"Well," said Milne. "But busy, as always."

"You must be," Ava said. "I hear your name often enough. You're making quite a splash."

"Not as much as this man," Milne replied. "You already seem to know everyone here," he said.

Eric laughed. "Just a few, and none very well."

They chatted absently for a while and Milne became gradually aware of how much distance there now existed between him and Eric. In some ways, Eric was exactly the same. In others, his mannerisms seemed to belong to somebody else entirely. The man that existed in Milne's mind and memory wore away, and a new person began to emerge. He had aged well, Milne thought, but he had certainly aged. He looked a bit more like his father, in fact. Milne had met him once during a trip to Eric's family home in Connecticut, years ago.

"Is everyone well? How's your father?" Milne asked.

"He's dead," said Eric. "He died two years ago."

"Eric, I'm sorry. I hadn't heard."

"It's alright," Eric said. "I should have told you. I really meant to, but you know how these things get. It's too easy to let intentions slip away. Things were a bit better between us at the end, in any case."

"That's something," Milne said. "How did he die?"

Ava cast a sharp look at Milne, which faded as Eric began to respond. "A heart attack," he said, "but, really, I think the war was just too much for him. Whatever faith he had left after the first one shattered with Pearl Harbour. He wasn't well for a long time."

"How's your mother?" Milne asked, hoping as he said it that she was still alive.

"She's the same as ever," Eric said. He looked absently through his own reflection in the window next to him. "We've always been good the two of us. My mother's only sin was conceiving out of loneliness rather than love." He topped up his emptying glass as he spoke, and Milne realized that he was fairly drunk by the unsteady pour. "Harold's moved in with her now," Eric continued. "He takes good care of her."

Milne nodded. He thought of his own parents. There was definitely love there, though it existed behind a facade of formality. Eric stood and walked over to the fireplace. He stared into the shifting light. "You know," he said, "I never could figure out why my father didn't like me. I used to think that it was because I studied literature or didn't stick it out at Yale but I think it started earlier than that. Maybe he just had children too late in life."

Ava glanced at Milne, who shifted awkwardly in his seat. Ava began to speak but Eric cut her off. "Ah, he was a bastard," he said. "Once, when I was twelve, I tried to sit with the adults at dinner. It wasn't allowed. I ended up making some kind of a scene in front of the president of Yale. My father didn't stir. My mother took me up to my room."

Eric crossed to the table and topped up his glass again. "Later, he came upstairs with disgust in his eyes like I'd never seen. He told me that I was right, that twelve was too young to act like a child. He stood me up and told me to be a man. Told me to hit him if I was angry. Instead, I just cried," Eric said. "I was scared." He stared at his reflection shaking in the light of the fire. "He took off his belt and thrashed me. Each blow was calculated, merciless. He taunted me as he swung. Finally, I hit him back, out of desperation, not anger. As soon as I did, he let me be."

He topped up his glass again. Ava and Milne looked at one another helplessly. "My mother never mentioned it, but she must have known," he added quietly. The room was silent but for the crackling logs. Eventually, Eric looked up from the fireplace and seemed to break from a trance, realizing that he was still in conversation. "Oh well, I'd made my name by the end so it wasn't all bad," he said. "He met Ava too. He loved her."

For some time, they sat awkwardly around the room. Eventually, Ava's clever manoeuvring brought the conversation back to life. Then, they talked carelessly for a while. They talked about the days before the war when everyone was an idealist and about people they had known who didn't come back—not about them during the war but beforehand, when things were right. Milne had not gone to war. Ava already seemed to know. The rain fell and the chimney cried.

When they ran out of topics, they began to discuss work. "Nicolas and Cliff are organizing funding for a magazine," Eric said. "It's one of the reasons I've been talking with them." He cleared his throat. "I'm moving to London after Christmas.

I'm going to launch the first issue and sit as editor for the time being."

"Well done!" Milne said. "Congratulations. Have you sorted out the details?"

"More or less," Eric said. "Nobody's been settled for the last decade anyway. Ava's just excited for the adventure. Mom and the house are safe with Harold."

They discussed the possibilities that come with running your own magazine—both wild and entirely possible—and came up with a list of contributors that Eric was sure to secure for the first issue. They reminisced about their plans to start a magazine in university, and then talked late into the night about those days too. Eventually, Eric excused himself to use the washroom and Milne and Ava decided that they should call it a night. When he finally stood up, Milne felt dizzy and his eyes clouded over. He realized how much he had had to drink.

"Thank you," he heard Ava say. "I haven't heard him talk about his father since the funeral." Milne turned and Ava stumbled backwards. He held out his arm to steady her and she grabbed his hand tightly. "How embarrassing," she said. "You must think that I'm such a child."

Eric came out of the bathroom as they entered the lobby. The three said their goodnights and Milne left Ava and Eric at the elevator door, dreading the climb ahead. He crossed the lobby, pausing on the thick rug to look back at his old friend.

It must have been something in the Paris night that affected him but as Milne stood alone in the lobby watching the elevator doors close from a distance and glimpsing, through the closing gap, Eric and Ava's eyes meeting in communion, he felt a hollow swelling in his chest a little below the heart. The rain had stopped and night had descended entirely upon the city. Moonlight cast across the fountain in the courtyard, and the reflection of the water shook and shimmered in the window beside him. He crossed the rest of the way through the empty lobby and took the old stairs behind the ballroom. As he walked back up the empty stairs to his room, the feeling of displacement set in again. He was in Paris, he thought. The Paris of so much poetry.

2

Milne woke early. It was cold—he realized that he had left the window open all night, but he was glad for the air. He sat up against the headboard and thought about the night before. Never, in all of the years that he'd known him, had he seen Eric as vulnerable as he had been then. He felt close to him, but also awkward. He wondered how Eric would feel. Ava had looked beautiful in her light blue dress, which was colourful and slim, as trends seemed to be turning. He thought about the warmth of her fingers in his hand.

Milne lifted his watch from the nightstand—it was 7:00. He got out of bed and stood by the window for a moment, feeling the cold air on his face and chest. Then, he went over to his briefcase and took out his notes. He was presenting in the afternoon and he looked forward to the task. He looked over his notes briefly. Then he showered and dressed.

He left his room. It was a long walk down. The walls seemed to close in around him, flight after flight, as he descended. When he finally emerged at the bottom and entered the lobby, he saw Eric and Ava sitting at a table drinking coffee in the restaurant. From the expressions on their faces, he decided that Eric must not have been happy about their conversation. He considered going back up, but Ava saw him lingering in the lobby and waved him over.

"Have you heard?" Eric asked when Milne sat down.

"Of course he hasn't," Ava snapped. "He's only just woken up."

"The Russians got the bomb," Eric said without pause. "Truman broadcast the news. They pulled off a successful test weeks ago."

Milne stared at Eric. He didn't know what to say. It had always seemed like a hypothetical fear.

Eric slammed his hand on the table, turning the heads of other guests. "Weeks," he said. "Fucking weeks ago! We've been sitting around entirely unaware, twiddling our thumbs and playing dress up. We could have been evaporated at any moment! We would have never seen it coming."

"Don't say that," Ava said. "And calm down. Acting like a fool isn't going to stop them from dropping the bomb."

For the next hour, the three sat in relative silence around the breakfast table. Ava tried to start conversation more than once and was met with nothing but empty words. The first event of the day began at 11:00. It was a presentation in a public square by two French philosophers and a British poet. Milne no longer felt like going. It seemed like a waste of time, all of a sudden.

After breakfast, Eric and Ava went upstairs and Milne stepped through the brass doors into the street and lit a cigarette. The morning air was hard and crisp. The Russians had the bomb—he couldn't push the thought from his mind. He wanted to think of his speech. He knew that, at the moment, that speech was the only way that he could help—his little contribution to the cause. He couldn't remember a word of it.

The Russians had the bomb. Without that advantage, he didn't know what they had left. He looked at the cobblestone beneath his feet and then just down the street to a bustling café. A woman, laughing, lay her arm across the table and touched the fingers of the man that she sat with. He thought of the woods back home, changing leaves in the fall. He thought back to a girl he'd once known, Isabelle. He remembered how it felt when he looked at her. He couldn't remember her face—it was too long ago for that. She had brown hair, he knew, and her eyes were brown as well. More than anything, he remembered the feeling.

Milne decided to walk to the square. It wasn't far from the hotel and he wanted the air. He turned to the left and headed down the street towards the café. He watched the young couple as he walked past. They were both laughing now, happy and seemingly oblivious to the news he had just heard. It was good, he thought, that they were peaceful still. The man had a book on the table in front of him—a new copy of *L'etranger* by Camus. The woman had a little brown birthmark, or beauty spot, on her cheek. The man glanced towards him and their eyes met—Milne looked away with embarrassment.

He hurried past the patio and turned the corner at the intersection. He glanced back—the couple was watching him. He averted his eyes again. He tried to glance casually past them. Just beyond the café, across from his hotel, a man in an oddly shaped homburg and a lengthy coat stepped out of a car which had been parked along the curb. Milne pretended to focus upon him for a moment and then turned and carried on down the street out of sight.

By the time Milne reached the square, the British poet, Carson Ward, was presenting from the podium. "Today, more than ever," he said, "it is time to resist. There can be no mistake any longer—the Russians are a threat of greater proportions than we could have ever anticipated."

The crowd was large, much larger than Milne had expected it to be, and they seemed, for the most part, to be focused intensely upon the presentation. He looked around for Eric and Ava but

32

could not find them in the crowd. Nicolas was standing close to the podium with a woman that he didn't recognize. Milne made his way through the crowd towards him.

"As Churchill said," Carson continued, "the United States stands, at this time, at the pinnacle of world power. This is absolutely true. Yet, this power is now being tested by the expanding Soviet Empire. This is one of the greatest conflicts in human history. Though the war is over, we live only in the shadows of peace—we haven't known real peace for half a century. I do not pretend that the United States is perfect; however, it must be recognized that America is, and will remain, the mainstay of freedom in the twentieth century. In this battle between freedom and totalitarianism, I have chosen my side. By standing here today, I expect that you have all done the same."

Milne reached Nicolas, who was keenly attentive to the speech. He acknowledged Milne with a brief nod. Clifford Bernstein was nowhere in sight. Carson spoke for a few more minutes, drawing applause and occasional jeers from the crowd. When he finished, one of the philosophers took the stage. He presented in French, with the occasional English phrase. Milne followed some of the presentation but many of the technical terms were lost on him. The philosophers spoke and debated for some time and then switched to English so that Carson could comfortably enter the conversation again.

A minor debate took hold between the three and, as Carson tried to rebuke a point made by one of the other speakers, someone at the front of the audience called out loudly. Milne could not hear what was said but the crowd erupted with applause and began to jeer as a disjointed unit. Carson and the philosophers attempted to limit the damage by stepping back from the microphones. The crowd did not die down and Nicolas climbed onto the stage from the right side to plead for patience.

"This is no way to go," he began, but was quickly muffled by the crowd. "We'll get nowhere like this," he tried again. "This is the time for meaningful ..."

Suddenly, three French women stormed the stage, waving a twisted banner. The crowd erupted again and Nicolas looked around in astonishment. One of the women yelled out, loud enough to carry over the jeers, "You can't find freedom at the barrel of a gun!" Another protestor appealed to the crowd for silence. When they heeded, she began to read from a piece of paper: "How can we look to the Americans for freedom when they give it out at home based upon the colour of skin?"

Police officers entered the stage from the back and roughly grabbed hold of the protestors. The crowd seemed to rise forward towards the stage, hurling vicious words at police and protestors alike. "No more war!" the youngest of the group yelled out, attempting to start a chant. She was quickly pulled backwards from the platform. For some time, police and audience pushed back and forth against one another. The protestors were hurried away and more police arrived. The crowd slowly dispersed.

Milne wandered aimlessly through the square, looking for somebody he recognized. When he found no one, he sat at a bench near the edge of the square and waited. Eric's presentation was delayed for an hour. By the time he was allowed to speak, he presented to a small, disinterested audience and a wall of police.

Milne sat with Ava and Nicolas in the side room of a restaurant beside the square, which was being used as a make-shift base for the day. Eric stormed in and slammed the door.

"The problem is that the French don't know a damned thing about America," he said. "And everything they do know about us is from second-rate Hollywood pictures or Steinbeck and Faulkner. They think of us as degenerate, backwards country-folk!"

Ava stood up and touched his arm gently. "It's alright, Eric. Nobody could have predicted that this would happen. You spoke wonderfully in spite of it all."

Nicolas smiled and looked at Eric. "It's true," he said. "The rest of the world is, at the moment, quite ignorant of American culture. You must remember, though, that the communist press is widespread in Europe. Waves of propaganda can't help but impact the general mindset of the public." Nicolas paused to light a cigarette. "A lot of these types still deny the existence of the gulags. It will take time to get through to them."

Eric threw himself into an armchair. "How are we supposed to get through that kind of idiocy at all? If they want to keep their eyes closed, they'll keep them closed."

"The way to get through to them is through the ones who have already turned away. This is what Clifford and I have been discussing. We need more ex-communists headlining these things—that would have a hell of an impact," Nicolas said. He set his teacup down on the saucer and looked past Eric, through the window into the square. "Ward was right. The time for neutrality is over. It will be increasingly hard for anyone to deny that. We just need to make sure that people end up on the right side. The next one of these won't be in Paris, mind you. I can guarantee that." He looked down at his watch and then quickly rose to his feet. "I better be going. I didn't realize the time. Good work today, Eric. And, Milne, good luck out there," he said. "I'll be up in the front again."

The next few hours dragged on slowly. Eric and Ava decided to see some of the other events to clear their minds, promising to be back in time for Milne's presentation. Milne decided to stick around the restaurant and practice his speech. He tried to read over his notes but couldn't focus on the page and simply skimmed the words absently. His mind was tethered to the surging crowd. He drank coffee and smoked cigarettes and looked out of the little window at the podium he would soon be presenting from.

After a while, he left the restaurant and walked up the street to clear his head and gather himself. When he got to the corner, he realized that he had no real destination in mind. He glanced carelessly back down the street toward the restaurant. A lady with a dog was chasing down a runaway child and a few birds scattered from a railing along the street. Just past them, a man was smoking a cigarette and leaning on the hood of a car. He looked familiar. His hat, an oddly shaped homburg, was more familiar still. Milne stared at him for what was probably too long and the man casually tossed his cigarette into the gutter, got into his car, and started the engine. Milne watched it pull away from the curb and disappear around the corner.

He continued down the street in the direction he had been heading. He stopped at a small bakery to look through the window. He kept walking and crossed the street to enter a little bookstore that he had noticed on his walk from the hotel that morning. The wooden door creaked when he opened it. The room was narrow, barely wider than a hallway. A small counter sat far at the back, beyond rows of shelves and books stacked in boxes on the floor. The scent of old paper and wood settled in the air.

He walked along the edges of the store and browsed the books—Zola, Flaubert, Dumas, Proust, He picked up a copy of *Journal du voleur* and flipped through its pages. From the corner of his eye, he saw an old man with a thick white beard peering over the edge of the counter at him, discreetly watching his every movement. Then, in his periphery on the other side, a

36

silhouette loomed, someone peering through the window of the shop. He turned—he recognized the man: Ignazio, the stocky Italian. He was squinting through the glass at a book on display. Milne put down the book he was holding, crossed the store, and quickly stepped outside to catch him before he moved on.

Ignazio looked up when the door opened. "Mr. Lowell!" he called. "Just who I was coming to see!"

Milne looked up at the storefront in surprise. "Here?"

Ignazio laughed. "No. I was on my way to the square ... for your presentation." He looked down at his watch. "It is at two o'clock, is it not?"

Milne checked his own watch. "It is, yes. I suppose I should be heading that way as well," he said.

"That would be well advised." Ignazio pointed through the window at the book he had been examining. "I believe that may be quite a rare edition," he said. *"Les Liaisons dangereuses."*

Milne looked at the book. Its cover was worn and it was difficult to read the title on the front. The name of the author was clearly printed along the top.

Ignazio shrugged. "We'd better be going," he said. "You can't be late to your own party."

Ignazio led the way. Milne followed closely behind. Across the street, two men in plainclothes trailed them at a slow pace. "The police," Ignazio said as he pointed them out. "They're a nuisance. Though, it is better than being knifed in an alleyway," he reasoned.

Milne tried to look at them without them noticing. "Why are the communists after you?" he asked.

Ignazio looked at him with surprise. "You don't know?"

"Only what Eric told me. Should I know?"

Ignazio smiled. "I was a founding member of the Communist Party of Italy," he said. "I'm a traitor."

"You quit the party?"

"Not quite. When the fascists took power, we remained active underground. For this, my brother was murdered by Mussolini."

"I'm sorry," Milne said. These men had been through much that he had not. The apology was heartfelt.

"I must admit that I am surprised that you don't already know this. I'm quite famous," he assured Milne. "After he was killed, I went to Switzerland. I helped the resistance from afar but I fell out with the party when the Soviets became what they hated. I renounced communism publicly. They never forgave me for it."

"It must be a relief to know that they're here—the police, I mean."

Ignazio glanced back and then shook his head. "There was a beggar here," he said, "a friend of Peret's. He'd lost his mind in Spain. He was a genius. I used to visit him on Rue Vercingétorix. Yesterday, I went to look for him. I walked and walked but couldn't find him anywhere, so I asked somebody on the corner: 'What happened to the beggar I used to see on this street? The one who drew on the walls,' I said. 'He was killed,' the woman told me, 'three days ago. He tried to stab a policeman in the eye.'" Ignazio patted his brow with a handkerchief, then folded it and put it back into his pocket. "Make of that what you will," he added.

They reached the corner and turned towards the square.

"What's the deal with Mr. Bernstein?"

"What do you mean?"

"You said that he wasn't a good face for the conference. Everyone seems to know him, but he's very hard to find."

"Ah, yes. I see. He feels that if he is seen around, the apolitical reputation of the conference will be tarnished. After the

38

mess they made in New York, the Soviets have their eye on things. Clifford is an easy target for propagandists—he worked with the American military for years." Ignazio stopped and stooped to brush dirt from his shoe. "People like Nicolas and myself are ... well, it is harder for the Soviets to discredit us."

At two o'clock, Milne stood at the podium overlooking the square. Nicolas and Ignazio were at the front of the crowd. Ava, Eric, and Carson Ward stood a few rows back. Milne recognized a lot of the faces—faces he was familiar with from newspapers and magazines. The turnout was far higher than he had expected, given the events at the previous presentation.

As he paused and looked out over the audience, he caught sight of two more familiar faces in the crowd. Fairly far back, several rows behind Eric and Ava, stood the couple he had seen at the café beside his hotel. They were watching him with an intensity that made his confidence falter. He looked down and shuffled his notes. When he looked back up, he couldn't see them anymore. He searched the crowd for them and then became aware of the hundreds of other faces looking up at him in anticipation. He realized that he had already been introduced. He cleared his throat and began to speak.

"A darkness looms over this century," he said, "but, historically, literature has thrived in times of darkness." His voice shook. They were lines that he had rehearsed countless times in the past few weeks but they felt weakened in light of the day's events. Despite his concerns, the rehearsed words spilled from his mouth automatically. "This is not the time for defeatism—though that has produced some decent literature in the past—it is the time for optimism. Optimism and discovery."

39

As he watched the audience before him, he realized that they were listening attentively. There were no jeers—there was no heckling. He began to speak with more determination: "We have, in these parts of Europe and across the sea, an opportunity to demonstrate that we have not been crushed by this century but that we have successfully defended those ideals and values which allow for us to be vibrant, to be creative, and which inspire genius in the population."

Milne paused and looked out over the crowd. Ignazio nodded to him. He spoke firmly and authoritatively and recited the rest of his speech without glancing back at his notes. He recognized a new manner in his own speech which no longer referred to largely abstract ideas but was authentic and grounded, and when he was done he was met with enthusiastic applause from the crowd before him. He felt revitalized. Nicolas beamed up at him from the sidelines.

He stepped down from the podium. Nicolas and Ignazio reached out to shake his hand and congratulate him. Ava, Eric, and Carson made their way through the crowd and congratulated him as well.

"That's the crowd you should have had," he said to Eric.

Nicolas laughed. "I suspect that the police put the fear of God into them after that stunt."

The group attended a short series of debates in the afternoon and then went back to the ballroom where the opening gala had been held. This time, the floorspace was devoted to twelve carefully arranged dinner tables, a small dance floor, and a bar. Carson, Eric, and Ava were placed at a separate table from Nicolas, Clifford, Ignazio, and Milne. At Eric and Ava's table, there were two prominent French writers and a labour organizer from Spain. At Milne's table, the two additional seats remained empty.

After they took their seats, waiters brought out a wine list. Throughout the course of their meal, the two empty seats at their table were filled, sometimes for five minutes and sometimes for half an hour, by a steady stream of writers, organizers, and journalists. Following the main course, the stream trickled off and Clifford seemed to relax.

Clifford spoke sparingly, and generally in the form of a direct question, but Nicolas spoke comfortably and freely. He'd known Clifford for decades, it turned out, but they'd only started to work together a few years earlier when Nicolas was assigned to the Morale Division in Berlin, where Clifford was also working. Nicolas composed and organized concerts to boost morale and help to revitalize the city in the wake of destruction. With Clifford's help, Nicolas boasted, he'd managed to oust and blacklist countless conductors, musicians, and singers with Nazi sympathies.

At a certain point in the night, Nicolas set his drink on the table. "Milne," he began. "We have a proposition. We've already discussed it with Eric and we're in agreement on the matter." Clifford nodded in support and Nicolas continued: "One of the reasons we invited you here to present was to get a sense of the way you took to things this weekend. I'm sure that Eric has mentioned it by now but he's moving to London in the new year to launch a periodical."

"Yes," Milne said. "He mentioned it yesterday."

"Well, we're building an organization—a kind of permanent structure dedicated to the promotion of cultural freedom. Eric's magazine will be the flagship publication. An executive committee, including Clifford and myself, will be based here running the administrative side of things—organizing funding, distribution and so forth. The plan is to organize a network of publications and conferences internationally, all run by people dedicated to

41

the same ideals as us—the same ideals as you." Nicolas looked closely at Milne. "Carson Ward will be co-editor with Eric," he continued. "If you're interested, we'd like you to do the same."

Milne was taken aback. "And move to London?"

"Yes," Nicolas said. "That's what it would mean, for the time being. We might eventually branch out into Canada but the idea, for now, is to work in Europe and export to neutral areas underexposed to American and European literature. London is the ideal location for this."

Milne looked around the table. Clifford looked back searchingly. Ignazio, who was listening intently, simply winked at him.

Milne left after dinner. He refused the offered car, deciding instead to walk back to the hotel alone. It was still early enough in the night and the square beside the restaurant was filled with French, American, and British intellectuals. Music carried to him from somewhere down the street.

He thought over Nicolas's offer as he walked. Could he move to London? Editing a literary magazine was a dream in and of itself. Editing a London literary magazine was something else entirely. He would join the ranks of London literature, which included not just the likes of Woolf, Eliot, and Auden, but also Byron, Dickens, Dryden, and Johnson.

A permanent structure dedicated to the promotion of cultural freedom, Nicolas had called it. They were waging war, he thought, on conformity, restriction, authoritarianism. Creativity, the human imagination—if that couldn't flourish, what did they have left?

Suddenly, he remembered: the Russians had the bomb. It was no longer just an arms race, an economic struggle. This was nuclear war. Where was the place of culture in that? Nicolas and Clifford thought it important, it seemed. Milne thought back to the man he had seen twice in the oddly shaped homburg. He thought back to the couple sitting outside the hotel, who then appeared at his presentation. Were these the Russian agents he had been warned of? Should he tip somebody off? He remembered the threat on Ignazio's life. Nicolas, Clifford, even Ignazio—they took it all in stride. Why did he feel so timid? This was their world, he supposed. It made him uneasy, but they lived for it. They knew that they were doing something important. At that moment, he was still on the sidelines.

He wondered if it was safe to be walking alone. He was just a writer. Ignazio and Clifford had reason to be targeted. Even Nicolas, a composer, had been involved in some kind of military activity. He felt a little more secure—he was the least likely target of them all, and none of them seemed worried. They had been in the war, though. They had been through it all. This was a world that he knew little of. The quiet Paris streets must seem so domestic after that, even if Soviet agents lingered in the shadows.

Irregular footsteps shuffled behind him—his senses heightened. He heard the scrape of a shoe on the cobblestones, the dust and grime of the city beneath the leather sole. Muffled sounds seeped from the buildings next to him. An echo carried from an alleyway. The soft music from the party was still audible, he realized. He heard the scrape again. Somebody was behind him. He could feel the presence, close. His back felt bare. He sped up. He needed to do something more, he realized. He tensed his body and stepped sideways quickly into the cover of a doorway. He held his breath and turned towards the sound with clenched fists. A man, drunk, stumbled forward along the street. His eyes were focused on the ground in front of him.

He muttered something as his foot caught a dip in the stone. He dropped a handful of coins and they rattled loudly across the ground. He stooped to gather them and fumbled. The tension faded—the fear dissipated. Milne exhaled. Of course, he thought. Of course.

Pigeons across the street ruffled their feathers. The streetlights were dim overhead. The sky cast a slightly blue light. Would he be able to move to London? He wasn't married. He had no family left in Montreal—his parents had retired to Prince Edward Island. The only person really left at home was Marguerite. He would be sorry to be apart from her, but friendships could withstand a little distance. How long would it be? A few years, at most? Another thought struck him: her publishing house had recently closed. If he was an editor, he could surely find her a position. Would she move to London? A magazine in defence of cultural freedom—who was better suited to the task than Marguerite?

The few courses that the college threw his way could be reassigned. They would publish quarterly, he assumed. That was steady work. Busy work. He would be working with Eric again. Carson Ward and his circle—some of the best writers in the English-speaking world. Even if the magazine failed, it would be worth it. He would be in London—fuel for a novel down the line. The best work was done away from home. Yes, he thought. It could work.

A door opened to his left and three Parisian women stepped into the street beside him. He lifted his hat and ran his hand over his hair. He straightened his jacket. The women spoke in rapid-fire French, oblivious to his presence. They weren't sure where to go next—he looked down at his watch. The night was just beginning for them, it seemed. He thought of his evenings at home—a book beside the fire, dinner alone. Laughter rang out. He longed for excitement and change.

44

He stepped from the alcove and wandered along the street. He had not been paying much attention to where he was going. He stopped and searched the area around him. It was familiar. He recognized a bakery—a bench—a wall. The hotel was just around the corner, he realized. He looked up at the buildings, the countless windows, mostly unlit. Life existed entirely in each. The hotel rose up in front of him again. *Novak Hotel & Suites.* He counted the floors to number thirteen. From here, it looked no different from the others. He walked towards it and crossed the street. He approached the heavy front doors—the gate entrapping that golden lobby glow.

Two people lingered in the shadow of the doorway. He stopped walking. Both looked directly at him. He should not have walked alone, he thought. He wondered if Eric and Ava were inside. He thought about turning and walking away but they had already seen him and he felt compelled to stay. He stepped closer. It was the same couple he had seen at his presentation earlier. They were both distinctive enough.

He approached slowly. They did not move from the doorway. Milne stopped a few feet away. The young man stepped forward.

"Excuse me, sir," he said.

Milne did not respond.

The man lifted something from beneath his coat. Milne flinched as his arm rose.

"Would you mind?" he asked, holding a book towards Milne.

Milne looked down and scanned the cover. Relief rushed through him—it was a copy of his first novel, *The Foxhunt.* For the second time that night, the tension and fear eased and he was left feeling foolish.

"Of course," he said. He reached for his pocket in search of a pen—the young women lifted her own arm and held one

45

out to him. "Who should I make it out to?" Milne asked, as he took it.

"Jules and Camille," the young woman answered, smiling. He opened the cover, scrawled a signature across the front page, and handed it back. Jules and Camille thanked him and then stepped aside to let him pass. He stepped into the lobby of the hotel. The couple spoke rapidly and quietly behind him. He passed through the lobby and made his way to the rickety stairs behind the ballroom.

The final day of the conference passed quickly. The disruption of Truman's announcement had people frightened or excited, or more often both. Milne ate with Eric and Ava in the morning, and then wandered the streets alone. He watched debates and listened to readings. He met Nicolas one more time and told him that he would give an answer as soon as he was able, though he had already decided what to do. He had hoped that others would stay on in Paris when the conference ended, and many did, but none that he knew.

3

London, 1950: *"Marguerite,"* Milne wrote, *"I miss you terribly. I had hoped to speak to you while I was home. Unfortunately, our paths did not cross."* He paused and looked at the thick black marks on the page in front of him. It was best to be direct. He touched pen to paper and continued:

> *I'm writing to invite you to join me in London. I've been given a magazine to edit with Eric (Felmore!). Carson Ward, the poet, is also on board. It is very internationalist. The magazine is dedicated to the promotion of freedom in the arts—much like the conference I attended in Paris. It is privately funded. Nicolas Babichev is a board member. Please write and we can discuss the details.*
> *With hope,*
> *Milne*
> *P.S. Need you on board!*

He put down his pen and read the letter over. He had met Marguerite in his first year of university. She was in an introductory political philosophy course he took as an elective, and then ended up being in two or three literature courses he took the following semester. She wrote a small amount of poetry at the time but soon shifted focus to politics.

When it came to politics, he tried his best to understand Marguerite. He knew the basic principles. He'd kept up with George Woodcock's *Now* during the war. He understood Woodcock—he was literary, academic. Marguerite read Russian anarchists—Goldman, Kropotkin, Bakunin—and spoke of vastly different evolutionary histories. She spoke of society as something innate to humanity and believed in the goodness of the human heart when unfettered by a society of imbalance. She was an idealist, he thought, in the purest of senses. And yet, she cared more deeply about life than anyone he had ever known. Not simply about life in the everyday sense but about life as a force in the universe, as a moment of being.

Milne dropped the letter into the outbox and lifted his coat from the back of his chair. Nicolas and Carson were taking him to a boxing match to welcome him to London. Freddie Mills, The Bournemouth Bomber, was defending his title at the Earl's Court Exhibition Centre. Mills was Britain's boxing poster boy—a scrappy, aggressive light heavyweight known for flooring heavyweights. He had an impressive record: in '47, Mills stopped the Belgian Pol Goffaux in the fourth round for the European light heavyweight title; in '48, he knocked out Paco Bueno in the second to keep the belt; later the same year he beat Gus Lesnevitch soundly; in '49, Mills challenged heavyweight champ Bruce Woodcock for all three of his titles—the British, Empire, and European Heavyweight Championships. Mills walked into the ring ten kilograms lighter than his opponent and went fourteen rounds before being knocked out cold. For the British public, this only heightened their esteem. Tonight, he was fighting a little-known American named Joey Maxim.

Milne took a cab and met Carson, Clifford, and Nicolas at a little restaurant in Kensington. They sat on a terrace at the

48

back, nestled beside the Chelsea Bridge overlooking the River Thames. On the other side of the bank, scars of bombing runs remained. Some collapsed buildings had never been cleared.

"It's going to be a hell of a fight," Carson said, looking out at the lights beneath the bridge. "Mills always puts on a hell of a show."

"We'll see if he can outfight the American," Clifford said. "If Mills was a pure boxer, it would be a fool's errand. With a brawler like that, you never know."

"I doubt that the American's ever been to war with heavyweights the likes of Jack London or Ken Shaw," Carson said. "Mills isn't just a brawler with a good chin, he has real heart."

"You know why they call him Maxim, don't you?" Clifford asked.

"I thought it was his name."

"Berardinelli is his name. They call him Maxim for the machine gun."

Carson smiled. "A British gun."

"A British gun invented by an American," Clifford said. "Used in every British war from 1886 to the Great War. Egypt, The Horn of Africa, The Philippines, The Boer, Rhodesia, China, The Balkans." He paused and gestured to the waiter. "Empires fell to the Maxim," he added.

"That may be so but unless little Joey is bringing one into the ring with him, I wouldn't worry too much about all of that," Carson said. He poured himself a glass of wine. "When he was fifteen years old, Mills tried to get in to watch the fights in Bournemouth. They wouldn't let him in—too young, they said. He walked to the back and climbed up onto the roof, crawled across the shingles, and over to the skylight above the ring. Watched the fights from right there—best seat in the house. Free of charge."

49

Nicolas tried to interrupt him but Carson was already committed. "In the first match," he continued, "one of the fighters was dropped. When he came around, the first thing he saw looking up was the face of this boy peering down at him through the skylight. Probably thought he was going over to the other side. When he regained his senses, he invited Freddie down and sat with him for the rest of the night. The very next day, Mills headed out to the fair and stepped into the ring. He was floored by a carnival man in two minutes but every day for the next four years, Freddie fought in carnivals and fairs against anyone who'd take him. They'd pay him with a hot meal and a beer. Then, the war broke out and Freddie joined the RAF. Before he knew it, he was an Army boxer fighting the toughest soldiers in the world."

Clifford shrugged and lit a cigarette. "It's a hell of a story."

"Do you follow much boxing, Milne?" Nicolas asked.

"No," he replied. "My father did. He used to talk about a man from his hometown, Sam Langford. He fought from lightweight to heavyweight. He said he'd have been a world champ but everyone was scared to fight him, even Jack Johnson."

"We should have brought the wives," Clifford said. "We'd have had better conversation for it."

"They do go in for a night like this," Nicolas replied. "As long as the fighters talk it out."

Carson laughed, and Milne realized that he was the only unmarried one in the group.

"I'll be leaving tomorrow," Clifford said. "Eric will be arriving next week, I expect. Right after he settles his contract with the college." He leaned back in his chair, watching the patrons around him. "You boys are doing something big here," he said. "Remember that. This is important."

"I know it is," Milne said. "Thank you, again, for taking me on board."

"Thank you for committing to this," Clifford said. "There aren't enough men like us to go around these days. Nicolas will be here for a week and then he's coming to Paris. While he's here, he can help you set up the office and get things sorted. Then you can get to work on the proposal."

"I've been through this with them already," Nicolas said. "For that matter, so have you."

"Well, I'll tell them again then," Clifford said. "We want the first issue done by June so that it can release at our conference in Berlin."

Milne was reminded of something someone had told him about Clifford in Paris, about his family and the war. His finger was constantly on the pulse of business. Socialization was shallow, it seemed. At any moment, during any conversation, he was liable to give directions, to speak about the importance of anti-communism, or simply to remind whoever he was speaking to of the work that they had yet to complete. He was friendly enough, though, and Milne had grown to enjoy his company. After dinner, Clifford footed the bill and the men caught a cab to Earl's Court to watch the fight.

The crowd was lively. Carson knew a promoter so the seats were only a few rows from ringside. When Mills entered the ring, the roar hit Milne like a wave. He could hear nothing else. When Maxim entered, the boos carried just as loud. From the start of the fight, it was clear that Mills was gunning for a knockout. He charged in at the opening bell and launched a series of heavy-handed hooks at Maxim, catching him off guard and sending him backwards into the ropes. Mills moved in and threw two sweeping hooks: the American stepped forward, slipped both, and peppered the Brit with punches. Mills stepped out of range and tried to regain his sense, but Maxim pressed forward again. Mills grabbed hold of Maxim's right arm and let loose with two dirty hooks to the body. Maxim weathered both blows and pressed forward, pushing Mills backwards.

The two fought back and forth, in a fairly even match, for two rounds. In the third, however, it was clear that Mills was losing ground. The American was fighting in a traditionally British style, standing tall and snapping quick counter punches, demonstrating craftmanship beyond the level that Mills was used to facing, or maybe Mills was simply wearing down. He began to rely upon clinching and throwing slapping hooks from the hold before Maxim could respond. His own sweeping style had taken a toll and he was gassing quickly. Late in the fourth, Maxim jabbed and parried until he had Mills on the ropes, where he began to snap out quick straight punches. Mills covered up when he could and wore the blows head on when he couldn't.

For the next several rounds, Maxim dominated the ring and wore Mills down even further. In the eighth round, Mills appeared to regain some strength and caught the American with two hard hooks to the body. Mills and Maxim traded shots, clinching, slipping, and pivoting in and out of dominant positions against the ropes until the bell ended the round.

In the ninth, Maxim rushed in aggressively. Mills stepped back and the two traded blows. Then, in a flurry of punches, fighting from a near clinch, Maxim caught Mills with a vicious combination—a left hook and a straight right, each landing on opposite sides of the jaw. Freddie Mills' knees buckled instantly and he fell forwards to the ground, crumpling against the canvas. He rolled back and sat up momentarily, holding his gloves to his eyes, and then collapsed sideways. The ref counted him out and his cornermen rushed into the ring. Staggering, he was carried to the corner. The doctor met him there, and immediately placed his fingers inside of Mill's mouth. He pulled his

52

lip up—Milne couldn't see from where he was sitting, but Carson looked sick. Nicolas shook his head. Milne looked over at Maxim's corner, his trainer had just removed something from Maxim's glove and was holding it in the palm of his hand. Clifford looked on with little change of expression.

"What's going on?" somebody in the crowd behind them asked. "Can anyone see what it is?"

"Teeth," another voice in the crowd said. "It's Fearless Freddie's two front teeth."

Maxim entered the center of the ring and raised his glove in triumph. He draped the heavy belt over his shoulder and looked out into the watchful crowd, surrounding the ring on every side. The Brit slumped in the corner, battered and exhausted.

4

Marguerite rested back in her seat. She tilted her forehead against the glass and looked out at the buildings lifting from the ground, stretching themselves around the tracks. She had thought that she would recognize London from pictures and movies but she recognized nothing at all. The beautiful, green countryside faded away and row upon row of building emerged—grey-brown blocks, uniform and dull. The excitement that she had felt since Milne's initial letter was absent. Instead, she was filled with unease.

To push it from her mind, she thought of Eric and Milne. Milne, who she'd known for so many years, and Eric, who she hadn't seen for nearly as many. She thought of London as it existed in her mind—London of Hyde Park Gate and Bloomsbury. London, where Mosley was beaten back on Cable Street. London: where Wollstonecraft and Godwin lived and breathed, where Rebecca West hosted Emma Goldman. Where Engels met Mary Burns ... no, that was Manchester. London, that was *Freedom Press, The Freewoman, The Egoist*. Imagism. Forget the fascist tendencies—Pound, Lawrence. Kropotkin, Reclus, Davison. Londinium, that ancient city, and yet it looked so ordinary. Not that ordinary was bad, of course. London was unfamiliar, that was all, and, as she watched the city emerge as a mass of industry, she longed for familiarity.

Then, the train blew past the first wave of buildings and rolled forward into the city. She watched life milling in the streets— people, buses, cars. Milne and Eric were waiting at the station. She would have an office overlooking these streets, new streets. Bookstores, coffeeshops, theatres, and pubs. Writers and radicals. The city stretched out on all sides. How many million lived in London? Seven or eight times that of Montreal, she reckoned. Coleridge, Gaskell, Rossetti. She was here to start a magazine. Freedom in the arts at a time when that seemed impossible.

A small woman on a seat across from her pointed out bridges and buildings to a young boy staring in awe. His face was pressed against the glass and detached itself only to ask about interesting things that he spotted. The immensity of it all began to strike her. Her fingers trembled slightly and she shifted in her seat, anxious to move. Something stirred inside of her. The worry faded away, and the excitement that had been harboured inside flourished once again. This was London, she thought. It was right here.

The train eased into the station. Marguerite stood and collected her bags. She made her way to the door. Peopled milled and bustled. Shoulders and arms bumped and jostled her. She held firmly to her bags and pressed herself against the wall. She peered through the window. Would she be able to find them in this crowd? The brim of a man's hat pressed into the side of her head. Why didn't he wait to put it on? She stepped back and bumped into an old lady who glared and muttered under her breath. Another man didn't seem to see her and stood on her toes. Eventually, the doors opened and the passengers around her began to pour out into the station.

When she stepped down from the train, she spotted them immediately—Eric, Milne, and a tall woman who she assumed was Ava. She rushed towards them with her bags in her hands and almost ran directly into a constable who was in the process of berating a young man he had firmly grasped by the collar. She stumbled to a halt, made a face behind the constable's back, and then rushed around him through the crowd towards the group.

She threw down her bags and wrapped the two men in a hug. "Milne! Eric! How are you?" she asked. "I can't believe I'm in London!" she added before either of them had a chance to answer. Milne started to speak but then Marguerite pulled back and looked at Ava. "This must be Ava!" she said, and embraced her as well. She pulled back and apologized, "I'm sorry! I'm just so excited to be here," she said. "I haven't really been outside of Canada before."

Ava laughed and began to reply but Marguerite was already speaking again. "Eric! It's been years. How are you?"

Eric smiled. "I'm fine," he said. "But let's move on from this train station and find something to eat. You must be starving." He grabbed one of Marguerite's bags and added, "I think that the policeman's friend might have seen that face you pulled so we'd be wise to move, even if you aren't."

They stepped out of the station and into the street. Four lanes of cars moved slowly up the road. Men and women on bicycles weaved through traffic. Pedestrians moved hurriedly up and down. A man selling fruit from a stall yelled at a passersby. Marguerite had never seen so many people in one place before. A red double-decker bus rolled to a stop in front of them and a produce van slammed on the brakes and the horn simultaneously. They crossed at an intersection and moved down a slightly smaller street. Vans, trucks, and buses were parked along the sides, and cars steadily worked their way down it. Men in hats and suits and women in long dresses and coats ran across the street when the traffic was slowed or stopped. At the end of the street, a policeman stopped traffic to let them cross.

Eric unlocked a car and loaded Marguerite's suitcases into the back. She put her smaller bag in beside them. He opened the doors and they climbed into his car. He pulled out onto the street and joined the flow of traffic moving past fountains, statues, trees, people, and endless towering buildings.

"So, what do you think?" Eric asked.

"It's so lively," she said. "So much bigger than home, and much more colourful than I thought it would be. I was worried when I saw it from the train, but it is amazing. I haven't seen so much activity in my life!"

"Yes," Eric said. "It's a little duller where we are but it's not a long trip in."

"How was your journey?" Ava asked.

"It was long but nice."

"You must be tired now," she said.

"I was but now that I'm here I feel so full of energy." She watched water flow from a statue, falling into a basin surrounded by people. At the bottom, clusters of birds ran for crumbs thrown by laughing men and women. Children ran and played amidst them, disturbing the feeding birds.

"Then we must go out tonight!" Ava said. "Do you dance?"

"Yes," said Marguerite. "That would be fun."

Milne watched Marguerite's eyes fill with wonder and excitement at the city. Eric parked the car again and they clambered back out of the vehicle. Milne straightened his jacket and Marguerite ran her hands through her hair. Eric locked the doors and pointed out a restaurant at the corner of the street. At storefronts and market stalls, people bustled and talked and laughed. Some hurried with their eyes hanging low, grim expressions resting on their faces.

They took a table at the back of the restaurant. They looked at the menus, ordered drinks, and chatted for a while.

"Eric says that you had to close your shop," Ava said.

"Yes, it was a tough operation to run. We had a lot of trouble from the police as well as some Albanian gangsters."

"Gangsters?" Ava asked in shock. "You're teasing me."

"No, it's true," said Marguerite. "We think they may have been paid by the police. They certainly didn't like having us in the neighbourhood. We had a few fires and a lot of broken windows. Alessandro, who worked with me, had a bad run in with them at closing one night." She stopped talking to accept her drink from the waiter. "Anyway, eventually," she said, "it was just too expensive to keep it running."

"That's horrible," Ava said. "At least it meant that you were able to come to London. You must tell us more about the gangsters later."

"Yes, I am happy to be here. It is a bad time for it, though. It's a mess back home."

"In what way?" Ava asked.

"Just last year there were very large mining strikes. Thousands of miners," said Marguerite. "Strike-breakers and police were sent in. The miners battled them in the streets."

"Thousands?"

"Yes. It was huge. They blew up a train track and barricaded asbestos mines and some roads into big mining towns. The police threatened to open fire on them so the strikers had to surrender. Many were beaten and arrested."

"What happened then?"

"They went back to work with few of their demands met. What could they do?"

"Yes, I suppose there isn't much."

"It had its impact. The people supported it—there were too many involved. Even the church was forced to speak up, a bit."

"And you were involved?"

"I did my best to support it. We printed communiqués and demands. It was a very busy time for us."

"They did warn me that you're a radical," said Ava, smiling. Eric shot a sharp glance in her direction.

"Only according to some," Marguerite replied. The waiter returned and they ordered.

"Was it hard to leave Montreal?" Ava asked, after the waiter left.

"No. I know that I'll be back."

"We were so happy that you agreed to come," Eric said.

"And, your parents are in Montreal, too?" Ava asked.

"No," Marguerite said. "But we don't speak much these days. My father's sympathies with fascism are an unfortunate reality."

"I'm sorry," Ava said. "Look at me interrogating you, and you're probably exhausted."

"Not at all. My parents are from a place called Cap-Rouge in Quebec. That's where I grew up. I moved to Montreal alone when I finished school. What about you? Where are you from?"

"New York," replied Ava. "Though, I lived in Vermont for a number of years."

Marguerite nodded. "And is New York much like London?"

"It's very different but busy too," she said.

"Oh! I had an idea on the journey over," Marguerite said, turning to Eric and Milne.

"What was that?" asked Eric.

"Why don't we reprint *Le Refus Global,* translated into English, of course."

"What is *Le Refus Global?*" Eric asked, looking to Milne.

"*Que ceux tentés par l'aventure se joignent à nous,*" Marguerite recited. "*Au terme imaginable, nous entrevoyons l'homme libéré de ses chaines inutiles, réaliser dans l'ordre imprévu, nécessaire de la spontanéité, dans l'anarchie resplendissante, la plénitude de ses*

59

dons individuels." Marguerite paused briefly, and then continued: "*D'ici là, sans repos ni halte, en communauté de sentiment avec les assoiffés d'un mieux être, sans crainte des longues échéances, dans l'encouragement ou la persécution, nous poursuivrons dans la joie notre sauvage besoin de libération.*"

"It's beautiful," Ava said. "But, what is it?"

"Paul-Émile Borduas," Milne said.

"And many others," Marguerite added. "It's a manifesto."

"What is it about?" Ava asked.

"I wonder if Paris will go for it," Eric said. "Maybe you could write a commentary on it."

"I can do that," Marguerite said. "It's about freedom," she added. "Have you heard of the Automatistes?"

After lunch, they brought Marguerite to the neighbourhood and showed her to the office. They took her to the Gargoyle Club that night and met with Carson and his wife Edna. She had a small apartment near Milne and soon settled into a routine which suited her. The first week went quickly.

5

The house was large and narrow. It was brick and stood between two others that looked nearly identical. It had a neatly manicured garden and a set of trimmed hedges leading to the front steps.

In the kitchen, Mary ran from the sink to the stove to stop a pot from boiling over. She lowered the heat and lifted the lid. She heard water running heavily and ran back to the sink to turn it off so that it would not overflow. She had been hired on as a maid but soon found herself filling all of the roles left behind by the now absent help. As she sank her arms into the basin in search of the mixing spoon that she had abandoned midwash, Edna entered the kitchen behind her.

"Mary! This heat is far too low," she said, feeling the pot on the stove. "I don't like having to watch over you like this."

"I'm sorry, Mrs. Ward. It's just …"

The doorbell rang through the house. Mary dropped the spoon back into the sink and began to dry her hands.

"Leave it, Mary. I'll get the door. Turn that heat up. It won't finish in time otherwise," Edna said as she hurried from the kitchen. She fixed her hair in front of the mirror in the hall and then entered the front hall. When she opened the door, Marguerite and Milne were standing on the stoop. She smiled at them.

"Come in!" she said. "Eric and Ava just arrived. They're in the sitting room with Carson."

Milne and Marguerite stepped inside and Edna closed the door behind them. They hung their coats on the rack beside the door and then she led them to the living room where Eric, Ava, and Carson were already comfortable. "Have a seat," she said. "Carson will get you a drink. I'll be in in just a moment."

Carson stood. "How was the walk?" he asked. "Not too cold, I hope."

"Not at all. It was lovely."

Ava stood and crossed the room to greet them. "It's great to see you again, Marguerite. Milne, how are you?"

They hugged and then sat on the empty sofa across from Eric. Ava sat next to him. Carson returned with two drinks and then took his seat as well. "Edna should be in in a moment," he said. "How do you like London so far? How many days is it now?"

"Five days," Marguerite said. "It has been a somewhat disorienting week. There is a lot to adjust to, but I love the city already. There is so much going on."

"When I returned to London it took me months to adjust," he said.

Marguerite smiled. "I hope that it isn't strange, but I went and bought one of your books after we met. I knew your name, of course, but I hadn't read anything you'd written."

"Not *Daffodils,* I hope."

"*Blind Surgery*—it was brilliant."

"Just what Carson needs," Eric said. "A little more fodder for the ego."

"Are you feeling neglected?" Carson asked. "They don't go in for pugilistic prose over here quite as much as they do across the pond."

"Isn't that why I'm here? To fix that?"

Carson laughed. "Well, I'll have to read some of your work now, Marguerite. You ran your own print shop in Montreal, isn't that right?

A sweet aroma began to seep through the hall and into the living room from the kitchen. Marguerite turned her head and breathed deeply. It was a scent reminiscent of Christmas dinner at home, in Cap-Rouge. As her parents had moved alone from France, Christmas was always a small affair. They tried to make up for it by going far overboard with decorations and food. She could picture the little blue house now, peaked roof capped with snow. For the first time in years, she began to miss her parents.

"Yes, I did," she said. "Until the end of the year. We couldn't keep it open any more. The atmosphere for that kind of work is not what it once was."

"What did you publish?"

"Political works, mostly syndicalist. Local and international—it didn't matter as long as it was relevant."

Carson looked confused. He glanced at Milne. "I knew a lot of trade unionists at one time. I was in Spain in '37."

"Were you fighting?" Marguerite asked.

"No. I was on assignment for the *Daily Worker*."

"You wrote for the *Daily Worker*?"

"Yes, I was a member of the party in those days."

"I didn't know that!" Marguerite exclaimed.

Carson smiled. "Most of us are ex-communists. It's one of the reasons why our magazine will be so important. We can serve as an example to the ones that haven't jumped ship yet."

"Serve as an example?"

"To demonstrate that communism is not conducive to cultural freedom," he said. "There is so much conflation now between communism and fascism that it's easy to forget that, at the time, we saw communism as the only hope we had of defeating fascism. When the democrats and industrialists were courting fascists, the communists were standing strong against it. We are the only ones who understand both the appeal and the disillusioning reality. We watched it unfold. Pure anti-communists can't communicate that sentiment."

"I was under the impression that this magazine is to be a celebration of cultural freedom, not of anti-communism," Marguerite said.

"It is," Carson and Eric said together.

"We oppose infringements on freedom of any stripe," Eric said. "Left or right."

"Don't worry," Milne said. "We're going to do this right, Marguerite."

"Marguerite's an anarchist," Ava said, looking at Carson.

Carson glanced around the room, unsure whether or not she was joking. "It's a beautiful ideal," he said politely. "I had my sympathies in years past, right enough, but now ... well, ideologies are best left to the nineteenth century, as far as I'm concerned. They haven't brought us much luck in this one."

Marguerite also glanced around the room. She looked at Eric and Milne, unsure whether or not she should engage. "Liberalism isn't an ideology?"

"Not a hard ideology—it's moderate, that's the strength of it. A mixing and meshing of various systems of the right and left—not dogmatic."

Ava interrupted with a wry smile. "Are you dogmatic, Marguerite?"

Marguerite laughed. "Staunchly," she said. "I am what you call a hardline dogmatist."

"There's a bookshop in Whitechapel that might interest you," Carson said. "It's called ... ah, I can't remember the name. Edna ... Edna!" he called.

Edna appeared around the door. "Yes? I have something on the stove … what is it?"

"What's the name of that bookshop in Whitechapel? You know, the one that Philip and Katherine were talking about last weekend."

"Kavanagh's," she said.

"Yes! That's the one."

"Thank you," Marguerite said, smiling. "Whitechapel … is that far?"

"I'll take you!" Ava said. "Do you know the address?"

"No," Carson said. "It's on Gunthorpe Street."

"Kavanagh's on Gunthorpe—we'll find it," Ava said. "Tomorrow?"

"Tomorrow," Marguerite said. Kavanagh—the name was familiar but she couldn't quite place it. Despite Carson's condescension, she knew that he meant well. Though it was not the hub that it once had been, London was still one of the world's centres for anarchist thought.

"Now," Ava said. "Can we talk about something other than politics?"

Edna re-entered the room and took a seat next to Carson. "Dinner should be ready very soon," she said. "I'm sorry if I'm repeating conversation but how are you enjoying London so far?"

"I like it a lot," Marguerite said. "Though, I was just telling Carson that it is quite a lot to adapt to."

"Yes," Edna said. "When I first came to London I had a horrible time adapting. Now, well, look at the life we have here. I wouldn't rather be anywhere else."

The music stopped. The crackling of the logs in the fire filled the absence left by Coleman Hawkins. Carson stood to turn the record.

"Leave it," Edna said. "We can eat now."

They moved into the dining room where the table was already set. The food was plenty and the meal was slow. They talked jazz and literature, city and childhood. Carson fascinated them with a story of Hemingway from Spain and Marguerite told them her story about Albanian gangsters. When they finished eating, Edna brought out coffee and cake.

"A name," Marguerite said suddenly.

"Yes," Carson smiled. "Nobody has dared to broach it yet, to make the first suggestion."

"Broach," Marguerite said. "That could be a good one."

"It's not bad!"

"It needs to be something that captures the spirit—no propaganda, no political bullshit."

"Pressing Matters," Carson said.

"It needs to be something exportable," Milne said.

"Export."

"The Truth."

"Too conceited," Ava said.

"Witness," said Marguerite.

"It's passive, isn't it?"

"Passive is good in this case," Eric said. "It makes it sound impartial, honest."

"I rather like it," said Carson.

"Milne?"

"It's good," he said. "The best so far."

The doorbell rang and quick footsteps moved from the kitchen down the hallway and into the entryway. Edna and Carson exchanged a glance. Muffled voices carried through the dining room walls. Carson set his napkin on the table and stood.

"I'd better go and check," he said.

"Leave it. She'll send them away."

Carson left the room. Edna sighed. When he reached the entryway, his voice carried loudly back to the group, though the words were inaudible. He came back through the door after a few moments with a stout man in a waistcoat and jacket.

"Carson told me that you had guests," he said. "I am terribly sorry to intrude. I was only stopping by to return a book."

"Harry, these are our newcomers from America and Canada," Carson said, gesturing around the table. "They're working on the magazine. This is Harry Pankhurst Jr., our member of parliament for the Labour Party. A dear friend."

"Do sit," Edna said. "It's no intrusion at all."

"I really mustn't," Harry said. "Sophie will be waiting. Carson would not allow me to leave without being introduced."

"You must both come by then. During the week."

"Of course," Harry said. "I am sorry, again, for the intrusion."

Carson walked him back to the door and saw him off. "Should we move in," he asked when he returned. "Now that we've been disturbed anyway?"

Edna agreed and they stood, abandoning the table, and moved across into the sitting room.

"I should have brought the wine," Carson said. "I'll be back in just a moment."

"No, no—everyone sit!" Edna said. "I'll bring it in." She left the room and returned with glasses. She placed them carefully on the table and stepped out again. Everyone else settled in. The seats were plush and soft. The fire burned, its gentle flicker swam in the dim light. Milne watched it. He was reminded of campfires as a boy. The soft feeling of damp moss on his feet. There was a certain smell the morning after a campfire—a certain sensation took hold of the air and lingered.

Edna tripped carrying the bottle back into the sitting room. When it hit the ground, it shattered. The sound pierced the cozy

67

atmosphere. Carson threw himself from the chair onto the floor next to the coffee table, his face drained of colour.

Edna stooped and knelt beside him. Tears crawled down her cheeks. "I'm sorry," she said. "Darling, I'm sorry. It was just the wine. I dropped the wine. I'm so sorry."

Milne shifted uncomfortably in his chair. He glanced at Ava, who squeezed Eric's hand. Eric looked into the fire. Marguerite watched Carson tremble. The puddle of wine spread itself across the hardwood floor, pooling against the carpet.

When they got off the Underground, the sun, cut by a roof across the road, cast a golden slant on the stone wall. Smoke rose from chimneys above.

Ava thought of Carson. "Some of them didn't really come back," she said.

"And some of them really didn't come back," said Marguerite. Her tone was sharp but she did not mean it to be.

"I'm sorry, di—"

"Thank you for coming with me today," Marguerite said.

"It's my pleasure," Ava said. "I've been looking forward to spending some time together, just the two of us."

A London Transport bus stopped at the corner beside them. They stopped talking and waited as a few people stepped off, then they got on. The bus carried them around the corner and onto a wide street with wider footpaths on either side. They slowly rolled past row upon row of semi-detached buildings and storefronts. Marguerite and Ava silently shared glimpses of bustling bookmakers and pubs. A group of old women crowded around a market cart selling fish. The sun was coming down.

The bus turned another corner and the road narrowed. The brick walls were cracked and dirty. Windows hung open and women and children hung from them. Men played dominos below. A low wall crumbled. A rabbi walked alone.

"It's the next stop," Ava said.

Marguerite nodded. She watched loose onions fall from the back of a market cart rattling along the cobblestones. When the bus stopped, they stepped out and wandered the narrow streets until they found the one they were looking for. The shop itself was down a little alleyway that twisted away from the road. They walked past it twice before noticing a handwritten sign with an arrow pointing down the lane.

The store was small. Pamphlets and leaflets were stacked neatly on a table next to the door. Bookshelves ran along all four walls and smaller ones sat in the centre of the floor. A bearded man sat behind a desk in the corner closest to the door. He looked up when they entered. Ava and Marguerite rounded the store. Ava recognized few titles. She flipped through books carelessly. Marguerite had an armful within moments: *The Selected Works of Voltairine de Cleyre*; *L'Homme et la terre*; *My Disillusionment in Russia*.

Ava lifted a journal from a shelf and opened it, scanning the titles: *RUSSIAN IMPERIALISM: How Menacing is it?*; *CHINA: Despair, Reform, or Revolution?*; *SEEN IN A CROOKED MIRROR: Nineteen-Eighty-Four by George Orwell*. She put it down and looked out a little square window into the alleyway. Pigeons strutted and wobbled on the cobblestone and along the rooftops. Marguerite laughed at some comment made by the bearded man. Ava turned and smiled.

For eight weeks, they drafted. It was immediately apparent that Nicolas and Clifford made a wise decision selecting Carson as an editor. Somehow, he secured an unpublished essay of Virginia Woolf's from her husband. T.S. Eliot sent a letter of support along with a poem "for consideration" within the first three weeks. The poetry section quickly filled with contributors from London. Eric struggled with Carson and managed to have two American poets included as well.

Marguerite translated excerpts from under-appreciated French works and included commentary of her own alongside. Milne and Eric co-edited fiction and essays. They read countless submissions and sent countless solicitations. Over dinner, coffee, and beer, they argued about writers and writing. Though the work was heavy, the weeks were enjoyable. Money flowed in, salaries were high, and benefits were many. Carson seemed to know everyone in London and the long days at the office were met with equally long nights in the city.

6

Eric and Ava sat in the front seat, driving through the countryside just outside of London. Marguerite and Milne sat cramped in the back. It was Friday morning and the first clear day all week. They had sent the first issue of *Witness* to the board in Paris the night before. They were heading out for a weekend in the country to celebrate.

A train curved smoothly across the landscape, pouring plumes of smoke into the sky. The smoke rose above the train and drifted backwards over it. Milne watched it move silently over the tracks. Up close, the train was jerking, clanking and rattling, screeching iron against iron when it turned sharply or let on the brakes. From the backseat of the car, it was a peaceful, serene scene.

The countryside grew. The buildings changed shape and became sparse. They drove for some time, chattering occasionally, but mostly in silence, glad for the break from work and the city. They passed through a small village and Eric stopped for petrol at the pumps. A tractor slowly and steadily rolled through the village beside them. An old woman pushed a little cloth bound shopping basket in front of her. Two old men, with sagging weathered faces, leaned against the wall and laughed.

After filling up, they passed through the village and continued on the road. The houses, shops, and barns faded away behind them. Further up the road, the little red two-door curled its way around a bend, overlooking the sweeping hills and checkerboard of fences and stone walls below. A stream ran perpendicular, trailing towards a small lake tucked in behind a field of sheep. Ava rolled down the window and Milne felt the air rush in against his face. He took off his hat and set it on his knee. Marguerite gazed out across the unfamiliar landscape.

"Is it like you remember?" Eric asked.

"Exactly the same," said Ava.

"Ava came here as a girl," Eric explained. "For a few months."

"You haven't mentioned that," Marguerite said. "What for?"

"To visit an aunt. My mother thought that I should experience English country life and sent me to stay with her sister. I was fifteen though, hardly a child."

"Will you visit while you're here?" Milne asked.

"God no," Ava laughed. "She was a horror."

"She's not joking," Eric said. "I've heard the stories."

"It was around here?" Milne asked.

"Yes. Somewhere very close by. It's why I thought of coming out here this weekend," she explained. "It's beautiful here. I've always wanted to come back, under better circumstances."

After driving a short distance further, Eric slowed to look at a signpost. "I think we've gone too far," he said.

"No," Ava said. "It's further still."

"No," said Eric. "I'm sure that we've gone too far." He turned his head and slowed the car even more. "Where's the map, Milne?"

Milne pulled the map from the side pocket of his jacket. Eric pulled over to the side of the road next to a bush. Ava opened the door and stepped out—she let Milne and Marguerite out of the back seat. Eric got out as well and walked slightly back on the road, as if it would tell him something about where they were.

Milne flattened the map against the hood of the car. Ava ran her finger along the road that they had taken from London. Marguerite lit a cigarette and stared across the countryside. Over the hill, a farmhouse stood beside a barn. A long path led down from the house to another road that she couldn't see. Shifting brown and white spots on the green indicated cows and sheep in distant fields. Between the hills, she spotted a series of green buildings tucked behind fences and barbed wire.

"What is that?" she asked, pointing to the cluster.

Eric looked out across the fields. "A military base," he said. "Probably abandoned. They built a lot of them out here during the war."

"Yes! It is further still," announced Ava. "We haven't come to this crossroads yet." Milne scanned the map and nodded. Eric slipped his hands into his pockets, shrugged, and said nothing. He walked around to the other side of the car and opened the door. They all piled back in. Ava would not allow Marguerite to refuse the front seat and squeezed into the back beside Milne. She leaned over to him as they left. "Eric will be a grump all weekend because he was wrong," she whispered, just loud enough for Eric to hear. Marguerite laughed. Dust billowed from beneath the tires as he accelerated along the road.

It was twenty minutes before they arrived at the crossroads. Eric followed the narrow, winding country road for another twenty. Then, Ava pointed out a side road leading up into the hills away from them. Eric turned the car. After a short climb, the car crested the top of the hill and they looked down over a valley. A lake lay in the middle, surrounded on two sides by a small forest.

"The inn should be just past that lake," Ava said.

"Should we stop for our picnic?" Marguerite asked.

73

Eric nodded and continued down the hill toward the lake. When they arrived, he pulled over at the side of the road. Marguerite got out and went around to the back to unpack their picnic. Milne and Ava squeezed out of the backseat and stretched their legs.

They walked down through thick grass to the rocky shore around the lake. The water was still and dark against the cool air. The trees across the lake blocked out whatever lay beyond. Past the little red car, the hills rose up to the sky. Marguerite set a basket down and Ava twisted the cork from a bottle that she had pulled from somewhere. Eric lit a cigarette and spread a blanket across the dewy ground. Milne stood looking on, feeling a little useless. He looked at the mud creeping its way up the side of his leather shoes. Ava sat on the blanket and Eric took off his jacket. He hung it over a fallen tree. Milne took off his own and did the same. He sat down on the blanket and accepted the sandwich that was handed to him.

Marguerite laughed to herself as she watched some ducks flounder at the edge of the lake. Then she gasped. "Look!" she said. "A swan!"

The swan glided slowly through the water, slipping into the middle of the lake. After a few moments, a second emerged from behind the cover of branches hanging over the shoreline. It followed the first at a short distance, which closed as the other slowed in the water. Ava lay her head on Eric's shoulder. Milne shifted his position on the ground—the earth was jutting beneath the blanket making it difficult to sit comfortably. He thought of the shared moments between Ava and Eric—the closeness that evaded him, despite having known Eric for many more years. There was an intimacy bound in the consciousness of both that was entirely unique to them. He watched Ava hold the bottle by the neck and drink straight

74

from it. Eric's sleeves were rolled up and his arm draped over her shoulders carelessly.

Milne watched the back of Marguerite's head as she watched the swans. Her hair was thick and short. He felt a smile grow involuntarily as he thought of the three of them in university. Marguerite had hated Eric at first, he remembered—a rich American boy with a senator father and Ivy League mannerisms. Eric had also had a tough time coming to terms with who Marguerite was. He wondered exactly when that had changed. Then he wondered, momentarily, if it ever had—they had never actually been that close, he thought. The swans circled one another in the center of the lake. Their long necks bowed delicately toward the water.

"Do you remember Leon?" Marguerite asked, suddenly.

Eric broke into laughter. "Leon!" he cried. "What was his last name again?"

"I can't even remember," said Marguerite.

"He was such as snob."

"It makes you realize how silly we are to watch them," Marguerite said as she looked out at the swans on the lake.

"And yet, look at what we've accomplished."

"Accomplished?" Marguerite replied, laughing. "Is that what we've done?"

"What would you call it?" Eric asked.

"Let's not get started," she said.

"No, please do," said Ava. "I'm intrigued."

"Don't listen to her," Eric said. "She thinks that the entire world is ugly."

"No," Marguerite replied. "That's where people mistake me. I think that the world is beautiful. I think that life is beautiful."

Ava smiled. "So, humans are the problem?" she asked.

75

Marguerite shrugged. "People are beautiful too," she said. "Our relationships. Our lives—there are so many beautiful moments. Thi—" she began, but then cut herself short. "Ah, I've started up again."

"Then you might as well finish," Ava said.

"No. I don't want to argue politics this weekend. Just look around—feel the world around us. It's when we alienate things so much that we get it wrong. When we live in this world of abstractions."

They sat for another forty minutes and ate their lunch by the lakeside. After that, they got back into the car and continued to drive. It did not take long before the little inn was visible on the road. It was a small, white, two-storey building. Large square windows stood out on the front and a brick chimney lifted from the slanted brown roof. The road narrowed as it neared. Eric slowed the car and rattled over the bumps—a strip of long grass ran up the center of the road. There were no other vehicles in sight but a pathway led around the side of the building to a coach house. Instead of following it, he pulled up along the front of the building.

They got out of the car and decided to leave their luggage in the back until they were checked in. A little wooden sign beside the door read *Pleasant The House.*

The main hall was large and comfortable. Tea tables and armchairs were neatly placed around it and a breakfast room sat off to the side. When they closed the door behind them, a little lady with curly hair looked up from the desk.

"Hello!" she called out with a heavy Irish accent. "Come in! You're the ones I've been waiting on, I assume."

They approached the desk.

"I'm Molly," she continued. "This is my inn. You're the American couples from London?"

"Well, we're from London but it's two Canadians and two Americans," Milne said.

"Grand," she said. "We have only one other couple staying with us this weekend—English. Three rooms, is it?"

"Yes, that's right."

After checking in, they brought their luggage to their rooms and then met back downstairs to explore the grounds. They walked through the gardens at the back of the inn and down to a little circular pond surrounding a small island, no more than ten feet across, which contained a bench and a sundial. A short bridge lay across one side of the pond. On the patio at the back of the inn, a few tables and a stone chess board sat out, weather worn but solid. The English couple waved from beside the coach house as they got into their blue four door and went out for a drive.

Marguerite took a book out to the little island where she sat in the sun to read. Eric went off to inquire about the stables and the horses inside. Ava, who was frightened of horses due to a childhood scare, challenged Milne to a game of chess. He agreed.

Despite his initial confidence, Milne knew that he was outmatched within three moves. Within six, he had lost. When she called checkmate, he tipped his King over on the board. With a toothy smile that evoked an irrepressible grin from Milne, Ava proclaimed her victory. She sat in the sun, leaning back in her chair, and he watched her beam. On her island, Marguerite turned the page.

Milne stood in front of the long mirror in his room. It had a slight waver to it—a defect of age or manufacturing—which left the right side of his body misshapen. He stepped to the side and his right arm and leg rippled in the reflection. He touched the baggy skin beneath his eye—it felt puffy and a little bit rough. He wondered if it had always been that way. His hair was starting to grey at the edges around his temple and ear. He felt too young for that—his father's had gone much earlier though, so maybe he was lucky. He adjusted the tie beneath his collar and brushed some lint from his thighs. Milne had spent much of his life wearing the same clothes almost every day. When he was young, it had been a financial necessity. Then, there was rationing. Now, it was habit. He wrapped his watch around his wrist—a pale strip disappeared perfectly beneath the strap. He put his wallet and cigarette case into his pockets and slid his arms through the sleeves of his jacket. It fit well, he was glad to see. He looked pretty good, he thought, besides the unavoidable signs of age. He wondered if Ava was downstairs yet—Marguerite and Eric too. Marguerite was an early riser on the weekend; he couldn't remember if Eric was.

He took the stairs and tugged at the breast of his jacket as he walked. When he stepped into the breakfast room, he saw Marguerite sitting alone drinking a cup of coffee. A twinge of disappointment hit him. She looked up. He waved to her and she smiled and nodded his way. He crossed the floor and sat down at the table with her.

"How was your sleep?" she asked.

"Good," he said. "I slept solidly the whole night. The country air must be doing some good."

She laughed. "I did too. My room has some character but it's of a good kind."

"Do the taps work?" he asked.

"Only the cold."

"Lucky," Milne said. "Neither of mine work. I think I might have broken something when I forced them."

78

Molly hobbled over to the table. "Good morning," she said. "Was everything to your liking last night?"

"Yes, it was just fine."

"Tea or coffee?"

"Tea, please," Milne replied.

"You'll have the full breakfast, I assume?" she asked, glancing disapprovingly in Marguerite's direction.

"Yes, that would be great. No tomato, please."

Molly looked relieved. "It's an awful thing to start the day on an empty stomach," she said. She turned to Marguerite. "Are you sure I can't get you anything else? Sausages? Eggs?"

"Coffee is fine, thank you."

"Toast? Fruit?"

"No, thank you." Marguerite said and shook her head. "I'm just fine."

Molly scowled and turned her attention back to Milne. "I'll be right back with your tea, sir."

When Molly walked away, Marguerite began to laugh. "You would think that I offended her," she said.

"I think you have," said Milne.

From the window, Milne could see the grass glistening with dew. The trees stood tall and prominently along the road. The lake was just visible beyond them.

"Do you miss home much?" he asked.

Marguerite looked out the window as well. "I do," she said. "But I'm happy in London for now. I was a bit worried before coming over that I might like it too much and never make it back to Montreal," she said. "But, I couldn't stay here forever."

Molly returned with Milne's tea and he thanked her. She topped up Marguerite's coffee.

"To tell you the truth," Milne said. "Things have been so busy that I haven't even thought about going back at all since

79

I came over. I've thought about home, of course, but not going back. I don't expect to stay forever either but if the magazine picks up, who can tell?"

Marguerite nodded and smiled.

"What have you been reading?" he asked.

"Colette," she said. "I finished *Cheri* last night before I went to sleep. I don't know why I had not read it before."

"I should probably confess that I've never read Colette."

"You have!" Marguerite exclaimed. "We read *La Vagabonde* in Contemporary French Literature with Dr. Lesage."

"Did we?" Milne asked with shock. "I don't remember that at all."

Eric and Ava came through the doors of the breakfast room. Eric leaned in and made some comment—Ava laughed loudly and squeezed his arm. Milne felt his chest sink. He averted his eyes. Some pulsing sensation worked behind them. He looked back up. Ava smiled.

Milne looked at Marguerite—she was looking back at him. He couldn't tell what the expression on her face meant. He searched her, and then the chairs beside them were pulled out and Eric and Ava sat down. Eric was sitting beside him—Ava sat across the table from Eric. Her eyes were green this morning, he thought. Something in the morning light. They had been bluer yesterday by the lake.

"Good morning," Marguerite said.

"Good morning," said Eric. "How did you sleep?"

"Great," she replied. Milne nodded and sipped his tea.

Molly approached from somewhere. "Full breakfasts, both?" she asked.

"Yes, please," Eric and Ava said simultaneously.

Molly nodded, then looked over at Marguerite and grinned. "Coffee? Tea?" she asked.

"Coffee for both," said Eric. Molly hurried away. Milne watched Ava adjust her necklace. Eric commented upon the morning as he looked out the window over the countryside. Molly returned and set down two mugs of coffee. The steam rose and curled between them.

. The other two guests entered the breakfast room and took the table next to their own. The woman, well dressed, said good morning as she passed. The man nodded and took his seat. Molly took their breakfast orders and filled their cups with tea. The man took out a newspaper and began to read from a section near the front. The woman made eye-contact with Ava.

"Are you staying here long?" she asked.

"No," said Ava. "Just for the weekend."

"Oh! You're Americans! Are you in England long?"

"Yes," Ava said. "Though only my husband and I are American. These two," she gestured at Milne and Marguerite, "are Canadians."

"Ah. I hear that Canada is lovely. What brings you to England?"

"Eric, my husband, and Marguerite and Milne are working on a magazine in London," she said, pointing respectively.

Eric broke in: "Don't let her modesty fool you. Ava is working just as hard as the rest of us."

"How exciting! What magazine? If you don't mind me asking."

"You shouldn't have said that," her husband said, folding his newspaper down and looking at Ava. His eyes explored her with unrestrained interest. "There'll be no stopping her now. She can't get enough of the things."

"Not at all," replied Eric. "It's a magazine for literature but it hasn't been released yet."

"Is that so?" asked the man. He set his paper on the table and leaned over. "Don't have much time for it myself but better that than fashion or gossip, isn't that right?"

The woman smiled weakly. "What kind of literature?" she asked.

"Elizabeth," the man said. "Let these people enjoy their breakfast." He cleared his throat loudly and then lifted his tea cup. "I'm terribly sorry."

"Don't worry about it," Ava said. "Mostly English or American literature. The contemporary stuff."

"And where are you from, Elizabeth?" Marguerite asked.

"We're from Leeds. We're down for a little holiday."

"How nice," said Marguerite. Molly returned with breakfast for the couple and they turned toward one another. They ate in silence as the morning sun streamed in through the window behind them.

After breakfast, they drove 15 km to the next village, following the crooked signs along the road. The windows were down and the air was cool. There was a single main road through the village, which parted around a church in the center. After the graveyard, the road merged and continued through the town again. Three or four side roads weaved away through tight buildings and cottages.

In the rear-view mirror, Milne caught sight of a blue car pulling in to the side of the road between a market cart and a statue. When he glanced back, the car was nowhere to be seen. Marguerite pointed out a bookshop and they parked a little further up. They wandered back to the store.

Inside, the musty smell of dusty tomes hung between wooden shelves. The air was heavy. A teenage girl sat behind the counter at the front, reading. She looked up and smiled as they entered, and then looked back to her book. Milne felt a sense of immense comfort as he watched Marguerite, Eric, and Ava browse the stacks around them. They fingered through pages and commented to one another about authors and titles. Marguerite lifted *For Whom the Bell Tolls* from the shelf.

"After the G.I. bill, all of my courses were filled with young Hemingways," Eric said.

"Look here!" Ava called from a row at the back. When they found her, she was holding up one of Carson's books.

"It's easy to forget how big he is over here," Eric said.

"Not when you're at his parties," Marguerite laughed.

"That's true," Ava said. She replaced the book on the shelf. "Should we get lunch?"

"Yes," said Eric. "Just let me pay for these." He bought three books and Ava bought one. When they left the shop, they wandered down the road in search of a restaurant. They couldn't find one, so they ate at a pub beside the church.

On the way back to the inn, the winding country roads left them feeling sick. They parked along the side and headed into the forest for a walk. They followed a little path through the trees and crossed a stone bridge above a stream. The fresh air felt nice. Leaves and sticks were strewn across the ground. Ferns and grass grew up beside the path. They wandered slowly and talked quietly. Birds sang, and the sounds of the forest surrounded them.

They reached a little clearing and the path began to fade. The undergrowth thickened, and the way ahead was lost.

"I think we'll have to turn back," said Eric.

They all agreed. As they turned, Milne looked up the hill beside them. Through the trees, looking down over the hill, he saw a little blue car. He could see the shape of a man through the window. "Look," he said, pointing to it.

Ava turned and looked at it. "That car belongs to the couple from the inn," she said. "It was parked beside the coach house."

"I thought I saw it when we were in the village too," said Milne.

"Do you think they followed us back?" asked Ava. "Why would they do that?"

Eric stepped from the path and began to climb the hill towards the car. Milne hesitated but decided to follow him up. As soon as they began to climb, the car began to roll away. Through the window, they could clearly see the face of the man they had spoken with that morning.

The sign beside the door read *Pleasant The House.* Willowherb grew wild along the edges. No vehicles were parked out front.

"Do you think they're here?" asked Ava.

"They could have parked in the carriage house again," said Marguerite. "Like yesterday."

Eric parked along the front of the inn and turned off the engine. He and Ava stepped out of the car, and then moved the seat so that Milne and Marguerite could climb out. As soon as they stepped inside the inn, they saw Elizabeth and her husband. They were sitting in the lobby drinking tea. The group stopped walking momentarily, and then Eric moved across the room towards them.

"Did you have a nice drive?" he asked.

Elizabeth looked up and smiled. "Yes, we did," she said. "It's a lovely village, isn't it?

Eric looked past her to her husband. "Is everything alright?" he asked.

The man looked up from his paper with confusion. "Yes, why?"

"You were watching us in the forest," Eric said.

He folded his paper down and smirked. "We weren't watching you. We saw your car along the road and wanted to make sure that you hadn't broken down."

"But you left when we started up the hill toward you."

"Yes," the man said. "I suppose we did."

"Did you have a nice drive?" asked Elizabeth.

"We did."

"The weather is almost perfect today," she said. "It would be lovely to take a picnic down by the lake. The swans are supposed to be beautiful."

Eric was caught off guard—before he could respond, she smiled and stood. "Good evening," she said, then she turned and walked away from the table. Her husband followed closely behind.

Ava, Milne, and Marguerite smiled as the couple passed, and then approached Eric.

"Well?"

"I don't know," Eric said. "They said that they were just checking if we had broken down, but they left before they could have known. And then she said something about the lake ... she mentioned the swans."

"The swans?" Ava asked.

"Yes, she said that the swans are supposed to be beautiful."

"That's odd. Who do you think they are? What should we do?"

"I don't know," Eric said. "What do you do in a situation like this?"

Ava moved to the front desk and rang the bell. After a few moments, Molly appeared from a little room behind the desk.

"Molly," Ava said. "What can you tell us about that couple from Leeds?"

Molly leaned across the desk with intrigue. "Why?" she asked. "What would you like to know?"

"They're just … unusual. They're making us rather uncomfortable, actually. We think that they might have been following us today."

Molly stood up straighter. She looked skeptical. "Following you? Why would they do that?" she asked.

"That's what we've been wondering."

Molly stared at her coldly. "What kind of an inn do you think I run?"

Ava stepped back. "No," she said. "It isn't that, it's …"

"They checked out just before you came in," Molly said. "They've already cleared out their room. I'm sure that they'll be gone within the hour, so you have nothing to worry about."

"Oh, ok. Thank you," Ava said. She looked at Eric. "Well, what should we do?"

"Let's just wait and see if they leave," said Marguerite. "It's probably nothing."

Ava nodded and turned back to Molly. "We'll just have some tea then, please."

"I'll bring it over to you," she said.

They sat at a low coffee table in the corner of the room beside a window. The sun was slowly slipping in the sky.

"They do seem rather harmless," Ava said. "More or less. Just unusual."

"Unsettling," Eric said. "I don't like that man."

"I liked her though," said Marguerite.

Ava nodded. "The husband wasn't very likeable. What was his name?"

Marguerite shrugged. "I can't remember."

The sound of an engine coming to life could be heard through the windows.

"They must have gone out the back," Milne said.

86

Eric stood and looked out the window. The little blue car came into sight around the corner. It passed the front door and then turned onto the road. It kicked up a trail of dust which hung in place and then began to settle. "Well, they're gone now."

"I think it's best to just forget them," Ava said. "We still have the whole evening ahead of us. Let's make the most of it."

Molly set a silver tray on the coffee table. She unloaded four cups, a sugar bowl, and a little jug of milk. "I'll be back with the pot in just a moment," she said. She returned with it shortly after.

They drank their tea and talked until Molly came back for their cups and told them that dinner would be ready in an hour. Then, they retired to their rooms.

Milne hung his jacket on the back of the desk chair in his room. There was a little shelf on the bedside table with a few books neatly stacked upon it. He stooped to look at them. The wooden boards creaked beneath his soles. The first book on the shelf was *The Wild Swans at Coole,* by William Butler Yeats; the next was *The Death of the Heart* by Elizabeth Bowen; the third was *The Heat of the Day,* also by Elizabeth Bowen.

Milne took the last book from the shelf and stood. His knees ached from crouching. The rain began to fall again outside, clattering against the roof and windows. As it did, he sat back on the bed and began to read: *That Sunday, from six o'clock in the evening, it was a Viennese orchestra that played. The season was late for an outdoor concert, already leaves were drifting onto the grass stage. ...* He felt the rough grain of the paper in his hands. He lost himself, forgetting about the cigarette that burned in his fingers until he turned the page.

He remembered things that no one spoke of anymore: women who found men when their husbands were away, women who hated men who did not go, lives that were full and

87

whole at home. After some time, he heard Marguerite leave her room. He looked down at his watch and realized that it was time for dinner. He marked his page and put down the book. He took his jacket from the chair and put it on, then went back downstairs.

Dinner was long and slow. They ate and talked and laughed. When it was done, Molly brought them coffee and they convinced her to sit with them. She brought out a pack of cards and taught them a game called 25. When the coffee was done, she found a bottle of brandy. She told no stories of the past and when they asked, she would not speak of it. It became dark and Eric began to yawn. Molly stood and cleared the table—Marguerite offered her help and was sharply rebuked, so they said thank you and goodnight, gathered their things, and slowly climbed the stairs back to their rooms above. Milne undressed and lifted the window to let in the air. Little droplets came with it, splattering against the wooden sill.

He could hear Molly tidying in the room beneath him. He could see the glow of the moon and stars outside. He picked up *The Heat of the Day* and continued from where he had left off: *She wanted to burn the lot—sorry for the petals of the roses for having fallen here at the end of their lovely life. …* He sank in and did not emerge again for several hours. He lived in its world—London, just a few years before when the bombs were falling. It was a wonder that this book found him as it did.

It moved him—it seemed entirely right and whole. It was a book about them, he thought—about an entire generation just a little younger than the century. If he had not come to London when he did, he would not have known this book at all. … *Robert was associated with the icelike tinkle of broken glass being swept up among the crisping leaves with the charred freshness of every morning. She could recapture that 1940 autumn only in*

sensation, thoughts, if there were any, could not be found again.
She remembered the lightness, after her son had left, of loving no
particular person left in London—till one morning she woke to
discover that lightness gone. ... his eyes were too tired to read on,
so he closed the book and set it on the bedside table.

Ava and Eric were talking in the next room. He pressed the
palm of his hand against the wall to feel the slight reverberations
through it. It was difficult to lie alone for so long, and he was
frightened by the thought that it could go on for much longer
still. When he drifted off, it was not the clatter of rain against
the roof that lulled him to sleep but the gentle murmur of voices
behind the wall.

In the morning, the golden country sun woke him. The curtains
were parted and a solid beam of light came through: its swell
filled the room. He washed his face and dressed and then went
down for breakfast. Marguerite sat alone in the breakfast room
with a cup of coffee, looking out over the garden. A book, *Native
Son* by Richard Wright, sat on the table in front of her.

Milne smiled and sat with her and together they watched the
sun rise a little higher. While he sat, Molly set a pot of tea on
the table and returned shortly with a full breakfast. When he
heard footsteps on the stairs, he tampered the feelings that rose
and greeted his friends with a smile. They ate together in relative
silence. He watched Marguerite across the table. He sometimes
wondered how they had ended up so close. They were worlds
apart, in many ways. They'd grown up differently. She'd grown
up Catholic, French-Canadian. To him, French-Canadians had
been neighbours and strangers. His world had been English—
not just in language, but in identity and allegiance. To his

89

parents and friends, war had been a matter of duty and valour. It had been hard for him after. Marguerite had made it easier.

When they finished, he stood and looked down at the table. His eyes lingered on the ring of colour left on the filter of a cigarette in the ashtray. He picked up his own case and slipped it into his pocket. Then, he went back upstairs, retrieved his coat, hat, and suitcase, and returned to the lobby. They settled up one by one.

"Oh!" Molly said when he reached the counter. "Mr. and Mrs. Haydon left something for you. I nearly forgot."

She disappeared into the room behind the counter for a moment and then returned with something in her hand. She held it out to him—his eyes fell. He scanned the cover of the book she held: *The Foxhunt.*

He took it from her slowly. Ava, Eric, and Marguerite turned to look in silence. His fingers trembled as he opened the cover. *For Jules and Camille,* it read. Beneath that, in a scrawling hand, was his signature.

7

In London, Milne took the stairs slowly. He dropped his luggage beside the door when he entered his apartment. He opened the suitcase and took *The Foxhunt* from it. He flipped through it again. Except for the first page, it was unmarked. Who were the Haydons? How had they come across this copy of his book? Why had they left it for him? He thought back to the conference in Paris. He had been concerned about the couple there, before they had asked him to sign their book.

He set the novel down and scanned the apartment. It felt odd. Every window left him feeling exposed. He looked down at the alleyway below and then into the windows across from him, capturing slivers of other people's lives. He wandered through the kitchen, the living room, and the bedroom. In the bedroom, he ran his hands along the rough, patterned wallpaper. A drawer on the dresser was open a crack—a piece of fabric was caught in the gap. He looked around the room and began to wonder if things were where he had left them. Could somebody have been in his apartment while he was gone?

He went back into the kitchen and took a glass from the drying rack beside the sink. He turned on the tap and tested the temperature. Then, he looked down at the glass. He eyed it. He ran his fingers around the rim and the inside. Was there a film inside, or was he just imagining it? He lifted another glass. It felt glossy. He took the rest of the glasses and cutlery from the drying rack and put them back into the sink. He opened the cupboard and removed the plates and bowls. He filled the sink with hot water and soap and scrubbed them all. There was not enough room on the drying rack so he lay hand towels across the counter and spread the kitchenware over them to dry.

He looked around the kitchen. Dishes and knives surrounded him on all sides. It was stuffy. It was small. He was losing it—he needed to get out. He grabbed his coat from the hook beside the door, left his suitcase on the floor, and left the apartment.

He wandered along the street, past postboxes, lights, and telephone wires. A woman hung laundry from a window. A worker leaned on the railing at a job site. A postman whistled past. Milne tried to remember if he had ever seen them before. He went into an antique shop and bought a jackknife. The blade felt small and weak. He put it in his coat pocket and left it there. It felt better to have it.

When he arrived at the office, Carson was already there. He told him what had happened in the country and Carson seemed troubled.

"I don't know who they were," Milne said. "At first, it just made us uncomfortable but the book has me concerned."

"How do you think they got a hold of it?"

"I don't know. Maybe they knew the couple in Paris."

"Have you spoken to Nicolas?"

"No," said Milne. "Have you heard from him yet?"

"Not yet," said Carson. "But I haven't been in all weekend, either. We were visiting Edna's parents."

Milne stepped over to his desk and picked up the phone: he dialed and listened; he spoke to an operator briefly; he listened;

the line connected, rang twice, and then Nicolas was on the other end. "Hello?" he said.

"Nicolas, it's Milne."

"Milne," he said. "How are you?"

"Concerned, to tell you the truth. We had a strange encounter this weekend."

"What do you mean by that?"

Milne sat down on the hard wooden chair and tried to work through the phrasing of what he wanted to say. "There was an English couple staying at the inn we visited in the country. They sort of followed us around while we were there, and when we checked out, we discovered that they left a copy of my book at the desk for me—it was one that I signed for a young couple in Paris."

"It wasn't the same couple?"

"No, I don't know how they got it," Milne said. He looked over at Carson, who was listening closely. "Do you think that they could have been working together?"

"In what way?"

"I don't know. Could they ..." Milne trailed off and glanced at Carson again, feeling somewhat foolish. "We were wondering if they could be Soviets, or something."

There was a pause on the other end of the line. Eventually, Nicolas spoke: "What would Soviet agents be doing following you around at an inn, in the middle of nowhere, with a copy of your own book?"

"I don't know, Nicolas, but I can't think of any reasonable explanation for this. You know better than I that the Soviets are all over literature right now."

"I'll see what I can find out, Milne. Did you try to ask them about it?"

"No. They left before we checked out. That's when we were given the book."

"Maybe they found it in a bookstore."

"That seems unlikely. I signed it in Paris a few months ago. They didn't mention anything about it and they didn't act like they knew who we were."

"It does seem odd," Nicolas said. He was quiet for a moment on the other end. "You know, I wouldn't put it past those bastards, either. I'll look into it."

"Thank you," Milne said, though he felt no relief.

"Listen, there's something else we need to talk about. Cliff thinks that the draft is too literary."

"Our draft?"

"Yes."

"What do you mean too literary?" Milne asked. "It's a literary periodical."

"A cultural periodical," Nicolas said. "We need more essays. This is the first issue. Readers need to know where we stand."

"Where we stand?" Milne asked, cradling the phone to his ear. "This whole thing was meant to be non-political—an expression of free culture."

"And we agree upon what type of society is necessary to enable that expression," Nicolas said. His voice was tinny on the other end, somehow strengthening his accent. "We need to make that clear from the beginning. The letter from the editor will do some of the job but we need two more essays clarifying things. When Marguerite's is done, I'd like to read it over."

"Of course, but why? We have three perfectly capable editors here," Milne said. He looked through the window beside him at the grey skies over the city. "Can we not let the content speak for itself?"

"It's an indirect game we're playing," Nicolas said, "but not that indirect. The readership are artists and intellectuals—the conscience of society. If you win them over the rest will follow

94

but for that to work, they need to know what they're buying. Make it easy for them."

Milne cleared his throat. "Listen, Nicolas. If you let us run this right, we can easily become *the* English language cultural magazine within a few issues—not just in Europe but in Asia and maybe even South America, where your neutrality issue is the strongest. With the writers and funding we have, we can be the idol of the intellectual world. If we come in heavy-handed, we'll turn them away just like we did in Paris." Carson raised his eyebrows and mouthed something. Milne held up a finger and listened to the other end.

"Freedom is fragile, Milne. Our job is to build a space in which it can exist. We need to erect boundaries—safeguard this space from things that threaten its existence. Carving out a pocket like that in this intellectual climate will require some heavy-handed digging. How else can we expect to outdo Soviet propaganda?"

"I understand bu—"

"Cliff was very clear," Nicolas said, interrupting him. "If you want the magazine to get out, you'll need to get this done. We don't have much time before the conference in Berlin, so the less time wasted the better." The line clicked and went dead.

Milne set the handset down and leaned back in his chair. Papers scattered the desks, books and journals were stacked on every other surface. He looked down at the draft in front of him. *Editors: Carson Ward, Eric Felmore, and Milne Lowell.* Clifford and Nicolas weren't mentioned anywhere in the entire issue.

"What was that?" Carson asked.

"We need to make changes or they won't put it out," he said.

"What changes?"

"They want more essays, in the interest of making our views clear to the reader."

Carson walked over to Milne and looked over his shoulder at the draft. "In order to add that much, we'll have to cut something significant," Carson said. "Essays take up space."

Milne flipped through the pages of the draft, searching for something that they could take out. It wouldn't be Eliot or Woolf. At least Marguerite was safe too. Carson had two poems in there. Milne was aware of Carson's eyes over his shoulder. He lingered briefly and then continued flipping.

"Too literary? Absolute bollocks," Carson muttered behind him. They heard footsteps on the landing outside and looked up from the desk. Eric opened the door and stepped inside.

"Morning, boys," he said. He hung his coat on the rack and turned to face them. "What's the matter?" he asked, when he saw their faces. "News about the weekend?"

"I just got off the line with Paris," Milne said. "They think that the draft's too literary. They won't put it out."

"Too literary?"

"Cliff wants to make room for political essays."

"He told you that?"

"Nicolas did."

"What the hell are they thinking? It's a literary journal, for Christ's sake." He strode over to the desk and picked up the draft. "What do they want cut?"

"They didn't say."

He threw the pages down. "Over my dead body," he said. He lifted Milne's phone and dialed. He spoke to the operator and waited. He twisted the cord impatiently. He slammed the phone back onto the receiver. He picked up a pen from the desk and tapped it. "We'll see about this," he said. "We'll see about this." He opened a drawer and took a piece of paper from Milne's desk. He brought it over to his own and wrote furiously for a few minutes, folded the letter, and sealed it in an envelope.

96

He stood up, grabbed his coat, and headed for the door. "I'll see to this," he said. "Don't cut a goddamn thing!"

The door slammed behind him.

The tile floor beneath the kitchen table was cold against her feet. Ava wished that she had worn slippers. The furnace in the corner burned so that the heat washed over half of her body but left the other side bare to the air. Papers and files littered the table. She lit a cigarette and leaned over them. She was glad to be done. She pushed aside the first sheet of paper to look at the list of contributors. These names had seemed mystic months before. They seemed nothing short of normal now—the artificiality of fame. It existed in the mystification itself. In the abstraction of the man—that was something Marguerite had said one night.

The kettle began to whistle and she stood to remove it from the burner. Steam rolled up the wall behind the stove. She turned on the switch and lifted the kettle onto a cold burner. She looked around the flat. It still didn't feel like home. She looked at the clock on the wall. She wondered if they would go out tonight. She had stayed in all day.

Eric climbed the front steps of the apartment building. What the hell were they thinking in Paris? This was *his* magazine—he was supposed to have control. What was the point of being the editor if you had to answer to someone else? He had been tasked with revitalizing and strengthening European culture—he needed authority to do so. He would take the train to Paris, he thought, to sort this mess out in person.

He opened the door and stepped into the building. He climbed the stairs to the fifth floor. He knew America—he was

97

American. Nicolas, Clifford—they had great respect for it, but they were not the experts that they thought they were. If they truly wanted to accept the leadership of America in the post-war world, it was time to step aside. More political? That was entirely contrary to the plan. It was necessary to win the mind in order to sway it. He turned the handle to the apartment. It was locked. He knocked. On the other side, he heard hurried footsteps and then the sound of the sliding bolt. The door opened. Ava's smile was wide.

"You're home early!" she said.

Eric stepped inside. "Those bastards in Paris rejected our draft," he said.

"They did? What for?"

Eric threw his coat over the back of a chair. "They thought it was too literary! Imagine that! They want it to be more political!"

"Too literary? It's a literary periodical!"

"I know, Ava. It's ridiculous."

"What are you going to do?"

Eric paused. He looked at Ava. For the first time, he realized that she might not approve of his plan. "I'm going to go to Paris," he said.

Ava was silent for several moments. Eric avoided looking directly at her. She waited for him to meet her eyes. After some time, she spoke. "You can't speak with them on the phone?"

"Milne already has."

"And?"

"They wouldn't listen to him."

"What do you think? That you'll stroll into Paris and throw your weight around and they'll just change their minds? It's their magazine, Eric, whether you like it or not."

"I'm the editor," he said.

"And they're the money," Ava said. She sat on the edge of the table and crushed her cigarette in the ashtray. She put her hand on his arm.

Eric didn't respond.

"You knew that this was the deal," she said. "You can make it work. Can't you?"

Eric stayed silent. He leaned on the table and stared down at the papers littering it. Ava sighed. She felt sorry for him—she knew how helpless he must have felt. She stepped forward and rested her hand on his tensed shoulder. "Can I at least come with you?" she asked.

He stood up, shrugging her hand off. "This is business, Ava. I'll be in and out. Only there as longs as it takes to sort this mess out."

Ava turned away. "You're so ungrateful," she said. "I moved to London for you."

"Oh, come on. You wanted to be here as much as I did."

"What about those people at the inn? Did Milne tell Nicolas about that? We could be in danger."

Eric didn't reply. Ava sat down on the bed and lit another cigarette. The blankets felt damp beneath her. Everything was damp in London. She looked at the glazed window beside her. Paint chipped from the frame. She twisted the curtain between her fingers absently.

Eric looked at Ava, sitting on the edge of the bed. Her face was masked with exaggerated distress. What was she really thinking? he wondered. In some remote part of Siberia, Russian engineers, huddled for warmth in a basement shelter, tirelessly worked calculations, establishing, to the most finite details, how to deliver nuclear fallout to this very city. Meanwhile, Ava crossed her arms on the bed and stared at him with distaste. Eric looked away. Small-minded, he thought.

Ava leaned back on the bed. Look at him, she thought. So lost in this work that everyone else fell away. If they forgot what it was all for—to protect these very moments, these relationships—what was the point? Marguerite was right, she thought. Abstraction was the crime. He didn't care that he was needed here in London. He wanted to rush in and do something impulsive. Save the day—be the hero.

"How are we supposed to deal with everything here if you're over there?" she asked.

"If I'm over there, you won't need to deal with anything here. I'll talk to them."

"Milne already has."

"Not in person," Eric said.

"We need you here," she said. "I need you here."

"I'll only be gone a few days."

The next morning, without mentioning it to anyone but Ava, he took the train from London to Paris. After two days, he wrote a letter informing them, amidst rantings about editorial freedom, that things were moving slowly—he would be in Paris for at least another week.

8

Milne leaned back from the pages in front of him. Ava set a cup of coffee on his desk. "Here," she said. "You look like you need a break from that."

"Thank you," Milne said, taking the coffee.

Ava had a cup of her own. Gingerly, so that she wouldn't burn her mouth, she tilted the mug and tested the heat of the coffee against her lips.

"Don't be too thankful," she said. "Cassandra made the coffee."

"I'll be sure to thank her as well," he said. He looked out the window behind him. "It looks cold out now."

"It is," Ava said. "I just came in. I can't get used to this English cold. It's different than the cold at home."

"It cuts right through your clothes."

Ava nodded. "How's the work going today?" she asked.

"It's tough. I still don't know what to take out. We worked so hard on the first draft."

"I know," she said. "I'm sorry about that."

"Hopefully Eric will have some luck in Paris."

"Yes," Ava said. Milne leaned back in his chair and straightened his tie. A strand of hair had fallen out of place and was hanging down his forehead, nearly reaching his brow.

"Here," she said, and leaned over the desk to smooth the loose strand back into place. Her fingers brushed his skin. He turned to look away.

"I'm sorry," Ava said.

"Not at all." He lifted his cigarette case from his desk and opened it. He offered one to Ava. She took it and he lifted his lighter. She leaned forward again and drew on her cigarette, holding it between her fingers and lips to the flame. Her left hand rested on the table, her ring against the oak. Her perfume was strong and sweet. She closed her eyes while she bent over the lighter. Her cigarette took and she leaned back. He lit one of his own.

Milne felt awkward. "You've travelled quite a bit, haven't you?" he asked.

"I suppose that I have," she said. "Not nearly as much as I would like."

He thought of Montreal, shaded streets and postmen, neighbourhoods and country towns. "I haven't travelled a huge amount," he said. "It's one of the reasons I took this job. So that I could see a little more of the world."

Ava smiled. "Where would you like to go?"

"Oh, I don't know. Places far away. China, Russia."

"The red states excite you?"

Milne laughed. "Maybe I will have to wait a while for those. Vienna, Prague."

"I love Vienna. I haven't been anywhere better."

"Really? What's it like?"

"Magnificent. Massive bright palaces, squares, statues. Fountains and gardens. The opera house is spectacular. You can feel something in the air there," she said.

"I'd love to see it someday."

"Maybe we should run away from all of this," she laughed. "Move to Vienna. Smoke Turkish cigarettes beneath the stars. Never think about a semicolon again."

Milne's focus melted away. He felt the pages beneath his hands. He caught himself staring absently past Ava. "Yes," he said, after a long pause. "Isn't that an idea."

"What is it?" Ava asked.

"I …" he shifted his gaze back to her. "Nothing. I just feel like there's a lot more to life than this," he said. "You make me envious is all."

"What are you envious of?"

Milne felt the warmth of her breath against his cheek. He hadn't realized how close they were sitting. "The travel," he said hastily.

Ava parted her lips to reply but the door opened. Marguerite and Carson entered the room. Ava leaned back quickly.

"Milne!" Carson announced. "Marguerite has figured it out."

"What has she done?" he asked. He rose from his chair behind the desk. From the corner of his eye, he watched Ava turn to the window.

"I think … well," he said, turning to Marguerite, "go ahead and tell them yourself."

"We should wait to hear from Eric first," Marguerite said. "If we ask for a small page increase, we can print one more overtly political essay at the start—something from the files. Then, instead of cutting anything, why don't the editors—you three—just write introductions to each piece which contains political significance."

Milne nodded. "That is a good idea. Carson could just write one introduction for the entire poetry section."

"I still don't like it," Marguerite said, "but I can't think of a better alternative. And besides, if it is your own honest literary criticism it won't be so bad. I can strengthen my own piece to counteract the intrusion. What do you think, Ava?"

Ava turned from the window. "It isn't my decision to make," she said.

"It's as much yours as ours," Marguerite said. "I'm beginning to think that it isn't ours either but I'd like to hear your opinion."

"I think it's a good compromise," she said. "If Eric is unable to change their minds."

Milne sat at his kitchen table late into the night. He read and re-read essays—nothing was a good fit. It was difficult to find even one new essay that didn't feel out of place. They had meticulously curated the first issue, and now the flow was interrupted.

He went over to the stove and lifted the kettle from it. He filled it with water and set it back on the element. He eyed the essay on the table, scratched with handwriting and editorial marks. It was overt, not subtle at all, but that was what Cliff and Nicolas wanted. He sat down at the table and set the essay aside. He took a blank sheet of paper and thought about Marguerite's idea. He took the draft of *Witness* from his bag and looked over the stories he had chosen for it.

The kettle began to whistle and he took it from the stove. He readied a pot of tea, then he sat back down and began to write.

A slight breeze entered the courtyard. Trees vibrated. Marguerite sat in the dewy grass reading. It was the story of Italy a hundred years before; of Risorgimento; of Revolution; of Arthur and Gemma ... *a soft spring night, warm and starlit. The water lapped against the stone walls of the basin and swirled in gentle eddies round the steps with a sound as of low laughter. Somewhere near a chain creaked, swinging slowly to and fro. A huge iron crane towered up, tall and melancholy in the dimness. Black on a shimmering expanse of starry sky and pearly cloud-wreaths, the figures of the fettered, struggling slaves ...*

She heard a rustle behind her. She looked. Milne stepped off the path. She held out her arm and he took hold. She used his grasp to stand.

"I went inside," he said. "When I couldn't find you, I came out here."

She smiled, slipped into her shoes.

"Do you need anything from inside?"

"No," Marguerite said. She slipped her book into her handbag. "I'm ready to go."

They left the courtyard. It was cool and the breeze was somewhat stronger in the street. They wandered slowly toward the cinema. They bought tickets at the door and sat in the middle near the aisle. The crowd was thin. The lights went down. Shapes shifted, danced. Vienna appeared. Harry Lime did not. It was bright when they left. They parted at the doors. Milne went to the office and Marguerite met a friend for dinner.

When he reached the office, he rang Paris and ran through the work that they had been doing. Nicolas told him that Eric would likely be returning home within a few days. Milne pitched Marguerite's solution to their problem. Nicolas told him that he would run it past Cliff, but that it seemed fine.

Milne began to thank him but Nicolas cut him off. "While I have you on the phone," he said, "there's something else that I've been meaning to mention. It's a little delicate."

"What is it?"

"You know we are very happy with Marguerite's work," Nicolas said, then paused. Milne waited in silence. After a moment, Nicolas continued. "There is some concern on the board about the number of lunches and dinners that Marguerite is taking with single young women."

Milne was stunned. He said nothing.

"It won't necessarily be an issue," Nicolas added. "As long as she remains discreet."

There were a few moments of silence on both ends of the line. Then Nicolas said goodbye and hung up the phone.

Milne placed his own handset back on the receiver. He rubbed his eyes with the palms of his hands. How did Paris even know what Marguerite was up to in London? Marguerite's social life should have been of no concern—hell, he thought, it was no secret that Carson had lived with a man for years before his marriage to Edna. He leaned back in the chair. He didn't know whether or not to bring this up with Marguerite. It would upset her.

He picked up his pen and tried to read the article before him. He wanted to push it from his mind. Nicolas had spoken as if the comment was a friendly warning, though he couldn't help but feel that it was some kind of threat. Had Eric said something to them?

Milne worked slowly and distractedly. He found himself reading the same sentences over and over without taking in any information. Late in the afternoon, Ava came to the office to do some work. She took the empty desk beside Milne. The presence of another person jolted him from his rut and, as soon as they settled in, he worked intensely. The hours passed quickly. At a certain point in the evening, when it was getting to be fairly dark, Cassandra, the secretary, came in and asked if they needed anything else before she left for the night. They assured her that they would be alright, and she sorted out her desk before leaving the office.

The next time Milne looked up from his article, the room was dark except for the little pool of yellow light pouring from the lamp on his desk and its twin on Ava's. Ava was watching him work.

"Sorry," she said, when their eyes met. "You looked so focused. I didn't want to disturb you."

Milne looked at his watch—it was 11:15. "Oh! I'm sorry. I didn't realize quite how late it was," he said.

"Not at all," Ava said. "I don't mind the company."

Milne stood and collected his coat from the rack beside the door.

"I don't mean to impose," Ava said, "but it's awfully dark. Would you mind walking me some of the way?"

"Of course," he said. "I wouldn't think of letting you walk alone."

Ava locked the doors as they left the office. They stepped into the street—it was a colder night than usual. A man stood in the darkened entryway a few doors down from their own. Though he knew it was ridiculous, Milne felt his arms tense. He eyed the man as they passed. He readied himself for harassment—robbery, maybe. His left hand slipped into his coat pocket and fingered the jackknife. They passed unimpeded and he relaxed, though he felt uneasy about the man behind him in the dark. He felt the cold air on his neck and face, and he saw Ava shiver beside him. He took off his coat and lay it across her shoulders, using the opportunity to look behind them. No one was there.

"You don't have to do that," she said. "We don't have far to go."

"It's only fair. I'll have it on the way back," Milne replied. "Besides, I have my jacket."

They turned the corner at the end of the block, walking absentmindedly toward a blue light outside of the police station a little further up the street. The glow of streetlights sparsely dotted the street. They drifted in a slow and steady rhythm in and out of the warm rings of light as they walked. The final destination didn't really occupy any space in his mind—the walk was too currently present. Ava smiled and shrugged her shoulders, burying herself in his greatcoat to stave off the cold. Milne put his arm around her shoulders and pressed his body against her side.

"It's beautiful in London," she said. "Isn't it?"

Milne didn't look around. "It is," he said. "I'm glad that I came."

"I am too," she said.

They walked slowly for some time. The streets were empty and quiet. When they reached the block that she lived on with Eric, Milne felt his chest empty out a little. They reached the front steps and he put out his hand to help her up them in her heels. Her fingers were thin and cold, and he thought that they lingered too long in the palm of his hand before she turned to unlock the door. She lifted off his coat and handed it back to him. He slid his arms into the sleeves and felt the warm weight of it press against him. A slight breeze swept up from the ground and lifted itself around his legs and back—he shivered and shrugged his shoulders. The chill remained beneath the warmth of the coat, and he shifted anxiously on the steps. Ava opened the door and turned to him. She reached out and took hold of his arm, and then kissed him on the cheek.

"Goodnight, Milne," she said, and then stepped inside and closed the door. He stared at the closed door for a moment that dragged on, and then looked up at the front of the building and then into the cloudless sky above, watching the dancing stars. He turned from the building and walked down the steps to the street, each step further echoed through him. His hands were buried deep in the pockets of his coat and he walked slowly down the street the same way that he had come.

He decided, mostly so that he could keep the night alive, that he should go back to the office and pick up the essays that he had been working on. Though he walked as slowly as he could, it seemed much faster on the way back. A clock tower chimed in the distance. When the bells faded, the wind carried a leaf across the ground, scraping and trailing loudly in the calm of the night. Milne rounded the corner to his office.

Immediately, he noticed that the man he had passed earlier was still leaning against the entryway of the building—the glow of his cigarette gave him away. Milne stopped walking and leaned against a tree. Another man stepped out of their office building and walked towards the first. He handed him a folder of some sort and kept walking. The first man stepped out of the doorway and walked down the street toward Milne. Milne quickly bent and pulled his shoelace loose, and then began to retie it slowly. The man slowed as he approached. He looked closely at Milne's hunched figure. Milne looked up. The man nodded to him and quickened his pace, clutching the folder beneath his arm.

Milne stood up and ran to the office building. The front door was locked. He looked down the street—the silhouette disappeared around the corner. Milne glanced the other way—the second man was also gone. He thought of the couple in Paris and the couple at the inn, still unexplained.

He let go of the door handle and ran toward the corner. Wind caught in his coattails and threw them behind. He listened to the clap of his hard soles against the ground. He slowed when he turned the corner and searched the next street. The silhouette ahead turned—he had heard the scraping of Milne's soles. Milne stopped and stared at the man. He could just barely make out his features in the dark. He did not think that he had seen him before. Then, the man turned and ran.

He crossed the street and quickly made it to the next corner—Milne ran after him. Leaves rustled. The man seemed to run silently but Milne's feet echoed through the night. He made it to the end of the street and turned again. He saw the man ahead and ran faster—his chest burned and he felt a stitch spread up the side of his stomach. His ankles were sore.

The streetlights throbbed overhead. The man looked over his shoulder and then turned down an alleyway. Milne could see the folder in his hands. When Milne reached the alley, he saw the man making his way down a steep set of stairs. He was either very lucky or he knew the city well. Milne slowed to take the stairs—he didn't trust his balance and he was out of breath. He rubbed his side and took the stairs two at a time. When he reached the bottom, he came out onto a well-lit street beside a park.

He looked up and down the street but could not see the man. He jogged to the entrance of the park. A pathway led to a fountain in the center. It seemed the most likely route for the runner to take, so Milne hurried toward the fountain. The path was well-lit but the rest of the park was dark. The man was nowhere in sight.

He carefully scanned the bushes and trees. The adrenaline had faded. His heart was racing. His side ached. He sat on the edge of the fountain and tried to catch his breath. The man was gone. He had let him get away. After a minute or two, he stood. He felt exposed sitting in the light, surrounded by darkness.

He retraced his steps back through the park, then followed the alleyway. It seemed much further on the way back and the stairs were difficult to climb. When he reached the office building, he unlocked the door and stepped inside. He climbed up the stairs with great effort. When he reached the office itself, he unlocked that door too. The lights were on. He searched his desk, then Eric's and Carson's. He looked through the folders and the papers on the shelves. He couldn't tell what documents were missing, if any. He looked down at his watch—12:55. He picked up the telephone.

The ringing in his ears—had it always been there? The doors faded to black. A wardrobe and flowered wallpaper became visible. The ringing was louder—the street came forward again, and then Nicolas became aware of the presence of dream. Consciousness was within his grasp—he opened his eyes. Slowly, he adjusted to the darkness. The ringing was loud.

"Nicolas," his wife groaned. "The telephone."

He reached for the table and knocked over the alarm clock. His hand felt the cord and he followed it to the receiver. He lifted it and pulled it to his ear.

"Hello?"

"Nicolas," the voice on the other end said. "I'm sorry to disturb you."

Nicolas sighed. "Who is this?"

"It's Milne. I'm at the office. I think some men just broke in here."

Nicolas sat up straight and pushed the blankets down. He reached over to the nightstand and lifted the alarm clock. He stared through the dark in an attempt to make out the time. "Are they still there?" he asked.

"No. I chased one of them."

"You chased one? Did you catch him?"

"He got away."

"Ok, hold on," he said. "Let me call you back from the office. Wait right there." He hung up and looked over his shoulder to his wife who was now sitting up in bed.

"What's the matter?" she asked.

"Nothing," he said. "Trouble in London. I have to go deal with it. Go back to sleep." He crossed his room to his wardrobe and began to change.

"Is everything ok?" she asked.

"Yes," he said. "Go back to sleep."

After he dressed, he went downstairs and picked up the phone in the hallway. He dialed a number and waited. It was picked up from the other end. "Cliff," he said. "I need you to meet me in the office. Right away."

He stopped in the kitchen and picked a pastry from a plate on the countertop, then went out the back door and locked it behind him. He left the yard through the back gate and walked up the alleyway until he reached a dimly lit side street. He turned to the right and followed it. As he walked, he ate. The pastry was flaky and sweet. His footsteps echoed off the walls around him.

Clifford made some calls and though nothing seemed to be missing, the police swept the area of the London office, prowling alleyways and knocking at doors. They sat outside the office at night to see if anyone returned. A few nights later, three newsstands were burned within a five-mile radius. There was no reason to believe that there was a connection, but the police drew a line and undertook a series of raids. They woke sleeping people in the night and searched their stores and homes and they shut down clubs and cleared out pubs in the middle of the day. Marguerite was arrested during a raid on Kavanagh's and Milne had to go in to vouch for her and take her home. Before long, Eric returned to London and things went back to normal, though sleep was uneasy and nobody walked alone after dark.

9

The crackle of gunfire across the water settled in. It was a steady, distant sound. The idea that men were out there sat heavy on them all. Here, it was calm. A series of faces—expressions. A redheaded boy from Manchester dealt a hand, somebody lit a cigarette, somebody else turned up the radio: *there'll be bluebirds over; the white cliffs of Dover; tomorrow, just you wait and see.* When the first shell dropped, he didn't know what happened; Vera Lynn sang on. The second blew the radio apart; faces shattered; Carson screamed.

He was awake—his eyes were wide. The room was dark around him. A stream of light poured in through a crack in the curtains. It was silent except for the ticking clock on the wall. His shirt clung to the sweat on his chest and back. He wondered if he had screamed aloud—he felt like he had, like he had woken up screaming—but Edna slept on, so it must not have been the case. He felt the pillow behind his head: soft, damp. He sat up and pushed the blankets aside. He crossed to the window and pushed the curtain aside. The blue night was still.

He pressed the latch and cracked the window. Cold air slipped in, expanding around him, slowly working its way up his hands, arms, chest, and neck. He breathed deeply. He scanned the street—a few cars, no people. Still and quiet. He turned and walked to the door, careful to tread lightly to avoid waking Edna. She was beautiful when she slept, he thought: her eyelids; her eyelashes. It was the contentedness, that blissful unawareness. She stirred slightly, shifted position. He wondered what was going on in there—in her unconscious mind. Was it as peaceful as it looked? Did sleep bring darkness for her, as it did for him?

He opened the door slowly, the hinges creaked. He looked over his shoulder—she wasn't disturbed. He stepped into the hall and closed the door, then took the stairs past generations of his family framed on the wall. He parted the curtains and looked through the window beside the door at the street in front of his house. There was nothing but a mass of shadows.

Who was watching? The Americans, the Russians, or his own? He ran through the possibilities, as he did night after night. Would the Crown stalk them? Break into their office? Unlikely. What would be the purpose? If the Americans ran the show they wouldn't need to. And so he arrived, once again, at the resolution that it must be the Russians.

He let the curtains fall back into place and went into the kitchen. He poured a scotch into the Waterford Crystal that Edna's mother had given them as a wedding present. He looked at the clock on the wall. Nicolas and Clifford would already be in Berlin.

He looked out of the kitchen window into the little garden behind the house. No movement there, either. He stepped out of the kitchen and entered his study. His grandfather's Holland & Holland was in a cabinet by the door. He'd moved his desk away from the windows to the corner of the room to feel more comfortable when he worked at night.

He turned his desk lamp on and looked over the finished edition of *Witness*. This is what it was all for. The magazine felt light in his hands.

✷

Ava watched Eric pack a suitcase on the other side of the room. "You were just gone for a month," she said. He didn't reply—the conversation was worn. Through the windows she could see the rooftops of other buildings. Light in some windows, darkness in others. She thought of New York, of her friends back home. What would they do on a night like this?

Eric stooped over the suitcase—the bumps of his spine trailed down his back, the scar on his shoulder where he was nicked by shrapnel in the Pacific. He was trying to figure out what he would need to wear.

"I don't understand why I can't come. I haven't been to Berlin in years."

"I'll only be there for a few days. I already told you that they aren't paying for the wives."

"The wives?"

"Oh, come on. You know what I mean. Why do you have to do that?"

She felt the cold air coming in through the window beside her. It felt like spring, not summer. It always felt like spring here, she thought. She lit her cigarette. Mist rolled along the street below. A slight breeze sifted through the light white curtain beside her. A baby began to cry in the apartment below. It would likely go all night.

What was Milne doing tonight? Who did he say goodbye to before he headed off? Marguerite was going, of course. Eric was folding socks and stuffing them into the sides of his suitcase. Whoever had broken into the office was still out there. Now, she would be alone in the apartment. What had they wanted? What about that strange couple in the country?

"Eric," she said. "I don't want to stay here by myself."

116

Eric stopped packing and turned. "You'll be alright," he said. "There's nothing to be afraid of."

Some unfamiliar, sickly smell floated up from the street. "Yes there is," she said. "You know that as well as I do."

The train pulled slowly out of Charing Cross Station. From the window of the carriage, Milne watched a woman kneel to hug her children. They waved at a window a little further back on the train. A father, he reckoned, heading out of the city. There was no one on the platform for him. No one left behind. There was Ava, and she wasn't his. He watched the little faces, then the platform, and then the station, disappear behind them. Bridges, factories, warehouses, vehicles, and people moved past. From time to time, the streets bore signs of bombing runs from the war. He remembered rations, radios, and refugees—he could not imagine bombs falling.

The train rattled on. Eric struck up a conversation with Marguerite about something insignificant. The city gave way to field and the countryside enveloped them. Milne watched trees and fences grow gradually in the distance and then blow past at tremendous speed. A lady with a trolley slowed at the door. He ordered tea and asked for an ashtray—as an afterthought, he ordered a sandwich. Carson bought cigarettes. Eric ordered coffee. She gathered their money, distributed their change, and then carried on her way. The sky outside darkened. It became difficult to make out the landscape beyond its shapes.

Over a period of three days, fifty-five American delegates landed in Berlin for the first International Congress for Cultural Freedom. As they were shuttled from one end of the city to another by military vehicle, two hundred delegates from across Europe arrived by train.

On Monday morning, the 26th of June, the radio pulled Milne from his sleep. Light poured through the windows. He pulled the blanket over his head. The room was stuffy. It drew him back. He lay in bed, fighting the urge to slip back into sleep, and the tinny words emitting from the radio began to sink in … *Korean troops have crossed the 38th parallel to begin what is expected to be a full-scale invasion of South Korea. For those just tuning in, we have received reports that at approximately …* Milne opened his eyes. He listened to the rest of the report without moving. When it finished, he reached over and switched the radio off. Another war, he thought. Déjà vu.

Berlin, 1950: The evening was bright and clear. The heat still hung in the air. He felt sweat trickling down his lower back beneath his suit. He ran a finger under his collar, scratching his neck. A bell rang. He stepped to the side to allow a cyclist to pass. Just ahead, a steady stream of delegates worked their way into the *Titania Palast*, a state-of-the-art theatre complex. He walked toward the delegates—artists and diplomats—and said polite hellos to those that he recognized.

"*Guten Abend.*"

"*Gleichfalls.*"

Nicolas and Clifford stood near the doorway laughing about something. Milne by-passed the line and approached them.

"Milne!" Nicolas said. "I was wondering when we would see you."

"Nicolas. Clifford. Are the others here yet?"

Nicolas shrugged. "They may be but we haven't seen them yet."

"I was supposed to walk over with them," Milne said, "but with this news about the war, it completely slipped my mind."

Clifford nodded. "Go on," he said. "Take a seat inside. If the others arrive, we'll send them to you."

Milne nodded and stepped through the doors of the *Palast*. He passed through the lobby and into the theatre. The seats were mostly full. He looked over the heads of the patrons for Marguerite, Eric, or Carson, but could see no one he recognized. He took a seat in the back near the aisle and kept an eye on the door. The room filled steadily. The lights flickered and dimmed. Milne turned his attention to the stage.

After a few moments, in an overly theatrical fashion, a clumsy looking man in a tight suit stepped into the center of the stage. He was the Mayor of Berlin, evidently. For several minutes, he spoke, alternating between German and English. Milne tried to focus but none of the words registered. He thought of Korea. How many would die in this one? How many would have to go? Would they impose conscription again? If China became involved—God forbid, Russia—would it spark another like the last? He heard the audience laugh and applaud periodically in the background. This could be the tipping point they had been waiting on. In Paris, it was the bomb. In Berlin, war.

When the Mayor stepped away from the podium, Nicolas approached it. Milne tried to clear his mind. He forced his attention onto his friend. Nicolas waited for the last few spatters of applause to die down and then began to speak:

"*Wilkommen*. Good evening. I would like to welcome you to the first International Congress for Cultural Freedom." The audience applauded. "Given the day's events, I hope that you'll excuse my brevity. As far as I am concerned, there has never been a more noble mission than the spiritual and cultural reorientation of conquered and occupied Germany." The audience began to clap again but he raised his hand to hush them. "However," he said loudly, "this morning, my sentiments have been somewhat shaken." He paused and waited for the audience's full attention.

"Not because the nobility of this task has been diminished in any way but because I believe that we have been blind to another task just as noble, just as necessary, and just as pressing as this one. What I am referring to, of course, is the reorientation—the reinvigoration—of the intellectual mind in Europe along staunchly anti-communist lines."

The audience burst into furious applause. Nicolas waited a few moments and then continued: "The containment strategy is cultural as much as economic or political. We know this. For this to succeed, the era of Soviet euphoria must come to an end. I do not wish for this Korean war any more than anyone else here today. However, I can say, wholeheartedly, that if it had to happen, it is better to happen now than at any other time, because now we are ready."

The audience applauded again, but he held up his hand and continued to speak: "Right now, as this conference signifies, we are in a position to fight back. As I look out over this crowd tonight, I can say with confidence that freedom is here in full force. It is time to get organized. Let's put this thing in motion. *Lass es beginnen.*" Nicolas stepped away from the podium. When the raucous applause died down, the curtain behind him rose and the Berlin Philharmonic began its scheduled performance of Beethoven's *Egmont Overture.*

Milne looked at the faces around him. The audience was rapt—proud. He scanned their features in the dark. How many Soviet agents sat among them, he wondered? He had no doubt that they were there, invisible in the crowd. His mind raced for the entire performance. They had put together a magazine— they had spent the last six months building an issue to showcase the strength of free culture. For what? Would it matter at all?

Then, the music began to grow, and the audience rose, and he found himself slipping into it. The individual—those distracted thoughts—faded. It was a stronghold. These were the minds of free people—intellectual people—dedicated to the protection of art for art's sake, of thought for thought's sake. This could be bolstered—strengthened. Eric had once said that creativity could not be fostered in a society of conformity. It was true, he thought. They could win the battle for the mind by simply displaying what they had that the Soviets didn't.

The performance ended and the audience erupted into applause. Milne rose with it and clapped loudly. It was a spectacular rendition—a work of art in its own right. The curtain fell. The lights brightened. The flow of the crowd took Milne from the auditorium into the lobby. He was bumped and jostled. He spotted Clifford and Marguerite standing to the side near the coat rack. He walked over to them and Marguerite smiled.

Clifford was in the middle of a sentence: "you've made some friends in London," he said.

"Yes," she replied. "I was lucky to meet some wonderful people very quickly."

Cliff nodded. "You have to be careful with those types," he said. "There are a lot of fellow travellers in London getting fat on Moscow gold."

Marguerite laughed, and then realized that he was serious. She glanced at Milne. "Don't worry, Mr. Bernstein. They are no more fans of Stalin than we are."

A man touched Clifford's arm as he passed. *"Bis morgen,"* he said.

Clifford glanced his way. *"Tschüss."* He turned back to Marguerite and shrugged. "Maybe they aren't but anarchists and socialists are not far removed from communists. It's best to keep an arm's length."

Nicolas laughed—Milne hadn't noticed him approach. "If we kept an arm's length from communists," he said, "we'd lose half of our speakers this week."

Clifford smiled. Delegates flowed past them out the doors and into the street. Milne motioned to Marguerite and they followed the crowd. The evening air melted over them, providing relief.

"What a performance," he said.

"Where were you?" she asked. "We waited for you for half an hour and then sent the bellboy up to your room looking."

"I'm sorry. I got distracted by this news and forgot that we were supposed to meet."

"It has filled everyone with excitement," Marguerite said. The crowd around them moved steadily. The constant drone of conversation carried through the Berlin street with it.

"And paranoia," Milne added. "Pay no heed to Clifford. It's good that you have friends in London. They'll be good for us too. With the others, it's all highbrow." They walked through the doors and followed the flow into the street. "Where are Carson and Eric?" Milne asked.

"They went ahead to the party—Carson knew some people. I told them I'd wait to see if you showed up."

"Thank you. Do you know where we're headed?" he asked.

"No," Marguerite replied, "but it looks like everyone else does."

"Somebody must," Milne said. The crowd parted beside them, and a car slowly pushed through. As it passed Marguerite and Milne, it rolled to a stop.

"Mr. Lowell!"

Milne looked over—Ignazio Brown, the Italian writer, spoke through an open window. "I thought that was you," he said. "Get in!"

"Is it not easier to walk?" Marguerite asked.

Ignazio laughed. "No," he said. "They don't know how far they have to go. Somebody started walking and they all went with him."

Milne shrugged at Marguerite and she opened the back door of the car. They got in. The driver turned around and smiled—his shirt was silk and his eyes were soft. "This is my friend, Angelo. He doesn't speak English."

"French?" Milne asked.

"Only Italian," Ignazio said. He turned and looked over the seat at Marguerite. "I don't believe I know you," he said.

"Marguerite."

"You're a …?"

"Writer. Editor."

"Of course," Ignazio laughed. "What else? How did you like the performance?"

"The orchestra was very good," she said. "I worry, though, that this rampant anti-communism is in danger of replacing the promotion of freedom."

"They see them as synonyms, you see," Ignazio said. "I already feel as if I need a break from this all."

"It can be pretty overwhelming," said Milne.

"Overwhelming … Yes, it can be quite overwhelming."

"I don't know how they never get sick of parties," Marguerite said.

"They're all sick of parties," said Ignazio. "This weekend is a fantasy for many of them. Particularly the ones who weren't in the war."

"What do you mean?" asked Milne.

"They're all very excited—dreaming of communist attacks from all angles. Berlin," he said with emphasis, "is where the action is. Communists on all sides—occupying half of the city. It's the first taste of blood for most of them."

124

"It's also the most fitting place for such a conference, isn't it? To make a statement?"

"Maybe," Ignazio said, sighing. "But, despite what Babichev says, the most noble task isn't propaganda warfare. It's liberating ourselves from the allure of gunfire all together."

"Yes," Marguerite said. "That is what I've been trying to say—not as eloquently."

"Have you seen the libraries yet?" Ignazio asked.

"No."

"They're all over. Libraries, reading rooms—whatever the official term is."

"I've heard about them. The High Commission finds them very effective."

"What are they?"

"They're rooms filled with English books and German translations of them," Ignazio replied. "The walls are lined: Tom Paine; Moby Dick; Leaves of Grass; Dickinson. Anthologies too ... biographies." Ignazio assumed an affected trans-Atlantic accent and began to list titles: "The Flowering of New England. The Story of American Literature. The New Deal in Action."

"They sure aren't subtle."

Ignazio laughed. "No," he said. "I don't know if they even mean to be. They were set up by the Office of Wartime Information—they're military libraries." He shook his head. "I have little patience for their types," he said.

"What type?"

"Ivy League, OSS types. The American High Commission is full of them—Berlin is basically run by them. They think that an intellectual aristocracy can save the world from decay. They want to save high culture as much as they want to save democracy— maybe more." He leaned back and offered Milne and Marguerite cigarettes. They both accepted. Ignazio lit his own and looked through the window at the crowd pouring down the street. "They know that they don't need to convince people to like American culture," he said. "They're terrified because America is Hollywood and Patti Page. They want their Sartre or Picasso."

Milne lit Marguerite's cigarette and then his own. "Don't you think it's good to promote better art?" he asked. "Patti Page will hardly stimulate change."

"It's not just the Americans, of course," Ignazio added. "I find there's little serious discussion at these things. It's much the same language and style as the other side." He pointed ahead and said something to Angelo in Italian. Angelo rolled to a stop. "We're here," Ignazio said. He opened the door. Milne and Marguerite followed him out of the car.

"Angelo isn't coming in?" Milne asked.

"No. Not tonight." Ignazio gestured at a tall building directly ahead. "Here it is."

The stonework was grey. Each floor was marked on the outside with a thin line of intricate molding. Milne couldn't make out the pattern in the evening light. The front doors were open, letting in anyone who knew to come. The lobby was tiled and tall. A staircase wound around the edges, and an elevator shaft ran up the center. The door and shaft were trimmed with an ornate brass weave. They crowded into the elevator and closed the thin wooden doors. Milne could feel Ignazio's breath creeping down the back of his neck.

The elevator rattled and creaked as it rose through the floors. Music drifting from above slowly grew louder. At the top, it stopped. Marguerite opened the doors and stepped out. Milne and Ignazio followed. An apartment door to the left of the elevator hung open. Jazz and laughter carried from it. Conversation without context. Milne looked to Ignazio who nodded. They stepped through the door and into the room.

The room they entered was large—bigger, itself, than Milne's entire flat in London. "Come on," Ignazio said, and stepped further. The room was full and the music was loud. Milne spotted Carson talking to someone in the kitchen. He tapped Marguerite's shoulder. "There's Carson," he said.

"Milne!" Carson shouted when he caught sight of them. "So, she found you at last."

"Yes," Milne laughed. "I'm sorry about that."

"You found your way here alright?"

"Ignazio ..." Milne turned to point him out but could no longer find him. "Well, wherever he is, brought us. He had a car."

"Do you want a drink?" Carson asked. "Help yourself—they have everything."

"Whose apartment is this?" Marguerite asked.

Carson shrugged. He turned back to the woman he had been speaking with. "I'm sorry," he said. "Isolde, this is Marguerite Allard and Milne Lowell, both from Montreal. They work on the magazine with me in London."

Isolde reached out and shook their hands. "It's a pleasure."

"I interrupted you, Isolde. What was it that you were saying?"

Isolde looked embarrassed. "I don't know how you feel," she said to Marguerite and Milne, "but it's just this conference. I don't know ... I feel like we shouldn't be standing around presenting to intellectuals and sipping cocktails. We should be rousing crowds—bringing people on to the streets to fight this battle head on."

Marguerite nodded. "It's elitist."

Carson shook his head. "Maybe, but it's necessary for the moment. The battle for the mind of the masses starts with those who influence the mass mind."

"Soviet propagandists litter our newspapers. We should be taking the fight to them—doing the same."

"There's too much focus on the Soviets, I think," Marguerite said. "There are other threats to freedom."

"Have you heard the news from Indo-China?"

"Nicolas," Carson said, looking past Milne. "How are you, old boy?"

Milne turned to look. "Good, you found them," Nicolas said.

"We did."

"Well," Nicolas said, joining the group and raising his glass, "here's to the changing world, and our part in it."

"Here, here," Carson said, raising his own.

"Cliff's around here somewhere," Nicolas said.

Carson set his empty glass on the counter. "Isolde was just telling us that she thinks we ought to be out on the streets."

"Many are," Nicolas said. "But that's not our part in this battle. We're part of a fraternity—the intelligentsia of Europe. Our battle is for freedom of culture and mind. The battle of the streets is for others to fight and, believe me, they are doing so."

"I wonder what my place in this fraternity is," said Marguerite.

Nicolas shrugged. "The liberal world—mixed society—is the place of reason and rationalism. We need to demonstrate that. We meet in debate and discussion—that allows for meaningful change."

"What do you think, Milne? You've been awfully quiet," Isolde said.

"The freedom of this society allows for creativity and artistry that others do not. I think that the most powerful thing we can do is demonstrate that."

Nicolas and Carson nodded. "But great art has often come of horror," Marguerite said.

"Russia might even be the prime example of that," Isolde said. "Think of Dostoevsky."

Milne turned away from the conversation and caught Nicolas by the arm. "I don't want to put a damper on the evening," he said, "but I've been meaning to ask. Have you heard any more about our break in?"

Nicolas shook his head. "No. What would I hear in Paris? Have the police come up with anything yet?"

Milne shook his head. "I haven't heard from them since I was interviewed."

"I know that it is worrying," Nicolas said. "I really don't know what more we can do, though."

"Nicolas, we're being targeted. I don't know if they're trying to scare us or ..."

"I think he's right," Marguerite broke in. "This isn't too different from the strategy the Albanians used to scare us out."

Nicolas looked confused. "Albanians?" he asked.

"This was in Montreal," Milne said. "She had trouble with a local gang."

"For work you published?"

"Agitation, I suspect. We think that they might have been paid by the police."

"Well, the police in London are looking out for us. They have their eye on things. When they find anything, they'll let you know."

"Nicolas, we're being watched ... followed."

"This is what we signed up for," he said. "We're on the front lines. If they are communists, what do we do? Let them scare us? Play dirty ourselves? No, the best thing to do is to keep course—do what we have set out to do. Look at this conference.

Look at the issue you've put together. So far, things have been a huge success. You've done great work. Be proud of that. We're even thinking of expanding—Latin America, maybe."

The night moved and the music and laughter carried with it. The group dispersed, shuffled, and regrouped in a seamless cycle. Marguerite found a group of Spanish artists in one of the bedrooms and spent most of the night talking quietly with them after that. Eric and Carson paired together, and Nicolas disappeared early. There was no sign of Clifford at all.

As the evening wore on, Milne found himself increasingly alone with Isolde. He found himself passenger to the atmosphere of the party. Where it went, he went. When the energy lifted, he rose with it. Isolde knew Carson from Cornwall but she now lived in Prague. Milne couldn't determine what she did for a living. There was passion in her—a grounded intellectualism that reminded him of Marguerite. She didn't seem to dance, and Milne was glad.

When the party petered out, and those who remained were sleeping or quiet, Milne followed Isolde onto the balcony. It was dark. In the distance, the faint glow of light leaked through the wall of buildings. Some rooms across the road were bright. From the balcony, everything below appeared as a silhouette. Trees reached up from the darkness, brushing the sides of the building. The leaves rustled with the wind—it carried through them, winding between the branches. Milne closed his eyes and felt the breeze against his skin. Something else brushed it—soft, smooth, carrying down his cheek, a gentle tingle with it. He exhaled and felt his chest sink and his breath leave him.

A set of blue eyes across the table—swirling steam from a coffee mug; a motion, the movement of a hand—the twitch of lips before the smile; a blue dress; a hand finding his in the crowd; a name lingered on the tip of his tongue, unspoken.

"I have to go," he said, opening his eyes. Isolde drew her hand back.

"What's wrong?" she asked.

"I'm sorry," he said. "I just have to go."

Milne stepped through the doors and back into the room, letting the sheer curtain flutter. Marguerite sat on a sofa with a new Spanish friend. Carson was nowhere to be seen. Ignazio drooped over the arm of a chair, asleep. Eric caught Milne's eye across the room and raised his glass.

Plush duvets and pillowcases covered the bed. Morning light crept through the curtain. Red leaves on green vines twisted their way up the embossed cream wallpaper. He ran his fingers over the grooves. His grandmother's house had similar paper on the walls of the bedroom. As a child, he'd trace patterns in the dark, listening to the crash of waves on the shore and the murmurs of adults talking in the room below. If the moon was bright, he'd creep to the window, trying not to let the floor creak beneath him, and look out over the cliffs. When he went back to bed, he'd dream of shipwrecks, pirates, and sailors.

He sat up. His shoes were beside the door and his jacket was thrown over the back of a chair. Vague memories of the walk home filtered through his mind. He went into the bathroom and filled a glass of water from the tap. It was warm. He emptied the bottom half down the sink. In the shower, he ran his hand across the loose skin on his chest and stomach. He felt a pain in his legs and lower back. He thought back to another time: dandelions and burning piles of leaves. He didn't know what caused it but nostalgia was brewing. There was a simpler time when war was war. He remembered parents in the neighbourhood conspiring,

131

girls being promised. Isabelle, who thought him a coward. He'd thought that it was love. He looked down at the water running into the drain.

Somebody knocked at the door. He got out of the shower and dressed quickly. "Just a moment!" he called out.

"It's me," Eric called back.

Milne finished buttoning his shirt and opened the door. Eric leaned against the wall with a cigarette in hand. "I was just going down for breakfast, are you ready?"

"Yeah," Milne said. "One moment." He stepped back inside and sat in a chair beside the door. He slipped into his shoes and laced them up.

"Hell of a night," Eric said.

"That's for sure."

"That Welsh one had her eye on you. You let her slip away."

"I don't know about that," Milne said. He grabbed his jacket from the back of the chair and stepped into the hallway. He locked the door behind him.

Ava closed her eyes. She felt the prickle of grass stems on the back of her neck; a tickle behind the ear. There was a slight breeze, cool and gentle. She opened her eyes. Dark clouds, clustered low, rolled quickly across the sky. She sat up. She'd better move before the rain, she thought. In the park around her, a group of children chased one another, wielding sticks like rifles. A small girl chased a puppy through the trees along the edge of the path. An elderly couple sat in contented silence on a bench. She felt the dampness of grass beneath her, slowly seeping through her dress. The grass was always damp in England.

She got to her feet and checked her dress for stains. It wasn't actually the grass, she'd heard once, that caused the stains—it was the weeds, the flower stems, the leaves, the clover. Eric had told her that, she remembered, in the Adirondacks. Just weeks after they first met.

She did not know what to do now that the first issue was done, the boys were in Berlin, and she was alone in London. The first few drops of rain fell on her shoulders and arms. She began to walk through the park toward the street. Parents tried to usher the running children in from the rain. The elderly couple raised an umbrella and slowly rose from their bench. She made her way through the park and stood on the footpath along the road. The rain started to fall heavily. She thought of Milne.

The magazine launch was largely uneventful. It was a relatively minor event in terms of the overall conference. Nicolas introduced them to a room full of students and delegates in the theatre complex. Carson spoke first. He gave a humorous account of the events leading up to the conference—not enough to let the fear show but enough to pique the interest of the audience and the press. Eric and Milne spoke in turn after him, giving a slight variation on the themes laid out. Marguerite attempted to say a few words but her microphone cut out and she could not be heard. Carson then closed with a reading.

Based upon the applause and questions, it was a success. There was a small reception at the end. Immediately, a group of students latched on to Carson and he was not seen for the rest of the afternoon. Nicolas introduced the others to the American representatives of the World Alliance for Democratic Youth, a powerful group in student circles. Marguerite spoke to them.

She asked how they liked the conference. "I'd like it better," one of the students replied, "if we had a little more freedom."

They finished the night off at another party. The next day, the main debates were followed up by a tour of the barricade. A line of Soviet troops stood guard along the border. Barbed wire trailed beside them, strung between concrete and steel barriers. The wind pressed against their faces and uniforms, casting the rainfall against them with force. They stood firm. Milne watched the faces of the men. Not all were young, several were much older than he was. The uniforms were impeccable, despite the rain. No doubt they knew about the tour in advance. American soldiers stood facing the border feet away from him. Most of the Soviet soldiers stood emotionless, like the Americans, though he saw traces of fear and nervousness on some.

The crowd chattered around him as the guides spoke in a multi-lingual presentation about the border. An English voice seeped through the general drone of the crowd: "Apparently, he had an entire second family in Yugoslavia." Milne turned and looked at the group with him. The English presenter was detailing the history of the erection of the barrier, of the Soviet and Allied blockades, and the hordes of East Germans who were crossing into the West day by day. Marguerite looked at him and gave a weak smile. Carson and Eric talked amongst themselves about the other side.

He heard Nicolas speaking just behind him. "The culture that we've brought to Germany has had a profound effect on the German perspective. For generations, they've considered America to be culturally barren. We've completely changed that," he said to a sceptical American official—the type of man that Clifford liked to say had built a career buying lunches.

Milne pushed his way to the edge of the group and walked absently down the street. For some reason, the weekend was wearing him thin. Ignazio might be right, he thought. Though important, it was incessant. A line of barbed wire ran as far as he could see ahead, spotted with checkpoints and guards. He turned up the street away from it. He passed by restaurants, coffee shops, apartment buildings, and storefronts. He bought cigarettes in a little shop and sat on a bench for a while. A lady further down the street fed pigeons crumbs from a sack. Down the street across from him, broken concrete was strewn across the ground. He got back up and walked towards it.

A man sat on the ground, leaning back against the wall. He wore a tattered and faded uniform. His eyes were sunken and his face was sallow. He looked up at Milne as he neared. He opened his mouth to speak but no words came out. Half of his teeth were missing or broken. The rest were yellow and brown. He lifted an old army hat and stretched it out. Milne reached into his pockets. He dropped a small handful of coins into the hat. The coins slid and jingled, and some fell through the bottom of the hat, where there must have been a hole, into the waiting hand of the old soldier.

Milne hadn't been in the war. He had found sanctuary at the university. He had studied and taught. It was, at times, an immense source of guilt. At times, it was an immense relief. He hadn't supported the war in its early years—it seemed like a step backwards, a plunge back into imperial conflict. It had been easy to find support on the left in Montreal. Marguerite and her friends had taken him in. It had not been as ideological for him as it was for them. He remembered sitting in an office without windows reading Milton when Tom Dixon knocked on the door and told him that it was all over. Then, survivor accounts of concentration camps began to emerge. Friends and family who went overseas treated him differently or didn't come back at all. A park across from him appeared like a bombed-out

135

scar on the face of the city. In some parts of Berlin, it was nearly possible to forget about the war entirely. Not here.

He stood at the edge of the street and looked out into the ruins beside him. A woman, following closely behind a shaggy brown dog, walked through the crumbled brick and concrete with her hands in the pockets of her coat. The dog stopped and sniffed around the corners of some collapsed structure. In the center of the wasteland, neatly confined by the clean streets around it, was the bottom half of a statue. Its legs and lower stomach stood proudly raised upon the platform, stretching up into a cracked torso and missing chest and shoulders. From where he stood, he could see a round piece on the ground which must have been part of the head at some point. The dog lifted its leg and relieved itself upon it.

He thought of the German woman he met in Paris. He couldn't remember her name. He couldn't even picture her face. Instead, all that he saw was that colourful blue dress and the plush scarf around her neck, just below the line of shortly cropped blonde hair. The cigarette—he remembered that now too. The loose, carelessly dangling wrist. The eyes—grey and cold, peering through thin wisps of smoke—hardened. He thought of her young sister. It had seemed too distant at the time—she had seemed so cold to him. It wasn't so distant now. He ran his hand over his mouth and felt the discomfort grow within him. *It doesn't matter,* she had said, and he had walked away. It did matter, though. It was something that she must think of on late nights when she couldn't sleep—maybe every time she saw a girl of about the same age.

"There you are," he heard from behind him. A French-Canadian accent. He turned and faced Marguerite. The rain eased around him.

"Do you think of your brother often?" he asked.

"Every day."

He nodded. "I met someone in Paris," he said. "Her sister died here after the war. I didn't really think about it until I came here."

"Yes," Marguerite said. "This place still has the stench of death."

They stood and watched the rain fall gently upon the ruins. The woman and the dog walked through them. Milne looked back up the street—the old soldier was gone. Marguerite touched his elbow. "We should go back," she said. "We will lose the group."

Without warning, thunder cracked, echoing across the sky. With little delay, lightning followed, stretching through the blackened cloud. Milne stared out over the rubble. Marguerite stood behind him.

II

The Foxhunt

I

London, 1951: The road wound through hills, trees, and fences. Acres of carefully manicured land passed them by. The trees were sturdy and pruned—the flowers wild but kempt. The early morning light carried through the trees at the end of the field with carefree ease.

"It's a brutal sport, I know."

Milne looked over at Carson, who had spoken suddenly and apologetically. "It's alright," he said. "They'll go ahead whether we're here or not, I suppose." He watched the fields roll past as they drove. "Who owns all of this land?"

"This is all his," Carson said.

"All of it?"

"Everything since we passed through the gate. This is Pankhurst Estate."

"How much land is this?"

"More than their due."

The road twisted into a cluster of oaks. They followed it, slipping momentarily into woodland. When they emerged around the bend, a stone manor stood out along the sky, carefully positioned on a hill.

"Have you thought any more about going to Colombia?" Carson asked.

"Of course I'll go," Milne said. "How could I pass it up?"

"Wonderful," Carson said. "It'll be a damned good trip. I'll let Nicolas know."

The road wound up to the entryway, where three cars were visible. A carriage house hinted at more. "It looks like most of the others are already here," Carson said.

The driver traced the path. He was emotionless and silent. His body was still except for the gentle shifting of his arms. When he rolled to a stop in front of the house, he quickly stepped out of the car and opened the back doors—Milne and Carson stepped out. Immediately, Milne felt the fresh air blanket his face. He breathed deeply: cool and hard, it filled his lungs.

He looked down over the landscape. An endless, cascading sea of green met his eyes. Forests and fields stretched in all directions. He walked around to the trunk of the car. The driver stepped in front of him: "Your bags will be taken care of, sir."

Carson was walking up the steps to the front door. He followed behind. As soon as they approached the door, it opened. They were greeted by a butler in a perfectly fitted uniform. "Good morning, Mr. Ward," he said. "Please come in." They stepped inside and their coats were taken from them. "I will show you to the study," the butler said.

He led them past a massive staircase in the entryway and down a large hallway hidden behind it. The ceilings were higher than any other house that Milne had been in. At the end of the hallway, light streamed in through a broad window. The rest of the hall was dark. They passed three doors and entered the fourth.

The windows along the outer wall ran nearly from floor to ceiling. Curtains hung the length, tied with frayed rope. Harry Pankhurst Jr. was in the corner next to the door, filling glasses generously from a decanter. "Carson, welcome! I'm glad you made it. Drop of brandy?"

"It's eight in the morning, Harry."

"It's hunt day, Carson. Everything's game." Pankhurst shifted his gaze to Milne. "Mr. Lowell, I know you're up for it."

Milne wanted to turn him down but the glass was full before he could.

"There's a good sport," Pankhurst said. "Let me introduce you to the rest." He threw his arm over Milne's shoulder and pointed across the room to two men chatting next to the fireplace. "That is Bill Prescott and Gregory Wallace. Bill's the one who looks like a polecat. Gregory's the stout fellow with bad hair." He then pointed at a group of men in the opposite corner. "Those three are Philip Muggeridge, William Molesworth, and Sir John Innes. Philip is the one spinning the globe with his finger, Molesworth is the one with ears like a lagomorph, and Innes is the other one."

He took Milne by the arm and brought him around the room. He introduced him to Bill, Gregory, William, and John. The other guest slipped out of the room before Milne reached him. Once the initial introductions were out of the way, Carson began chatting with William, who he seemed to know the best. John was fascinated by Canada and asked countless questions about wildlife and culture. Bill, who was on his third brandy, challenged Milne to an arm wrestle.

When Muggeridge reappeared, Milne watched him with fascination. His manner shifted with ease. When he spoke to Pankhurst, his host, he was charming—pandering—and when he spoke to the other guests he slipped into dry contempt. At times, his presence filled the room and he seemed to breathe the very energy he built. At other times, he seemed to fade into the room itself, seeming no more present than the animals mounted on the wall.

"Philip Muggeridge," he said, with an extended hand, when Milne approached.

"My God, yes! I am terribly sorry," Pankhurst interrupted. "I forgot to introduce you."

"Philip, this is Milne Lowell. He's a Canadian writer—a friend of our Carson's."

"Milne," Muggeridge said, "what an interesting name."

"Isn't it?" Pankhurst said. "Where does it come from?"

"What do you write?" Muggeridge asked.

"Novels, essays."

"Poetry?"

"Hardly ever."

"That's a shame," said Muggeridge. "The search for the perfect metaphor is the only truly honest task."

"Who said that?" asked Milne.

Pankhurst interrupted, holding two fresh glasses of brandy. When they took them, he pointed to an ivory plated rifle mounted above the fireplace. "My father's souvenir from the Boer," he said. "Well, that and a festering …" Somebody bumped a table across the room, sending a set of crystal glassware to the floor. It shattered. Shards scattered.

"Bill!" Pankhurst screamed. "That's the second time you've done that!"

Bill collapsed into a chair, laughing. Pankhurst sighed and threw back the rest of his brandy. "That's as good a cue as any, I suppose. Let's mount up. Somebody better strap Bill to his horse."

The riders followed the trail through the grounds and into the forest. Four foxhounds ran with them. They trotted calmly along the dirt path, stirring dust and building clouds over the trail. The trail became narrow and they rode in single file for some time. The trees thickened and then thinned again. After some time, the riders passed through them and entered a meadow. The pattern shifted and the line dispersed. They rode together across the fields. Pankhurst called out and the horses moved faster. The dogs ran alongside. They climbed a hill and something moved close to the earth. Pankhurst cried out again.

The foxhounds bolted. Their paws threw dirt behind them. Strong thin legs carried them over grassy knolls. The horse's hooves beat into the soft earth—a swarm of thick legs battered the air. Ahead, a red fox, *Vulpes vulpes,* darted across the ground. A morning mist still hung faintly. The fox's tail flicked through it. Milne watched the faces of the men around him—the hard cheeks and sharp noses on some, the doughiness of others. Starched collars and riding caps on all. He was rooting for the foxes, he realized.

Besides the party and its prey, the morning was quiet and calm. Birds in the distance called out to the day. A wooden fence partitioned a field from the meadow to their left. The hounds bore down in silence. A horse whinnied as its hoof sank briefly into the edge of a foxhole. It recovered quickly and carried on. The horses were large and powerful—thick skin and short hair, sleek brown and black coats, taut over muscular legs. The riders laughed and shouted like boys. The fox slipped beneath a bush and disappeared momentarily.

There was likely no animal more beautiful than the red fox, he thought. No animal more loved in folklore across the world. Reynard, cunning and sly. It emerged again and they pursued the animal across the hills and through the undergrowth at the edge of the forest. Tailcoats blew in the wind as the sound of hooves beat across the field. The hounds spread and began to close distance. "Atta' boy, Mountain!" a rider called.

The fastest of the hounds caught up to the fox. The dog lunged and grabbed the fox by the back of the neck. The fox stumbled and rolled across the ground. As it rose and steadied itself, the dog lurched at its throat and swung it limply through the air. The other hounds reached the fox and pounced.

Cries pierced the air. Empty meadows, forests, and fields stretched out in all directions. Only the cheers of the riders met the sounds of anguish seeping from the captured animal. He could not block the sounds, so Milne stared at the back of his horse's neck. From the corner of his eye, he saw the thrashing hounds around the struggling fox. He looked to the trees. Tears trickled down his cheek. He wiped them quickly. Fortunately, the rest of the riders were watching too closely to notice. He could feel the pocket of elation beside him. It was different to them, he realized. The yelps eventually waned to whines and a breeze carried them through the silence. He wondered how far it could be heard. From here, it seemed like no one else was listening—that no one could be even if they wanted to. The dogs sniffed. They poked and prodded the limp and bloody fox.

The riders dismounted around the kill. Milne swung his leg over his horse and stepped back onto the earth. Pankhurst was already approaching the animals. He shooed the dogs. One lingered too long and received a kick from his heavy boot. He stooped and dipped his fingers into the dripping gash in the neck of the animal. He stood and walked toward Milne.

Milne looked across the group at Carson, who looked away. Pankhurst slowly wiped the blood from his fingers on each of Milne's cheeks. Some of it spread smoothly—some clumped and dripped. Milne suppressed a gag. He tasted vomit. He held

146

as still as he could. The grey eyes of the hunter stared through him. His own eyes betrayed him, he knew. The fingers lifted from his cheeks to his forehead and made the sign of the cross. He smelled the brandy on Pankhurst's breath. Another hand clapped his upper back. The hunter wiped his hand on a rag that he pulled from the pocket of his coat. The dogs tore into the carcass.

2

Carson,

We received the draft you sent our way. I am uncertain about the cover. The poetry and fiction selections look strong. We will not be publishing Kean's piece on Korea. The last thing people need right now is some cheap dig at the behaviour of American soldiers. Remove it entirely. I take your point about the potential of Allard's essay to draw sympathizers away from more subversive currents—redactions to follow.

As a side note, do not concern yourself so much with sales. We are primarily concerned with impact. Distribution can be taken care of on our end.

C.B.

Carson put the letter down. He opened the top drawer on his desk and removed several sheets of paper. He lifted a pen from the corner of his desk. *Cliff,* he began. *We will look no better than Stalinists or fools if we continue to screen in this way.* He stopped. He crumpled the sheet and dropped it in the bin next to his desk.

Cliff, he began again: *I am unsure of what you mean when you say to concern ourselves with impact rather than sales. Is one not the measure of the other? In any case, the impact will not be positive if we censor all criticism of the free world.*

Again, he stopped. He folded the page in half and dropped it into the bin. Through the window, he watched mist roll over the rooftops. He opened the bottom drawer and took a bottle of Bushmills from it.

Neon strips flickered in Piccadilly Circus—signs lifted from curving walls: Prince of Wales; Coca-Cola; Craven "A"; Guinness Time. In alleyways, women leaned against doorways smoking cigarettes. Policemen lurked nearby. Milne stepped back from the road and scanned the faces emerging from the steps of the Underground in twill and kidskin. Black cabs and red busses stopped and started behind them.

Marguerite appeared on the steps wearing a narrow corduroy skirt and a plaid coat. Milne called out to her. She looked over and waved. He pulled his cigarette case from his coat and offered one to her when she neared. She took it and thanked him; he lit it with a match as she blocked the wind. They crossed the road to the fountain.

"How was the hunt?" Marguerite asked.

"It was about what you'd expect," Milne replied.

"Did Carson enjoy it?"

"I don't think so."

Marguerite stopped and sat on the edge of the fountain. The breeze came in strong gusts and blew short strands of hair across her forehead. She looked out absently at the people passing by. "Was it absolutely horrible?" she asked.

Milne watched the water cascade from the top of the fountain behind her. He thought of Pankhurst's eyes staring into his own. When he swallowed, he could taste the putrid iron of blood. "Yes," he said. "It was."

Marguerite stared at him from where she sat, one leg crossed over the other. "Do you regret going?" she asked.

Milne didn't respond. Marguerite finished her cigarette and stubbed it out. They walked the square and followed the curving road beneath a sign for Gordon's Gin. They passed through a narrow alleyway where boys hung from windows above, looking down over the street. A black Bentley rolled to a halt at the entrance ahead. A wrinkled face peered from the back window at them, and then the car slowly carried on.

They went into a restaurant that Carson had suggested. The ceiling was low and the room was dark and quiet. They were seated near the back and ordered martinis. Milne looked around. He wondered about the people around them. A woman in a wool dress sat alone at the table beside them, drinking wine and watching the door. A waiter brought their drinks to them.

"Have you talked to Nicolas about Colombia?" Marguerite asked when the waiter left.

"I spoke to Carson," Milne said. "I'll write to Nicolas about it this week."

"You said you would go?"

"Of course."

Marguerite flicked the ash from her cigarette. "Can I admit that I'm jealous?" she asked.

"I'd know you were lying if you said that you weren't."

Marguerite smiled. She sipped her drink and watched other people in the restaurant. She wondered what it must have been like just a few years earlier—were restaurants like this open during the war? Probably not, she thought. Many still had shortened hours. She spotted the woman in wool sitting alone and wondered about her. The waiter returned. Milne ordered fish and Marguerite ordered the steak.

"Did you go to ... that event you were talking about?" Milne asked.

"The rally?"

"Yes, the anti-war one."

"I did," Marguerite said. She stubbed out her cigarette and left it in the ashtray. "Two from Liverpool came up and spoke in Trafalgar Square. They speak every Sunday morning down there, apparently, right in the center of town."

"Did you know them?"

"No."

"How did it go?"

"They were arrested."

Milne nodded. "Good turnout, at least?"

"It was alright," Marguerite said. She lit another cigarette and rested her elbow on the table. "It's been twelve years since the outbreak of the Second World War—this is what they said—twelve years. This means that the conditions of war have been ever-present for every child. Before this, they said, war was tolerated only as a temporary measure. Now, it is just a factor of life. Peace has taken on this temporary character." She drew on her cigarette and then cast a cloud of smoke into the air. She stared absently through it. "We've embraced this state of permanent war, or permanent war preparedness ... they said."

The sun was low in the sky and cast its slanted evening glow through the window at the front of the restaurant. Marguerite watched the light slide away as the sun dipped further behind the buildings across the road. She watched Milne play with the olive in his glass. "Do you think that we could do better?" she asked.

Milne looked up. He dropped the olive-laden toothpick back into the glass—droplets splashed onto the tablecloth. "What do you mean?"

Marguerite shrugged and began to play with the olive in her own martini. "I don't know," she said. "The magazine, I suppose." She rolled the toothpick between her fingertips, sending tremors across the surface.

"We're doing very well," Milne said.

"I know," Marguerite said. "It can just feel detached or something, at times."

"There's nothing detached about art," Milne said. "If politicians paid a little more attention to it, we'd all be better off."

"Of course we would," she said. "Don't get me wrong, I'm very grateful to you for bringing me over. It's just ... I received a letter from Alessandro yesterday. They're organizing again—it made me think, is all."

Milne nodded. "I haven't been in touch with anyone at home for too long," he said. "It's easy to forget." He paused to watch a waiter pass by with a plate of fish. "The work here might not be as dramatic," he continued, "but it might be longer lasting. The impact is difficult to chart."

"Maybe I'm just impatient," Marguerite said. "Time goes by so quickly—I'm scared to wake up someday and realize that it was wasted."

"This isn't a waste," Milne said.

"That's not what I meant."

"I know. I didn't mean to sound sharp. I meant that you are doing something worthwhile."

Marguerite lifted her olive and bit into it. The smooth shell ruptured. She chewed it slowly. "Who do you think it was you chased that night?" she asked.

Milne shook his head. "Communists, of some colour," he said. "Stalinists," he corrected himself, "or local sympathizers. They were too sophisticated for common criminals. If I hadn't stumbled across them, we wouldn't know that they had ever been there."

"I think about that often," she said. "You have to wonder what we miss."

Their food arrived and they ate and talked until the candle on the table burned low in its cradle. After dinner, they walked the short distance to Soho. Dusk pulled down at the sky. Lanterns hung over the streets, casting a flickering yellow glow. They passed restaurants, tailors, cafes, and newsstands. Men in patched coats smoked cigarettes in front of closed shops. Children begged on the streets. Someone called to Milne, offering rationed meat in any amount. A crowd passed in blackface, screaming and dancing, casting echoes. The lanterns cast their subtle light on wooden signs: Twinings; Imperial Tobacco.

Milne and Marguerite walked in the lamplight and avoided alleyways until they reached a club on Dean Street. The doorman let them in. Inside, they were engulfed in its folds. The rooms were small and the groups were select. They went upstairs and Milne saw Eric and Ava in the corner. He touched Marguerite's arm and pointed across the room. Ava glanced their way and saw Milne through the crowd. She tapped Eric and said something to him. Eric looked over and then they stood and crossed the room through the crowd.

Eric clapped him on the shoulder and put a drink in his hand. "I can't tell you how glad I am to see you," he said. "I'm ready to put my foot up the ass of the next poncy Brit to use the phrase 'American domination.'"

"He's a truly gifted cultural ambassador," Ava said.

"I'm sure they're well used to the Oxford treatment," he said. "Speaking of, how was the hunt?"

"It's not much of a sport, if you ask me," Milne said.

"Good to get a little local flavour though, isn't it?"

Milne took a drink. He glanced around the room. "No sign of Carson and Edna tonight?"

Ava shook her head. "Not yet, anyway."

Milne's eyes lingered on Ava. She looked at him briefly, then reached out and took Marguerite's hand. "Will we dance?" she asked.

"Let's," said Marguerite.

Milne closed the door and hung his coat beside it. He turned on the overhead light. The room drifted, slipped, around him. He took a beer from the fridge and opened it. He sat down at the table and lit a cigarette. He lifted a submission from the pile in front of him and began to read from somewhere halfway through the first page:

The European immigrant's familiarity with an alienated government—a state dedicated to somebody else's interests—made him sceptical of the democratic process. Initially, he rejected its institutions entirely but, slowly, as the increasing mass of immigrant bodies was steadily matched by the increasing representation of immigrant interests in party platforms, the possibility that the power of government could be a force for good began to take hold ...

His eyes drifted from the letters on the page. He set the essay aside and lifted the one beneath it. He scanned the page: *The World Wars left us in a position of benefaction ... begrudgingly embraced ... the survival of Europe, of Western Civilization ... and yet American influence in Europe is at once sought after and condemned ....* He put the submission down and flipped through the pile beneath it, scanning titles: *Democracy and the Avant-Garde; The Poetry of William Carlos Williams; The Music of Aaron Copland; The Mixed Society; Individualism and the*

Poetic Technique of e.e. cummings. He took one from the pile at random and began to read: *Man was given a blank slate; he created America.* He dropped it back onto the table.

Winter waned and flowers blossomed: forsythia, foxtail, and monkshood. The woolly remnants of a Russian fixation faded from fashion. Reports from Korea continued to flow, bringing news of starvation and slaughter, and the Rosenbergs went on trial. The spring was long and damp and often colder than the winter before it.

3

A blackbird perched on the windowsill. Milne watched it through the glass. The party was quietening. The room slowly emptied out—dispersal at the end of the night. The board in Paris was planning to establish a magazine for Latin American audiences. Carson and Milne were going to Colombia to meet with a prospective editor, Eduardo Munoz. Edna organized a farewell. It had been slow and tedious.

"What have you been working on?"

"A series of dialogues," Marguerite said.

"Do you ever think of writing in English?" Eric asked.

"No," she said. "Why should I?"

"You do for us. It would increase readership, wouldn't it?"

Milne listened to the conversation between them. His mind drifted. The flutter of a tablecloth near the open window—sifting, dancing fabric. He had seen fabric move like that before. The tails of a dress, sometime, somewhere. Plates clattered in the background. He listened to fragments of other conversations. He watched the faces of the people around them. Marguerite's voice returned: "and if it is natural? Solidifying that is ... good?" Milne poured himself a glass of water and sipped it slowly. Eric's voice hung in the air, unanswered. Milne glanced back up and met his eyes. He smiled and nodded at whatever had been said.

"There you have it," Eric said. "It's about reining in. Controlling passion and impulse."

"You want a dispassionate society?"

"In terms of politics, yes!"

Milne picked at the crust of a sandwich. The meat inside sickened him. Eventually, Eric excused himself. Milne and Marguerite sat at the table and watched the remaining people circulate around them.

Eric adjusted his collar, eyeing his reflection in a decorative mirror on the mantlepiece. He turned and bumped directly into one of Carson's friends. He could not remember her name.

"Sorry," Eric said, stumbling around her. "How are you enjoying the party?"

"It's a bit of a bore, isn't it?" the friend said. "Nothing like the parties they used to have."

"Is that so?"

"Have you tried the caviar?"

"I haven't," Eric said.

"Don't bother."

Eric leaned against the wall. He unbuttoned the cuffs of his shirt and folded them back, before rolling them half-way up his forearms. Across the room, Ava and Milne were talking. Carson's friend lingered awkwardly for a few moments and then wandered off to find somewhere else to perform.

London was full of that type, Eric thought—as well as every other. He smiled as he watched Ava and Milne across the room. They were getting along well. He was glad. He leaned against the wall and watched his friends laugh. He sipped whiskey. He rolled the ice in his glass. He had wondered whether or not they would get along. Ava would get along with anyone but Milne was more particular. And yet, here they talked away like they had known one another for years. Almost—there was a search, in fact, an exploration that did not exist in old friends.

He felt somebody's hand on his shoulder. He turned. A tall man in a tweed jacket was trying to reach past him. "I'm sorry," the man said, "I'm just trying to retrieve my glass." Eric stepped to the side. The man picked up the half empty glass of scotch and thanked him. He wore thin, circular spectacles and was balding on the top, though the hair that he had was long and wild—it was deep black and lifted from his scalp in all directions.

Eric put his own drink down on the table. It wobbled. "Aha!" the man said. He held his glass out to Eric with one hand and lifted Eric's glass from the table with the other. "Hold these," he said. He positioned himself in front of the table and grasped it tightly between his fingertips. "There's a simple mathematical solution to this," he said. Then, he slowly rotated the table. Gently wiggling it with his fingers as he did. After about a quarter of a turn, the table stopped wobbling and sat securely on the ground.

He stepped back and raised his eyebrows at Eric. Eric handed back one of the glasses. "Impressive work," he said.

The man grinned. "Stieglitz," he replied, holding his hand toward Eric.

Eric accepted the handshake. "Eric," he said.

"How do you know Carson and Edna?"

"Carson and I work on a magazine together."

"Ah! So this is your party then—you're off to Colombia."

"No," Eric said. "Just Carson and Milne Lowell. I'm staying in London."

"That's a shame," Stieglitz said.

"How do you know the Wards?"

"We moved in the same circles when he was teaching," he said.

"What do you teach?"

"Quantum mechanics," he said. "At least that's the easy answer."

"Sounds impressive," said Eric. "I avoided science all I could but I'm glad you boys are on our side to keep us a step ahead of the Russians. What is it that you work on?"

"It's a little complicated ..."

Something about Milne and Ava drew Eric's attention. Stieglitz was already in the middle of the sentence: "keep in mind that the objects which emerge from the disturbance ..." Eric glanced back at Milne. Immediately, he began to recognize something in his mannerisms—subconscious shifts, glances, and expressions. He recognized in them some commonality that they shared with mannerisms of his own. He moved his focus back to Stieglitz, aware that he was being rude.

"... the rearrangement of the collision products is consequent upon the disturbance. You are familiar, no doubt, with the term atomic spectra?" Eric nodded absently. Milne and Ava were deep in conversation, oblivious to the rest of the room. "... a-particle of the substance," Stieglitz continued. "Of course, there is another circumstance which you may have thought of yourself. Think back to the basic ideas of Rutherford and the measure of nuclear matter ..." Milne laughed, his eyes lingered. There was attraction—was Milne aware? He knew the effect that Ava could have. His focus shifted to Ava. She was relaxed, comfortable. Were the manners reflected? He couldn't tell.

"... not deflected but slowed gradually! The element of time is still missing!" Stieglitz was becoming excited by his words. Eric tried to return focus to him. As Stieglitz spoke, he waved his arms erratically for emphasis. "The behaviour is not directly predictable in detail," he said. "So, by introducing the element of time …" he gestured with a particularly frantic flourish and the fountain pen that he was holding flew from his hand. It sailed through the air and landed across the room. He looked at Eric quickly and then crossed the room and dove beneath a sofa with surprising grace in pursuit.

Eric used the opportunity to slip away. He turned his attention back to Milne and Ava. He was being jealous, he knew. They were friends and it was good that they got along. He had hoped for it. Milne laughed at something else Ava said. His eyes softened, intensified. Milne touched her arm gently as he laughed. Eric watched her react. Ava looked over—he made eye-contact with her. She stiffened, smiled quickly. Milne looked over, following her gaze. Eric raised his glass to him and then crossed the room.

"Cecil Day-Lewis was here," Ava said when he approached. "But you missed him, he was only just stopping by."

"Is that so?" Eric asked.

The fire crackled—embers throbbed red in the charcoal and ash—rain poured steadily on the other side of the window. The panes were glazed with running water: sheets, streams, and droplets.

"Read it to me again," Ava said.

Milne held the book in his hands. The pages shook with the light of the fire. She settled in against his shoulder. *"Among twenty snowy mountains,"* he began, *"the only moving thing was the eye of the blackbird."*

It was evening all afternoon.
It was snowing
And it was going to snow.
The blackbird sat
In the cedar-limbs.

4

Bogotá, 1951: Milne sat at a table outside of the little coffee shop. Cars and people moved up and down the street in front of him. A tall, dust-crusted bus rattled past, working its way through a street far too narrow for the width of its body. An old man sat just inside the door, mumbling quietly to himself. An impossibly round grey bird sauntered along the curb in front of him.

They'd arrived in by plane that morning. It was the longest flight he'd ever been on. He knew that it must have cost a fortune. He ordered another coffee. Then, he heard a voice call out from his right. "Milne!" He turned and looked down the street—Carson was hurrying up the road towards him. "I'm sorry," he said when he got close. He was out of breath. "I got held up. Have they arrived yet?"

"No," Milne said. "You made it in time. Don't worry."

Carson fell into the seat across from Milne. "Oh, thank God," he wheezed. "I ran across the entire bloody city. The bank really was no help at all."

A man came out with Milne's coffee. *"Gracias."*

"Café, por favor," Carson said. The man nodded and disappeared. Carson breathed heavily and took a notebook from his bag. "Ok," he said. "When they get here, they will probably ask

about distribution, editorialship, and funding." He looked up at Milne. "In all departments, they'll be practically the same as us. Editorial authority with the same kind of approval from Paris. They select their own content. They differ from us in that they will handle their own distribution internally. Internationally, Paris will take care of it. In terms of funding, I have approximate numbers here," he said, tapping his notebook, "if they ask."

Two men stepped out of a building across the road and walked toward the table. Carson had his back to them. Milne tapped his arm. "I think that's them," he said quietly and nodded in the direction that they were coming from. Carson turned his head. One of the men waved. He had a thick black mustache and perfectly parted hair. His clothes were neat and expensive. When he reached the table, Milne and Carson stood and shook his hand.

"Eduardo," he said. The other man shook both of their hands as well. He introduced himself as Hector. Milne and Carson introduced themselves and sat down. The two men joined them.

"How do you like Colombia?" Eduardo asked.

"We just arrived yesterday," said Milne. "It is beautiful. I've never seen a view like that from a plane before."

Hector lit a little cigar and waved away the man who approached with Carson's coffee. "We spoke to Nicolas," he said. "We expected him to come."

Milne looked at Carson. "I thought he told you that we would be coming. We're the editors of *Witness*, the magazine in London."

Eduardo laughed. "It's ok. It's better to talk to other writers anyway."

"Do you also write?" Carson asked, turning to Hector.

Hector smiled. "No," he said. "I am more organizational, like Nicolas."

Carson nodded. "What do you do?"

Hector drew on his cigar. "Are you familiar with the *Organizacion de los Estados Americanos*? OAS?"

"Somewhat," Carson replied.

"What they do in offices, we do on the ground."

"What is that, exactly?"

"Pave the way for progress."

Carson looked confused. "What does that entail?" he asked.

Hector looked directly into Carson's eyes momentarily, searching for something. When he spoke, his voice was calm. "Fighting," he said.

Milne was caught off guard. He glanced at Eduardo. He wondered if he understood correctly. "You're a guerilla?"

Hector laughed. "What do you know of guerillas?"

Milne felt his heartbeat quicken—he tried to smile but couldn't contain his unease. "Just what I see in the newspapers."

"And what is that?"

He decided to be honest. "Kidnappings," he said. "Bombings."

The poet looked amused. Hector smiled. "Did you plant no bombs in the war? Did you take no prisoners?" he asked. "You like to act so principled," he said. "We know who you are—we know who you work for." He paused and watched their faces. "Maybe, you do not know who you are," he said. He was laughing but it no longer seemed lighthearted. "It might surprise you how quickly your principles fall away when it suits you." He stood up from his chair. "We're done," he said. "Tell them we need more guns. Not money, not books. Weapons."

The poet smiled awkwardly and stood as well. "It was a pleasure to meet you," he said. The two men stood together, looked up and down the street, and then walked away from the table. Carson and Milne sat silently, watching the backs of the men disappear down the street. The waiter returned with Carson's coffee. Carson stared down at the dark liquid in the mug. "I'll need something stronger than this," he said.

They left their cups at the table and went across the road to a bar. Though it was early in the day, the bar was nearly full. "Whatever's good," Carson said. Milne held up two fingers. Two men along the bar smiled and spoke quietly. The barman spoke no English. He took a bottle from the top shelf.

"What now?" Milne asked.

Carson shrugged. He drank slowly. Milne drank as well.

"Have you always lived in Montreal?" Carson asked, eventually.

"No," Milne replied. "I was born in Nova Scotia. My parents moved to Montreal when I was young."

"Why did they move?" Carson asked.

"My father worked for a shipping company. He moved from one port to another."

"What did he do?"

"Logistics—numbers," Milne said. "He hated it, I think."

Carson nodded. "Naturally," he said.

"What about you? Have you always lived in London?"

"No," Carson said. "Cardiff, Oxford. We moved around. I was in Europe for some time."

"That was before?"

"Before. During."

"Where in Europe were you?"

"All over," Carson said. "You name it, I've been there. One way or another. I lived in a villa in Ferrières-en-Brie for a while with a friend but he popped off one night in Paris after drinking too much absinthe."

"What do you suppose we should do now?" Milne asked.

"Get on the line with Nicolas, I suppose."

"Do you think he knew who we were dealing with down here?"

Carson looked around the bar. He leaned over to answer but the barman approached. Carson nodded to him and held up two fingers. A breeze rattled the door in its frame. Milne and Carson drank in silence. One of the old men at the bar stepped down from his stool and moved close.

"You're from England," he said.

"I am."

"And the United States," he said, looking at Milne.

"Canada," Milne replied.

The man sat next to Carson. His friend moved down the bar and took the stool beside him. For a while, they didn't speak. Milne watched the clock. Carson ordered another round. The old men spoke together in Spanish.

One of the old men looked to Carson. "Englishman. What are you doing here?"

Carson glanced at Milne with a crooked grin. "We came down to help set up a magazine," he said. "But it turned out that you crazy bastards were just looking for a crate of machine guns."

The old man burst out laughing. "Watch how you speak," he said, wagging his finger.

Carson loosened his tie and leaned down the bar toward him. "I should warn you. I boxed in the army."

The man laughed and said something to his friend. He slapped Carson on the back and turned to the bartender. *"Otro trago,"* he said, "for my favourite Englishman. Listen, I know somewhere you will love ..."

Milne glanced over his shoulder. Two men in uniform, soldiers or police, sitting at a low table along the wall, watched them silently. He nursed his drink. They were being too loud, he thought. He tried to make out what the uniforms signified. He wondered, suddenly, if Hector was pro- or antigovernment.

What about themselves? Carson and the men spoke amongst themselves. Milne traced the grain of the wood on top of the bar with his finger. The bartender offered him another drink. He shook his head.

The bar closed early. They left. The old men stayed behind. The uniformed men left with them. In the evening air, Carson and Milne walked back to the hotel. When they arrived, Carson took a bottle of rum from his suitcase and set it on the dresser.

Milne opened the door to the balcony and they stepped out onto it together. The sun was beginning to fall behind the buildings across the road. The night was long and warm. They sat out enjoying one another's company, without much talk. Milne thought about the conversation with Hector. He wondered if the magazine would still happen. Some of their money was coming from the Americans, he figured. There wasn't much doubt about that. He thought of the couple in Paris; the couple at the inn; the break in; Berlin and the war; Hector and his guns.

When the stars began to flicker, Milne felt his eyelids droop. He thought of the stars above London—the stars above Ava. He said goodnight to Carson and stepped back inside. From the window of his room, as he changed for bed, he saw Carson pour another glass of rum, light a cigarette, and lean on the railing, looking out into the night.

Milne woke. His head ached and his stomach turned. He looked out the open window next to him. The sun was heavy in the sky. The clatter of a typewriter beat into the room from behind the wall. He drew himself from the bed and yawned. Through the open window, the sun filled the room. Tears crept from the corner of his eyes. He wiped them.

Carson sat at the desk in the next room over, an empty pot of coffee and an empty bottle of rum beside him. Ashes spilled from the tray and onto the sheets of paper littering the desk. His face was pale. The skin beneath his eyes was loose and bruised.

"Jesus," Milne said. "Did you sleep at all?"

Carson didn't look up. "I've got it," he said.

"You've got what?"

"I've got it," Carson repeated. He continued to type.

Milne took the coffee pot from the desk and brought it into the kitchen. He rinsed the pot and put the kettle on. He listened to the beat of the typewriter. *We know who you are,* Hector had said. *Tell them we need more guns.* Milne watched steam rise from the kettle and spread out against the wall. It shifted as it rose. *Maybe you do not know who you are.* The water began to roll in the kettle and a low whistle grew. He took it from the stovetop.

He pressed the coffee and poured two cups. He brought one to Carson. "What are you writing?" he asked. Carson didn't answer.

"Are you alright, Carson?"

Carson didn't reply. Milne eyed the bottle.

"We need to get some food into us," he said. "Let's get breakfast."

"I'm really on to something here."

"You'll be onto it when you get back. You need to eat."

Carson looked up. His eyes were bloodshot.

"Jesus, Carson. You look like you haven't slept in a week." Milne grabbed him by the arm. "Let's go," he said.

Carson hesitantly got to his feet. He seemed to regain his senses when he rose. He went to the bathroom and closed the door. Milne looked down at the scattered papers on the desk.

He was either too groggy to read or there was no coherence at all on the page. It seemed to be the workings of a novel but it was entirely disjointed and rambling.

When Carson came out of the bathroom his hair was combed and his face was washed. He was still pale but looked far better than before. "Are you ready?" he asked.

Milne set down his cup and nodded. "I need to get out of this room," he said. "Let's go."

They walked down to the street and stepped outside. Milne immediately felt better. He breathed deeply. It hit him properly then: they were in Colombia. Before taking this job, he had been throughout Canada, New York, and Connecticut.

He looked around. The buildings were beautiful and tall. Even though their work was ruined, they could enjoy the week ahead, he thought. It was free now. "What should we do after we eat?" he asked.

"What can we do?" Carson asked.

"We're in Colombia. One of the most beautiful countries in the world. We can go out to the plateaus, the mountains, see the savanna, explore the city. We have an empty week."

Carson stopped walking momentarily. He stared at Milne. "Do you not understand?" he asked. "Doesn't it bother you at all?"

"What?"

Carson turned away and continued to walk. They walked silently along the street though neither knew where they were going. A young man stopped them and asked for a match. Milne took a matchbox from his pocket and held it out. The man took it from him and lit his cigarette. He offered one to Milne and asked him where he was from. Milne told him that he was from Canada but was working on a magazine in London. The man told him that he was a doctor in training, but that his true dream was to write as well. He lit Milne's cigarette and then returned the matches. Milne asked him if there was a good restaurant nearby.

They carried on down the street in the direction that the young doctor had pointed. The street was incredibly wide and framed on either end with immense Spanish buildings. When they reached the restaurant, they sat at a table inside away from the heat bearing down from the midday sun. Milne ordered a coffee and water. Carson ordered a cocktail. They ate *changua* and fruit and talked sparingly. Carson's mood shifted after eating—he became high-spirited, lofty. He ordered another drink. Milne ordered another coffee.

Milne excused himself to go to the bathroom. When he returned to the table, it was empty. He waved the waiter over. "Where did my friend go?" he asked. The waiter shrugged. Milne was not sure that he understood the question. He pointed to the empty chair. The waiter gestured to the door.

"*¿Se fue?*"

The waiter nodded. "*Sí.*"

Milne left the restaurant. He looked up and down the street outside. There was no sign of Carson. He looked for somebody to ask. An old lady was sitting alone in a doorway across the street. He crossed over to her.

"I'm looking for my friend," Milne said. "Have you seen an Englishman pass by? *Inglés.*"

The woman shook her head and said something to him in Spanish. A young boy leaned out of the window. He pointed across the street to a two-storey building.

"He went in there?" Milne asked. "*¿Ahí?*"

The boy nodded. Milne thanked him and crossed the street. The front door of the building was unlocked. It opened into what had clearly been the lobby of a hotel at some point. A woman sat on a chair beside a curtain leading past the empty front desk and into the back room.

"Did an Englishman come in here?" Milne asked. The lady ignored him. "I'm looking for my friend," he said. She shook her head and didn't move. Milne passed the woman and pushed the curtain aside. There was a waiting room, of sorts, on the other side. He stepped through and looked around. A wooden bench ran the length of one wall. A series of doors ran across the others. All but one were open. A man in a dark shirt sat on the bench reading a magazine. When Milne entered, he looked up. Milne walked toward the closed door.

Before he could reach it, the man stood and stepped in front of him. Milne stepped to the side and tried to pass the man—he grabbed Milne by his shirt and pushed him against the wall. Milne tried to break free of his grasp. "I'm just trying to get to my friend," he said. "He's in there." The man stared at him blankly. "He's married," Milne said. *"Casado."*

The man laughed. He let go of Milne's shirt. "Ok," he said. *"Ser rápido."*

Milne opened the door. Carson lay across a sofa half dressed and half conscious. A woman sat across the room on a table, fixing her makeup in the mirror. Milne shook Carson's shoulder. He looked up and opened his eyes. "We need to get you out of here," Milne said. He looked over his shoulder. The man was leaning against the doorframe behind him.

"Carson. Let's go." Carson began to sit up. Milne pulled on his arm. Carson pushed him off and fell backwards onto the sofa. Milne tried to lift him again and then felt the arms of the other man on his back. The man pushed him to the side and grabbed Carson by either side of his unbuttoned shirt. Carson pushed back at him but the man lifted him and dropped him off the sofa onto the floor. "Go," he said to Milne. "Now."

Carson stood uncertainly. Milne supported his arms. They walked to the door and passed through the lobby. The man held the door to let them leave. Milne turned to thank him. Carson slipped free from his grasp. He broke into a run and headed across the square.

"Carson!" Milne yelled after him. "Where are you going?"

Carson didn't respond. Milne looked on in horror as he stripped the remainder of his clothes in the street. He ran toward a horse statue in the center of the square, trailing his pants, which clung to his ankle, behind him. Everyone else looked on with wide eyes—some laughed, some shook their heads in disgust. Milne called after Carson and then began to chase him, but he was already too far. Carson made it to the statue before Milne could catch him. He grabbed onto the side of the horse and slipped on its sleek surface, falling into the shallow water beneath. On his second attempt, he successfully mounted the horse and raised his fist triumphantly in the air. "I am Caesar!" he announced to the onlookers. "Caesar of Colombia!"

Milne reached the statue—he did not know what to do. He put his hand on Carson's calf and spoke softly to him. "Carson, we need to go. You need to come down." Carson didn't lower his eyes to Milne. "Avenge O'Lord, thy slaughtered saints!" he yelled from his pedestal above the square.

Three men in uniform crossed the square from the other side. Milne grabbed Carson's arm and tried to pull him from the horse. Carson shook him off. "God damnit, Carson! Get off that horse," he said, grabbing his arm again. The crowd backed away and the uniformed men approached. One of them drew a pistol from his belt. The other two seized Carson by the leg and pulled him from the horse. He fell to the ground and one of the men kicked him in the ribs.

Milne ran around to the other side of the horse to plead with the men. The one with the pistol raised it and shook his head. Milne put his hands up and stepped back. The men lifted Carson and began to drag him away. The man with the gun stepped behind Milne and directed him to follow.

They walked through the square and were pushed against a wall. The guard with the gun went inside and made a phone call. Shortly after, two cars pulled up. The uniformed men spoke to the occupants. Milne and Carson were pushed into the cars. Two men sat in the front of Milne's car. His bladder felt weak. The cars drove. Though the drive was short, it felt long.

When the car stopped, the men stepped out. The back door opened and Milne was pulled from it. He was still in the city. He felt relief. The men led him into a large building—police or military. They took him into a concrete room. He did not see where Carson was taken. He hadn't seen him since they got into the cars. He sat at a metal table in the center of the room. There was no clock inside. His hand was cuffed to the chair. A dim lightbulb hung from the ceiling above the table. He felt dizzy.

Eventually, the door on the other side of the table opened and a different uniformed man entered. He sat down in the chair across from Milne and lay a folder in front of him. Something was written across the front in pen. Milne couldn't make out any of the handwriting. The man began speaking to him in Spanish. He opened the folder and looked through it. Milne saw photographs of himself and Carson amidst documents and reports. There were photographs of their passports as well. The man spoke quickly.

"No hablo espanol," Milne said. "Ah ... *no entiendo."*

The uniformed man stared.

"Do you speak English?" Milne asked. The man stood up and closed the file. He said something that Milne couldn't understand and then left the room. Milne sat alone at the table for a long time. The cuffs cut into his wrists. It was cold. He couldn't tell whether he was shaking or shivering. He took.a deep breath—tried to calm himself. He thought of Montreal. He thought of London. He thought of Ava. Of her chestnut hair; her eyes. He thought of her laugh and of her smile.

The door opened and the uniformed man returned. A younger man came in with him. He placed the file back in front of Milne and opened it to a photo of Milne, Carson, Eduardo, and Hector.

"What is your purpose in this country?" he asked.

"Business," Milne said. "I'm a writer. I work for a magazine."

"These men," he said, tapping the picture. "How do you know them?"

"That is…"

"We know who they are. How do you know them?"

"Business," he said. "We wanted to work on a magazine with Eduardo."

"What magazine?"

"Literature. Poetry."

"Politics," the officer said.

"Culture," Milne said. "A little politics."

"We don't want your politics here."

Milne didn't respond.

"Who else did you meet here?"

"Nobody," Milne replied.

He was questioned for a long time. Eventually, the officers either believed that he had no information or gave up trying to find it. He was taken from the room and put into a cell. Carson was already lying in the corner, bloody from the beating he had taken. His clothes lay around him. "It's all over, Milne," he mumbled from the floor.

Milne knelt beside him. "What is?" he asked.

Carson stayed silent. Before too long, Milne heard the slow steady breath of sleep—the unconscious sigh. Carson was right: the world was still at war. It had been one of the first things that he had ever heard him say. As far as he could tell, everyone else thought the same. There were no bystanders, there was no neutrality.

His clothes were damp with sweat. He thought of his mother and father. He thought of life. He thought of places and people, of experiences. Really, it was emotion that came to him—a diluted gesture at feelings he once felt, and which now lay on the other side of some wall, some abyss—some unknown. He wondered if this was all he would ever feel again: fear, terror. He thought back to the naïve and beautiful lie he had lived. It was all ridiculous. They had the option and capacity to feel so much. Instead, they chose pain; violence; domination—Fear. He looked at Carson. It was easy to blame him. He lay there, weak and pitiful.

There were no windows in the cell but the walls were thin. He could hear the sounds of the outer world through them. He closed his eyes. The suffocation that he felt—that claustrophobic sense—faded as he listened to the steady breathing of his friend and the world beyond the walls. The voices of guards carried into the cell. Opening and closing doors shook the floor beneath him.

He was alone. He sat in the cell with his eyes closed and scenes from the past year swarmed him. He tried to beat them back but they were overpowering. Crowds on the streets of Berlin; a plane of animated faces; a fleeing silhouette; the eyes of a soldier, scared, old; Ava on the shore; swans in the water; a broken neck limp in the jaws of the foxhound.

✴

Marguerite put down her pen and went out onto the street. It was quiet and still. Total darkness was kept at bay by the occasional streetlight and the glow from windows above. Sitting alone too long was becoming tiresome. The apartment was temporary, and it felt it.

Of course, she was not entirely alone. There was Milne. There was the crowd down at Kavanagh's. There were the few women at Kavanagh's or the welcoming pub next door who she slowly and anxiously tested, felt out, and then invited to lunch or coffee. Occasionally, there was something more. It was a loneliness borne from being out of place—from being unsettled and away from home. At the bookshop, they teased her for her work at the magazine. At the magazine, they seemed uneasy. In neither place was she entirely accepted.

Some nights when she couldn't sleep, she wandered the streets, as she was doing now. Some evenings she rode the Underground, expecting its displaced lull to be welcome, though it hardly ever was. She kicked a pebble with her toe and listened to it skitter across the ground. She saw someone, a man, standing at the corner ahead, well-dressed and dimly lit by the streetlight. She turned and went the other way.

She missed her homes—Montreal and Cap-Rouge. The forests, hills, mountains, and lakes of her childhood were not something she often missed before but here they were yearned for. She missed the freedom that she had. The independence. She had thought that she would find freedom here, but it was not the case. Here, people were disenchanted. There was no hope.

Two of her essays had been rejected in the last three issues. The other required heavy editing. Every time she fought and every time she lost. In order to publish, in order to get paid, she had to do what she was told. She was beginning to learn what she could get away with and what she could not. She tested the boundaries. If she dealt in the abstract, if she worked philosophically or referred to works of art or literature, she was generally fine.

In recent months, wandering had become frequent. When she slept, she dreamt. When she dreamt, it was frightening. Some nights she lay in bed fearful of the sleep ahead. When she woke in the morning, she felt relief.

Milne woke to the sounds of the cell door opening. He wondered the time—there was no way to tell. Two guards entered the cell. One of them prodded Carson with his boot.

"Stand up."

Milne got to his feet. Carson rolled over, waking. Milne stooped to help him up. "He needs clothes," he said.

"He has clothes," the guard said. "Help him dress."

Milne picked the torn clothes from the ground and helped Carson into them. They hung loosely on his frame. The guards escorted them through the building. Sunlight poured through the windows. When the front doors opened, it hit them like a breaking wave. Carson looked up into the light. Milne shielded his eyes. The guards pushed them through the doors and into the street.

"Where are we?" Carson asked.

"I don't know," Milne said. He looked around—none of the buildings were familiar. A voice, American, called out to them. Milne turned. A man in a light suit stood next to the door. His red hair was combed back over a balding spot in the center of his head. Milne took Carson by the arm.

"Are you …"

"I'm here to take you to the airport," he said. He seemed vaguely familiar but Milne couldn't place him.

"Have we met before?" Milne asked.

"I doubt it," the man said. He stepped away from the wall and opened the backdoor of a maroon four door. "Please get in the car."

"My friend needs a doctor."

"He'll be fine."

"Who sent you?" Milne asked.

"In the car," the man said. "Please."

Milne helped Carson into the back seat and the American got into the front. Carson slumped against the window and groaned.

"He needs a doctor," Milne said. The American didn't respond. He shifted and pulled away from the building. Milne didn't see beyond the inside of the car. His gaze shifted between the expressionless American and Carson's battered figure. Shadows, cast by buildings and trees, passed over the face of the driver as they drove. Milne felt a pain in his side for the first time. His head began to ache.

They left the shadows of buildings and the harsh glare of the sun pierced the windshield. The driver lifted a pair of sunglasses from the dashboard and put them on. Milne turned his eyes down. Hardened vomit coated the toe of his shoe. He didn't know where it came from. He scraped at it with the heel of his other foot.

The car rolled to a stop. Milne looked up—hangars and metal boxes surrounded them. A small plane rolled to a stop in the distance. Next to them, another plane sat ready for takeoff. The American turned and leaned over the seat. He took his sunglasses off and looked into Milne's eyes. For the first time, Milne saw compassion in them.

"This plane's been waiting for you," he said. "Hurry up and get on. You're going home."

"What about our things?"

"Forget them. You're lucky to be alive."

"Thank you," Milne said. "Who are you? Who sent you?"

"I don't know what connections you two imbeciles have," he said, "but they must be damn good." He turned and placed his glasses back on the bridge of his nose. "Go on now."

Carson sat up and opened the door. He struggled to his feet. Milne stepped out from the other side and rounded the car to meet him. He helped him stand and they walked to the plane. A man in a pilot's uniform helped them up the steps. It was half full of people who eyed them with confusion and irritation as they entered. Whispers swept through the seats as Carson's tattered form passed.

They took their seats. A man sat across the aisle from them with a holster on his waist. The sun streamed down from behind the plane. The stairs were lifted. The propellers began to spin. When the plane slowly rolled forward, the American's car was already gone. Milne watched the hangar slide backward—the grass and trees moved with it. He took his eyes from the window.

The plane lifted from the ground, shaking. Milne stared straight ahead, counting down each second until the plane levelled out. Green mountains and rows of buildings faded beneath them. They passed through the first thin layer of cloud cover. Milne turned and watched the beauty below disappear. He looked over at Carson, who cradled his head in his hands. He was asleep or unconscious. Milne wanted to feel anger. Instead, he felt pity.

Hector's words echoed in his mind: *Tell them we need more guns.*

5

London, 1951: When, on the final plane, the cloud cover parted revealing coastline jutting from the sea and a misshapen checkerboard of green and brown, Milne expected to find relief and comfort. Instead, he found himself looking out over the Dockyards—a shattered grid of factories and council estates—with unease. Pillars of black smoke rose from the city.

When they touched down, they were taken from the plane and separated. Milne was driven to an unfamiliar part of the city and brought into a building that looked like any other. The uniformed police disappeared and he was led into a small room on the second floor. It was too familiar.

He sat in a chair across from two men who questioned him. For two hours, they went over the details of his trip. They questioned him on everything from the moment he touched down to the moment he left Colombia. He tried his best to repeat the events exactly as they had occurred. They showed particular interest in Hector, the man who had accompanied Eduardo to the meeting. They showed Milne a series of pictures to try to identify him but none of them matched.

They shifted focus and asked him about his own life. They asked about his past and about his activities during the war. They asked him about people in Montreal—they had names and addresses. They asked about Marguerite. They asked him how long he had known her and why he had offered her a position in London. They asked him if he had ever visited Kavanagh's Bookshop and if he was aware of Marguerite's connections in anarchist circles. They asked his views on homosexuality.

Then, they shifted focus again and began to ask him about Ignazio Brown. They wanted to know if Marguerite and Ignazio had any contact before their meeting in Berlin. They wanted to know if they had maintained contact afterward.

Eventually, there was a sharp knock at the door. One of the men stepped out of the room. When he returned, he told Milne that the interview was over. They took him from the room, led him back through the building, and left him at the door. Milne stepped outside. He tried to get his bearings. It was cold. He didn't know where he was and had no idea how to get home. He needed a shower. He needed to eat.

A car door opened next to him and a man stepped out. Milne moved to the side to avoid him. As he did, the man reached out: "Milne!"

Milne looked back. "Cliff," he said. "What are you doing in London?"

Clifford looked at him and smiled. He didn't reply. He nodded towards the car. "Get in," he said. Milne looked back at the building, then walked around to the other side of the car. He got into the passenger seat. Clifford sat back into the car and closed the door. He ran his hand through his hair. "That was a real mess, Milne," he said.

"I know," Milne replied. He didn't know what else to say about it. It had been a real mess. "Have you spoken to Carson?" he asked.

"Yes, I went to him first. Sorry for leaving you in there for so long."

"How did you get me out?"

"I had someone pull some strings," Clifford said. He started the car.

"You saved us down there," Milne said.

Clifford didn't respond.

Milne tried to read his face. "How's Carson?"

"He's going to be taking some time off."

"Does Edna know what happened? Is he home?"

"He's home."

"Will he be back?"

"I don't know. Probably. He's a good name on the bill."

Milne nodded. He thought of Carson sprawled across the concrete floor. "That was a hell of a thing down there," he said.

"We'll have to talk about what happened with Eduardo," Clifford said.

"They asked me a lot about that. His friend in particular. Who was that? Did you know he was connected to guerillas?"

"What else did they ask about?"

"Myself, Montreal, Marguerite and Ignazio, mostly."

"Did they tell you why?"

"Why what?" Milne asked.

"They were asking about Ignazio."

"No. Why?"

"He defected," Clifford said. He was watching Milne's expression closely.

"What do you mean he defected?"

"I mean he went over to the other side. Maybe he was over there all along. We're trying to figure it all out—we'll talk more about it later."

"Is he in Russia?"

"Yes. Moscow, we think."

"Jesus. We were just with him in Berlin. I would never have guessed …"

"We need to talk about that too. You spent some time with him there, right before he went over."

"He didn't mention anything about it."

"Were there any indications?"

"Not that I can remember," Milne said. "Is Nicolas here as well?"

"No, he's still in Paris," Clifford said. "You must be exhausted. Close your eyes. I'll take you home."

Though he was filled with questions, Milne said nothing for the rest of the drive. Clifford left him at his apartment. He promised to call by in the morning to talk things through. Milne went inside, collapsed on the sofa, and drifted off. It was dark and empty. He did not dream.

He awoke feeling disoriented and unclean. A bad taste clung to his tongue. He went into the kitchen, put on the kettle, and then made his way into the bedroom. He unbuttoned his shirt and went over the interrogation in his mind. Why were they so interested in Marguerite? What was her connection to Ignazio?

He watched water droplets trace paths between the wooden crosses on the windows. Behind them, the foggy silhouettes of factories beyond the houses were just visible. There was a knock at the door. He buttoned his shirt and stepped out of the bedroom. He looked in the hall mirror and ran his hands through his hair, then he answered the door.

Edna stood in the hallway in a dripping coat. "Hello, Milne," she said. "May I come in?"

"Edna … of course." He stepped back and opened the door further. "How are you?"

"I'm fine."

"Is Carson …"

183

"He's home. Sleeping," she said. She stepped into the apartment. The kettle began to whistle. He apologized and hurried into the kitchen. "Cup of tea?" he called back.

"Yes, thank you," Edna said.

He returned with two cups and set them down on the coffee table in the living room off the hall. He took her wet coat and umbrella and hung them by the door.

"They may do better by the heater," Edna said.

"Of course," Milne replied. "I'm sorry." He took them from the hook and draped them beside the heater.

Edna looked around the cluttered little room and shifted awkwardly. "Milne, I don't exactly know what happened down there. I want to talk to you about it."

Milne looked down at the floor. "Yes," he said. "Please sit down."

Edna dropped into the seat. "Oh, I knew that he was in no state to go," she said. "I should never have allowed it."

"What do you mean?" Milne asked. He sat on the sofa across from her.

"I've been worried about him for a while now," she said. "I don't know who else to talk to about it. I don't know how the others would take it."

"What have you been worried about?" Milne asked.

"First, you should know, and please don't tell him that I told you this, that Carson was very unhappy with the way he was treated by Nicolas and Mr. Bernstein after they took him on. He thought that they weren't being forthright with him." She sipped the tea and glanced around the room again. "He really believed in the cause. He just wanted honesty."

"In what way?"

"Oh, I don't know," Edna said. "He thought that the Americans were more involved than they were letting on—the government, I mean. The three of them met with some people from the State Department early on. He didn't mind the idea of working with them but, like I said, he didn't like the dishonesty."

Milne sat back. "He met with the State Department about the magazine?"

"No, it wasn't anything like that. They met at a pub. It was nothing official, really. He just got the sense that there was more to it than they were letting on."

"There are always rumours," Milne said. "I try not to pay them heed."

"They're not all rumours. Some of them were involved in similar things in the war. With the Office of Strategic Services and all of that."

Milne nodded. "Yes, but that was unrelated. Things are different now."

"It may be. It is hard for me to keep it all straight in my head. When Carson was asked to approach Mr. Brown, for instance ..."

"Ignazio Brown?"

"Yes, Ignazio."

"What was he approached for?"

"For the job," she said.

"He was offered a position?"

Edna paused and looked at him oddly. "Yes," she said. "I assumed that you knew. He turned down the position they gave to you."

Milne thought back to Paris—the conference. He shook his head. "I didn't know."

"Oh. Well, it's a good thing, of course. It makes you wonder what would have happened if he had taken it."

"I don't know if he could have done much harm—we don't have the kind of information everyone seems to think we do."

"In any case," Edna said. "Mr. Brown was involved with the OSS during the war. He worked on the France-Swiss border with the resistance. Nicolas mentioned it to Carson when he asked him to offer him the job, as if it was relevant in some way. Carson found it all very unusual."

Milne nodded. "Ignazio was a complicated person, it seems."

"In any case, this is all beside the point. The point is that Carson has had a difficult time with all of this, despite how it may appear. He's become very closed off and temperamental." Edna wrung her hands. "He has bouts," she said.

Milne felt sorry for her. "Look, I don't know what you know and I don't want to upset you or cause trouble ..." he looked into her eyes—he thought of Carson half dressed in the brothel, naked in the streets, "... things went very badly down there."

"I think that I know most of it."

"Do you know that we were arrested?"

"Yes," she said.

"Do you know that they beat him?"

"Yes," she said. "He could not hide the marks. He was through worse in the war—he'll be alright with that."

"Do you know why he was imprisoned?"

Edna looked away. "Yes," she said.

"I think you know most of it then," Milne said. "I'm sorry." They sat silent for a while. "Carson is a good man," he said eventually. "It will be ok. Clifford will look out for him."

"To be honest, I don't trust Mr. Bernstein. Will you look out for him?"

"Yes," he said. "I'll do everything I can."

"He doesn't sleep," she said.

Milne nodded.

"Do you think there is any truth to it?"

"To what?"

186

"The Americans."

Milne looked at Edna for a long time. "I will admit that I've considered it," he said, "particularly over the last few days. And, I don't know how Clifford managed to get us out of there—things are certainly murky—but, if American politicians are anything to go by, the State Department has little knowledge or appreciation of art at all. I really can't see them justifying the cost, frankly."

Edna nodded slowly.

"If everyone who lifted a rifle in this century was suspected of carrying on his wartime duties when he returned from the front ... well, we could trust just about nobody." He stared at the cup of tea on the table. He did not feel certain.

"You're right," Edna said. She stood and stooped to pick up the teacups.

"Leave them," Milne said. "I'll take care of that."

Edna crossed the room and picked up her coat and umbrella. She looked scared.

Milne followed her to the door. "Nobody left it behind, Edna. The war, I mean. They all just carry it differently."

She smiled weakly. "Thank you, Milne. Carson likes you," she said. "More than most."

Milne nodded and opened the door. "Any time," he said. "If you need anything at all, just ask."

"Just one last thing," Edna said, before stepping out the door. "Have you ever heard of something called the Pearson Foundation?"

"No," he said. "I don't think that I have. Why?"

"It's just something that Carson has been rambling about. He's off the deep end, you see. I don't know—I thought that it might mean something to you."

"No," Milne said. "Unfortunately, I can't say that it does."

"Ok," she said. "Goodnight, Milne."

Milne closed the door behind her. He stared at the chipped paint along the edges of the frame.

6

Clifford arrived at 8:35 in the morning. Milne was sleeping solidly when he heard the knock. He answered the door and invited Clifford in to wait while he dressed. Clifford wore a blue blazer and two-tone derbies. When they left, it was 8:55 and the sun was rising quickly above the rooftops. The rooftops were black and grey and the sun was warm and bright. They walked for a while between the flat-stone buildings and stopped in a park where the grass was short and green and stretched out between the streets.

They sat on a bench between hedges and flowers looking out at the fountain in the square and Milne began to recall the events in Colombia for a third time. Clifford smoked Camels. He didn't interrupt or ask any questions. When Milne finished talking, they sat silently. The space was filled with chirping birds and rushing water from the fountain.

"Who led?" Clifford asked after a while. "This man, Hector, or Eduardo?"

Milne thought back. He eyed a magpie on the hedge. "I would say that Hector did," he said.

Clifford nodded and drew on his cigarette. Milne watched him. He wondered what he thought—what he knew. "Do you know what he meant?" Milne asked. "Why he thought we could find him guns?"

Clifford shrugged. "They figure that any American can get them guns down there."

"We're not even American," Milne said.

"It's all the same to them."

"He thought we worked for the government," Milne said.

"It seems so," Clifford said. They sat and watched the birds play around the fountain and young couples pass, giggling behind false composure. "They can't imagine that anyone would do this for the right reasons," he said. "It's why the communists have such luck down there."

"Some here think the same thing."

"The fact that intellectuals and the state share certain commitments isn't a bad thing. It simply means that government represents the people," he said. "A few years ago, people knew this." He sighed. "Everyone's been out for blood since the Rosenbergs," he added.

"People don't like to see a woman on the block," Milne said. They sat for a while longer and then continued to walk through to the other side of the park.

"How do you feel?" Clifford asked.

"A little shaken up," he replied. They rounded the corner and began to walk back up the path towards Milne's apartment. "We made a mockery of their country," he added.

"We shouldn't have sent you down there. I'm sorry about that."

Milne nodded. "It's alright. Nobody could have predicted that."

"No, they couldn't have," Clifford agreed. "We'll take care of Carson. Don't worry about that." They reached the end of the park and turned. They walked back towards Milne's apartment along the street.

"What do you know about Ignazio?" Milne asked.

"Nothing yet," Clifford said. "It was a shock to us all."

"What happened?"

"He kept an apartment in Berlin and stayed there much of the time," Clifford said. "He was meant to be somewhere and didn't show up. When they went looking, his apartment was cleared out. Somebody claims to have spotted him crossing the border in the backseat of a car."

Milne shook his head. "What would compel you?" he asked.

"Delusion or Power," said Clifford. "Sometimes it's a woman but, with Ignazio, I doubt it."

It began to get colder and the leaves fell from the trees. Nicolas organized a festival in Paris: for every day of autumn, a symphony, opera, or ballet performed—orchestras arrived from Vienna, Boston, Rome and Berlin. Work on the magazine continued with little break. Though he didn't come into the office, Carson's name stayed on everything. The magazine grew and every morning brought with it submissions and queries.

In the evenings, they sat together drinking wine and gin, and playing cards or dancing. They ate together and laughed and Colombia stopped weighing so heavily upon them. It was distant and peripheral. They missed Carson but did not call upon him out of pity or shame. Eric said that he had noticed Carson taking Benzedrine before the trip and felt like he was to blame. The nights were cool and the parks began to empty out. The leaves were golden on the ground and the vines turned against the brick and stone. And then, slowly, the colour faded and the leaves began to melt into the ground, and the rain came more frequently and brought a bitter chill with it, and the autumn slipped away.

When winter came, the branches were brittle and bare, and wind howled through the alleyways at night. Inside, fires crackled and coal burned. Dark plumes rose from smokestacks and chimneys and lingered, trapped, beneath the cold layer above the city. Particles drifted down and stained the earth and stone.

7

The morning had been cold and wet but, by noon, the sun emerged and the skies cleared, and little flurries fell upon the city. Marguerite looked up into the falling snow and then closed her eyes to feel the flakes melt gently on her cheeks. She heard laughter from children close by. Then, she opened her eyes and kept walking. The cobblestone was wet beneath her feet. She moved carefully. Ahead, she saw her bus. It waited at the intersection. The stop was just on the other side of the road. Through the little windows, passengers sat, waiting. If she ran, she might make it, she thought. Just as she decided to try, traffic slowed and the bus crawled through the intersection. It was warm, and she wore a wool cardigan beneath her coat, so she decided to walk. It wasn't far, in any case. When the bus stopped across the road, she let it go. It carried on without her.

Clifford was in London and she did not like it. He was cold, bitter. He was paranoid. Since his arrival, things had changed. She felt exiled from the group, simply because her idea of freedom didn't involve sidling up to one power bloc or another. Clifford didn't think that was possible. To him, the world was black and white. It had to be.

Marguerite stepped from the footpath into the street. She crossed it quickly. She watched a woman who'd stepped off the bus stoop to take a pebble from her shoe. Behind her, a man in a brown suit lingered. He'd stepped off the bus as well. He lit a cigarette and then stopped a couple passing to ask for directions. Marguerite wondered if he was following the woman. He was of average height and build, with the look of a civil servant. But the woman stood and crossed the street and the man passed the other way.

Marguerite walked in the same direction the bus was headed. The streets were more familiar now but they did not feel like home. The city was impersonal. Beside her, a mother pushed her daughter in a little blue buggy. She looked tired. The child smiled and reached up to the falling snow with splayed fingers. She grasped hopelessly for the flakes and then giggled when her palms remained empty. Her blonde hair was short and curly. A man passed with his head down. His face was drawn and dark. A young girl passed, laughing.

Marguerite watched the city, swelling with life in all of its forms. She drifted within it, alone. She thought of Hiroshima—of detachment and the seduction of power. Of swelling life eviscerated. She thought of the desire to know, the power of knowledge. She thought of those scientists for whom it was little more than an experiment, or worse, a job. She thought of the men and women around her, and she thought of Churchill and Stalin.

They credited war with progress—medically, economically, technologically—in blind ignorance of the fact that advancements were ignored until their value could be harnessed, perverted, for domination and power. She crossed the street again and entered a cafeteria where she ate lunch alone. When she finished, she took paper from her bag and began to write.

Henri,

Yesterday, after I wrote to you, I went to the sea. I looked out over the harbour to the fishing boats and thought of your friend in Newfoundland. The sky was dark and grey, and I was melancholy looking into it. Then, I remembered something you once told me, about the patterns in a cloudy sky. I found them and I found their beauty.

It started to snow today. It will not last but it brought me joy.

I regret how gloomy my last letter was. I began this one with the intention of leaving things a little bit brighter. The truth is, it will no longer be that letter. I wonder, daily, if I made a mistake. In my heart, I think I know the answer.

Things are not good in London. In London, there is deep sorrow. A sentiment of longing. People claw desperately for the crumbling empire. They desperately need to believe that America will set things right—that America will unify the colonies and recover the sphere of power, the sphere of extraction.

Perhaps they are right and things are slipping East. Perhaps people are simply breaking free.

Marguerite wrote and she felt some comfort. She wrote for pages and she railed against her job and her magazine. She stopped when it began to take effort. Then she left the cafeteria. She did not buy a stamp, and she placed the letter into an envelope and dropped it into a pillar box as an act of catharsis. It did not need to reach her brother—it could not reach her brother. It just needed to be written. When she turned away from the box, she caught sight, once again, of the man in the brown suit who'd stepped off of the bus. He walked alone and did not seem to notice her. She watched him for a moment, and then she began to walk through rows of textile shops and made her way to Kavanagh's.

✪

Snow drifted past the glass. Milne turned on the radio and adjusted the knob. Bing Crosby sang out the last few notes of a song. The kettle began to boil. He took it from the stove and poured the water into the teapot, which he left on the counter to steep. The night before, Milne had gone to dinner with Eric and Ava. When they finished, they cabbed home. Dusk fell as they drove, and the light played across Ava's face, revealing and hiding as it traced contours. "Tomorrow," she whispered to him as she stepped from the car. He did not know what time she would arrive, but he knew that she would come. The thought left a tremor in the pit of his stomach. The uncertainty gave him jitters.

Milne cleaned. He swept the floors and wiped down the countertops. He thought about Marguerite and her brother. About Eric. He felt untouched, relatively, by war. Some had lost parents, siblings, and friends. He had been a child during the first. An uncle had died—he had never met him. He grew up between them. During the second, he didn't serve. Friends had gone over. Most came back. Those that didn't simply disappeared.

Milne glanced over a pile of unread books in the corner of the room: *The Naked and The Dead; The Oasis; Escape From Freedom; Death in Venice*. He arranged them on the shelf. Eric swore that *The Naked and The Dead* was the greatest American novel since the war. One night, during a card game, he discovered that Milne had not read it. The next afternoon, Milne found a copy on his doorstep. He lifted the ashtray from the table and emptied it in the kitchen. He felt almost no guilt. Because that was better, he didn't ask why. He replaced the ashtray on the coffee table and looked around the room. Then, he went into the bedroom. It was clean. The bed was fresh. The window was cracked slightly, allowing cold air to filter through the room. He would have to remember to close it soon.

Milne stepped back into the hall and closed the bedroom door behind him. An oil painting of a gloomy dockyard hung on the wall. He'd bought it at an estate sale the year before. The former owner claimed that it was an unsigned Atkinson Grimshaw. It seemed unlikely but he bought it cheap. He didn't know how to check whether or not it was real. Carson probably would.

He moved back into the sitting room. His own book, *The Foxhunt*, sat at the end of the shelf. He walked over and lifted it. He opened the cover. Inside, it was signed. He traced the signature with his finger. There was a subtle texture to the page. He thought of the couple at Molly's inn—of the couple in Paris. He wondered about them for the first time in a while. Time had passed. They seemed less important. Who were they? What had they wanted?

There was a knock at the door. It was hard, loud—formal. He felt his chest contract. He looked at his watch. It couldn't be her, he told himself. It was early yet. He crossed to the mirror and checked himself. Then he moved to the door.

He opened it. Clifford stood in the hall. Snow dusted the shoulders of his Savile Row coat. He looked serious. "I'd like a word," he said. Milne looked past him down the empty hall. He tried not to look disappointed. "I'm sorry," Clifford added, "I know it's early."

Milne shrugged and opened the door fully. "No, please. Come in."

Clifford stepped inside. He looked down at the letters beside the door, scanning the small pile. He didn't bother making an effort to hide it. He hung his coat beside the door. He draped a scarf over it.

197

"Come in," Milne repeated. He closed the door and the two went into the sitting room together. "Sit down," Milne said. "I made tea but it's probably cold."

Clifford sat on the sofa. "That's alright," he said. "Do you have anything stronger?"

Milne checked his watch again. It was early, he thought. It was Christmas, though—or close enough to it. It might help the nerves, in any case. "I suppose," he said. He went into the kitchen and took a bottle of Irish whiskey from the cupboard. He poured out two tumblers and brought them back in. He checked his watch again. It was early yet. Unless Clifford stayed long there was little risk of overlap.

"Mind if I smoke?" Clifford asked, though he had already opened his case.

"Not at all," Milne said. "There's an ashtray on the table."

Clifford offered Milne a cigarette, which he declined. Clifford took one himself. He tapped it on the wooden arm of the sofa. "A flat was raided in Bromley a few nights ago," he said casually. He put the cigarette between his lips, then paused to light a match.

"Raided?"

Clifford nodded. He waved out the match and dropped it in the ashtray. "By the police," he said. "A lot of incriminating documents were found. False passports." He lifted his tumbler with the same hand that held the cigarette and sipped slowly. "A gun," he added. "A Tokarev TT-33."

Milne shifted uncomfortably. He felt nervous. He wasn't sure why. "What's that?" he asked. "Russian?"

Clifford nodded. "Pretty standard issue."

"How did you hear about this?" Milne asked.

"The police contacted me. It seems like they think these might be your guys."

"The ones who broke in?"

Clifford nodded again.

"They caught them?"

"Two. Both in custody."

Milne leaned forward. He thought back to the night of the break in. He'd seen the man's face as he walked Ava home. "Where are they being held?" he asked. "I might be able to identify the one I chased."

Clifford's face shifted into a faint smile. "They didn't get a night in the drunk tank," he said. "We can't see them. The police don't need you to anyway."

Milne stared. "Who are they?" he asked. "Russians?"

"Russians," Clifford confirmed. He tapped his cigarette in the ashtray. Ash fell from the end and crumbled in the glass. "They'd been here for a while."

"What were they doing?"

Clifford shrugged. "I just thought you might like to know that we got them," he said, watching Milne closely. He opened his cigarette case again and held it out. Milne took one absently. He wondered what documents they had on them when they were caught. He picked up the matches and struck one. The flame wavered. He thought of that night, walking Ava home in the dark.

"Do you see much of Marguerite these days?" Clifford asked.

Milne had a sense that he already knew the answer—that he wasn't asking out of interest. He recalled the questions about Marguerite after he returned from Colombia, after Ignazio's defection. "Of course," he said. "Whenever I can."

"How's she doing?" Clifford asked. "She never really settled in here, did she?"

Milne shrugged. He leaned back and rested his right ankle on his other knee. "I don't know," he said. "Well, I reckon."

"We need to be careful," Clifford said, "with who we speak to. Who we associate with. Friends of friends sink ships."

Milne didn't respond. He eyed the man across from him. He wondered about the implication. Clifford's brow was sharp, pointed. Milne wondered about Estonia. About the place and the people. He wondered about the history. It had broken free from the Russians, he thought, or maybe the Poles. It had tried to remain neutral during the war.

Then, there was another knock at the door. It was lighter, calmer. Milne jolted in his seat. He had nearly forgotten that Ava was coming over. He checked his watch. Clifford seemed to sense his unease. "Expecting anyone?" he asked.

Milne shook his head. "No," he said. "Not today." He put down his drink and stood. Clifford didn't move to get up. He took another sip of his drink and set it back on the table. As if to make a point, he drew slowly on the cigarette.

Milne felt his hands tremble. Clifford's eyes were on him. He didn't want Clifford to see who was at the door but he also didn't want Clifford to think that he was hiding something. He stood still for far too long. Clifford said nothing. Eventually, he crossed the room to the hall. He could see the shadow of feet in the hall through the gap beneath the door. There was another gentle knock. He walked to the door and opened it. He tried to think up an excuse as he did.

Marguerite stood in the hall. She was smiling. She took the hat from her head and shook the snow from it. "Hello," she said. "I was just passing and thought I'd drop in." She registered the surprise on his face. "I hope it's not a bad time."

Milne felt an unusual mixture of panic and relief. "No, not at all," he said. He glanced over his shoulder. "I wasn't expecting you, is all. Clifford just dropped by as well," he added.

Marguerite's face fell. "Should I come back later?" she asked.

"Don't be silly," he said. "Come in." He opened the door wider. Marguerite smiled and stepped through. "I can't imagine he'll stay long," Milne said quietly when she was close. She took off her hat and coat. Milne took them and hung them next to Clifford's. "Go on in," he said. "I'll fix you a drink."

"A drink?" Marguerite asked, checking her watch.

"Or tea?"

"Well, maybe I'll have just a splash," she said. "It is Christmas, after all." She stepped into the living room, where Clifford sat on the sofa in a blue and grey bespoke suit.

"Marguerite," he said curtly.

"A bit early for business on a Saturday, isn't it?" Marguerite asked.

Clifford frowned slightly. "How do you know it's business?" he asked.

"I haven't known you to do anything else," she replied as she scanned the bookshelf along the wall. She stooped to read a title. Clifford sipped his whiskey slowly. Milne returned to the room with a drink for Marguerite, and then invited her to sit.

"How was your night out yesterday evening?" Clifford asked, looking at Milne.

"It was fine," Milne said. He glanced at Marguerite. "I'm sorry," he said, "it was a last minute thing."

Marguerite gave a nonchalant shrug that was nearly convincing. "Don't think twice about it," she said. "I was out myself."

"Is that so?" Clifford asked, running his hand through his thin hair. "Where did you go?" he asked with convincing nonchalance. Marguerite did not respond. Milne glanced at his watch again. This morning he had hoped that Ava would come early. Now, he hoped that she would not arrive until evening. He shifted his gaze from Clifford to Marguerite. She stared coldly at Clifford. Clifford pretended not to notice. The room was silent but the ticking clock.

Milne's mind drifted. He thought about the sound of Ava's laugh. He took a sip of whiskey. A numb heat flooded his tongue. He suddenly remembered what Clifford had been telling him before Marguerite knocked.

"Marguerite," Milne said. "Clifford was just telling me that they might have caught our burglars. Russians," he said. "Spies."

"That's a little dramatic," Clifford said, "but, yes."

"Russians?" Marguerite asked with surprise. She leaned in closer. "What would they want with us?"

"Quite," said Clifford.

"They got them in Bromley," Milne continued. "Raided a flat. They had a gun and false passports."

"How do they know they're the same people?" Marguerite asked.

"I don't know," Milne replied. "They must have found something," he added. He looked at Clifford.

"The police are fairly certain," Clifford said. "I should think they know what they're doing."

Marguerite seemed to be deep in thought. Clifford watched her closely. Milne wondered what he was thinking. Once again, the room was silent. Milne's thoughts returned to Ava. If she arrived while the others were here, Eric would find out. Not immediately, perhaps, but eventually through some casual comment or slip of the tongue. Questions would be raised. Or, would it matter at all? He drank slowly and quietly and watched Marguerite do the same.

Eventually, Clifford stubbed his cigarette in the ashtray, finished his whiskey, and stood. "Well," he said, "this has been a pleasant visit but I'd better be on my way."

Marguerite looked up as he buttoned his jacket. "Oh, are you terribly sure you can't stay?" she asked. Clifford's face shifted to a smirk but he did not respond.

"Thanks for stopping by," Milne said. He stood and walked Clifford to the door. He let him out and said goodbye, and told him that he should drop in more often. Then he went into the kitchen and stood at the window and looked out over the empty laneway below. After a few minutes, Clifford passed by on the street at the end of the laneway, his collar pulled up to stave off the cold. Milne stood and watched and muffled voices from below carried up to him, though their words were lost along the way.

Marguerite came into the kitchen behind him. "What an awful man," she said. Milne did not respond. He was thinking about Ava. There was something about her that instantly drew people in. Her presence was intoxicating, entrapping. He wondered if she lied to Eric—he knew that she must. He wondered how they spoke when he was not around. He wondered if she lied to him.

Milne felt the whiskey clouding him and wanted Marguerite to leave. There was another knock at the door. It was unmistakably her. His face flushed. Momentarily, his heart stopped beating. He turned to face Marguerite. She could read his face, he thought. She had to know.

Marguerite glanced towards the door, and he stepped past her. He moved into the hall and closed his palm around the brass handle. He sensed Ava's presence through it. When he opened the door, she stood there in the hallway, solid and real, and her dark hair was damp with snow, and she wrung her hands together to relieve the chill. She stepped forward towards him. He could smell her perfume and the smoky wetness of her thick wool coat. A cool smile gently lifted the edges of her lips,

203

and her eyes burnt beneath her brow. Then, some colour in her pale skin changed, and her heavy lids widened, and her lips slowly parted, and he knew that Marguerite stood behind him.

"Ava," he said. He tried to sound surprised but the name left his lips too quietly and so, instead, he sounded lost. Ava recovered before he did and stepped through the doorway, brushing past him.

"Marguerite," she exclaimed. "What a surprise!"

Marguerite embraced her. "Ava! Were you just passing by?" she asked, extending an olive branch. "I just dropped in myself," she added.

"Yes, I was passing by," Ava said. "Eric told me you'd be in," she added, looking to Milne.

Milne smiled weakly. "Of course," he said. "It's cold. Come in, have a drink."

Ava checked her watch. "I suppose I might," she said. "Just to quell the chill." She took off her coat and Milne hung it on the rack.

Marguerite looked at Milne. She searched him. Milne thought of Eric. He felt selfish and guilty—he was willing to ruin it all to quell loneliness and boredom. She would hate him for it. "I should be going," Marguerite said, eventually.

"No!" Ava cried. "I'm interrupting. Do stay."

"Please," Milne said. His pounding heart began to slow. He felt his head clear. Marguerite nodded and agreed. Milne wondered if she actually suspected anything, or if he was simply being paranoid. Ava and Marguerite went into the front room. Milne went into the kitchen and returned with a drink and the bottle of whiskey. The three sat together and the wind outside rattled the windows, and the apartment was warm, and Milne was glad that Marguerite was there.

"Clifford dropped in earlier," Milne said.

"You've had a busy morning," Ava said. Her eyes found his. Her eyes were green and he was taken again. Painter's brush streaks of deep hazel crept in at the edges. Her lips, tinted red by something with a name like Red Sequin or Precious Ruby, rose and parted as she spoke. Something dark and subtle hung on her lids.

He laughed. It sounded unnatural. "He came by to tell me that the police think that they've found the men who broke into our office," he said.

Ava sat up. Intrigue settled in her eyes. "After all this time?" She took the drink that Milne had poured for her and turned the glass gently in her hands. "Who are they?" she asked. Something that Ignazio said in Berlin came back to Milne, something about those who dreamed of communist attack—who longed for the excitement.

"Two Russians," he said. "They had a flat in Bromley."

"How did they find them?"

"Some other case, I'd bet. He didn't say."

"How do they know it's them?"

"He didn't say."

"Well," Ava said. "It's a relief, of sorts. Russians!" she said. "Imagine that."

"It's something," said Milne.

"It makes you wonder," said Marguerite. She was looking directly at Milne. He couldn't read her.

"About what?" asked Ava.

"Ignazio, Colombia, the whole deal."

Milne topped up his whiskey. "I was just thinking about him," he said. The snow outside had stopped falling. He watched the clear skies through the distant window. "I wonder what made him go over," he said.

"Disillusion," Marguerite said. "It's the same thing everywhere."

205

They sat for a while longer. They played Cluedo and listened to Thelonious Monk. It was cozy in the apartment. Milne no longer wondered when he and Ava would be alone—he no longer cared. When the air in the room began to feel heavy, the three friends stepped out together and went down to the cinema, where they watched a *Scrooge* matinee. From there, Ava went home. It was early in the day so Marguerite and Milne made their way further into the city. They walked along the Thames and stopped on Fleet Street for a drink and something to eat. They walked up to Doughty Street, where Dickens used to live, and they stood in front of his house, which looked just like any other. From there, they headed down to Bloomsbury and walked past the British Museum. Marguerite spoke about Gertrude Stein, who had once lived close by.

A light snow fell on wreaths and ribbons, caught in the golden glow of streetlamps. The evening began to darken and a chill began to grow, and their feet were sore from walking, so they went a little further to the Fitzroy Tavern, where they stayed and warmed. It was busy. Laughter and conversation settled into the background, and they sat in the corner and half-listened to the tall tales a man was telling at the bar. They talked and drank until the night carried them across to the Newman Arms. It was an error of judgement. A fight broke out in the doorway before they even stepped inside. A couple of cosh boys set in on some Oxbridge lads who passed judgement on their drape coats. The barman got involved and the night ended then and there.

8

Next year, she would go home for Christmas, Marguerite decided. It didn't matter if she was in London or Montreal—she would go home. She wanted to hear a train roar past on the trestle bridge, casting a heavy mist over the town. She wanted to watch children fly through heaps of snow on toboggans. She wanted to hear skates carve and sticks clatter as boys in Canadiens jerseys played hockey on a frozen lake. She hadn't been home for Christmas since her brother died. She wondered if it was anything like it used to be. She wondered if her father still brought in a tree and if they bothered with Christmas dinner at all.

She turned away from the carollers. She walked the rest of the way down the street and went up to the office. Marguerite paused in front of the door. She had come to London for adventure and freedom. She had found a degree of both—she had also found suspicion and restraint. She took a deep breath and opened the door. Everyone else was already there.

"Sorry I'm late," Marguerite said.

"Can we begin?" Clifford asked. Marguerite nodded. She sat in the empty chair beside Milne. Her head hurt from the night before. "I'm sure you've all been wondering, so I'll address this first," Clifford said. "Carson is staying on the masthead.

We can't afford to lose him. For the time being, he will remain on hiatus. Luckily, we've managed to keep it under wraps so far. I'll be playing a more active role here to pick up the slack."

Marguerite, Milne, and Eric nodded in acknowledgement. He leaned across the table and continued: "There will be some changes moving forward. From here on, we need to start actively engaging with magazines which thrive on neutrality and soft-spoken ambivalence. *Les Temps modernes* and whatever communist-friendly bullshit they spew should not be engaged with directly. We just need to be better than them."

"All this talk of neutrality and ambivalence ..." Marguerite said. "This isn't a black and white thing."

Clifford shifted his gaze to Marguerite. "What isn't?" he asked.

"I don't know," Marguerite said, "the world, I suppose. To criticize one does not necessarily mean support for the other."

"In the battle between liberal-democracy and totalitarianism, there is no neutrality," Clifford said. "With communism, cultural freedom is not possible. In order to foster an environment which makes cultural freedom possible, we need to protect the space in which it can exist," he continued. "So far, we have been focused upon building a liberal, transatlantic intellectual milieu. This was necessary to build a strong base. Now, we need to present these ideas to intellectuals across the globe, especially in areas that are susceptible to neutrality or communism. That was what was meant to happen in Colombia. Now, we need to re-evaluate."

Marguerite shook her head in dismay. "So, what? Now that the colonies are becoming independent, we need to find a way to divide them up among the new imperial powers?"

Clifford looked at Marguerite with disgust. Eric glanced at Milne. "What now, then?" he asked, before Clifford could reply.

"We've been in communication with the Foreign Office here for some time," Clifford said. "We've made a deal. The Foreign Office will purchase and distribute copies of our publication through the British Council in Asia, India, and other areas beginning in the New Year."

"Do you think that it's wise to work directly with the Foreign Office?" Marguerite asked.

Clifford leaned back and sighed. "Why would it be unwise?"

"We're already losing credibility with a lot of people on the ground," Marguerite said.

"She's right," said Eric. "We have been hearing that lately."

"And what do 'people on the ground' think?" Clifford asked.

"They think that it's a rag," Marguerite replied coldly. "They think that we sell American propaganda, and that the veneer is rather thin."

"Then working with the British Foreign Office should reassure them."

Marguerite laughed. "That is ..."

Clifford cleared his throat and interrupted: "This magazine, this entire organization, was started with a purpose. We recognized a threat to cultural and intellectual freedom worldwide and we decided to do something about it. We overcame fascism and we can overcome communism too. The British and American governments are our greatest allies in this struggle."

Marguerite began to speak again: "I un–"

Clifford spoke up, louder than the first time: "Extreme, dogmatic ideologies do not allow this freedom to exist. That is the bedrock of our organization. Everyone else agrees on that. Milne brought you on board and we went along with it because he really fought for you but you are not an editor and you are not an administrator. You are a contributor. As far as I'm concerned, your presence is not even required at this meeting."

Marguerite stayed quiet. Clifford looked around the room, making eye-contact with Eric and Milne. He lowered his voice. "I apologize if I'm being harsh. Everyone needs to toe the line right now. It is of utmost importance that we all see eye to eye. I'm spending my Christmas here instead of with my family because of that mess in Bogotá. I don't want to have any further issues. From here on out, things need to run smoothly."

They talked through preparations for the upcoming issues and changes to be implemented in the New Year. Eventually, Clifford stood to signal the end of the meeting. Eric, Milne, and Marguerite left the office. They walked down the street in uneasy silence. Without Carson, with the presence of Clifford, things were entirely different. It was only when they reached the corner that Marguerite spoke. "I don't even know what to say," she said.

Eric nodded gravely. "He's tough but he does have a point. This is a battleground." He waved out his match and threw it on the ground. "Should we go for a drink? Figure out where to go from here?"

Marguerite nodded. She looked down at her watch. "Murphy's?"

Milne realized that he had forgotten to bring his articles with him from the office. "Go on ahead," he said. "I'll catch up."

"Ok," Eric said. "We'll see you there."

Eric and Marguerite walked down the street and Milne re-entered the office building. He took the stairs back up. He walked through the open door of the lobby and past the secretary's desk.

The office door was ajar—he looked through the gap. Clifford was on the phone, facing away from him. "The name is Baron," he said. Milne pushed the door open. Clifford turned quickly. He lowered his voice. "One moment," he said into the phone. He put it to his shoulder. "Do you need something?"

"Just my articles," Milne said.

"Alright then," Clifford said. "Close the door when you leave."

Milne took the folder from his desk and quickly left. When he closed the door, he heard the sound of Clifford's voice speaking quietly on the other side.

He walked to Murphy's. They stayed late into the night because the atmosphere was right. Eric fed coin after coin into the Wurlitzer in the corner, playing song after song on demand. Stories flowed and long dead memories were resurrected. Marguerite danced alone in the centre of the floor.

Ava sat on the edge of the bed and watched Eric's chest rise and fall beneath the thin sheet, damp with the scent of whiskey sweat. Scars cut through thick black hair. The breeze through the open window was gentle. The patter of droplets falling on the gutter played behind it. White walls shifted with the clouds.

She had decided against children when Eric was in Japan. In those years, boys grew up with no expectations but to become soldiers. War did not shake from them like army particularities. When Eric returned, civilian life did not sit well with him. Without command, without mission—without a battlefield—he was at a loss.

Ava left a note on the table and went out. She walked because the morning was fine. After dropping a letter in the box, she dropped in to the butcher, and then stopped in at the bakery next door. When she stepped out of the bakery, the sweetness lingered in the air and followed her. She walked over the thin layer of stone and felt her feet slide along the cobblestones. Some shops were closed and some were packed with people. Bells rang above entryways as bodies flowed. Notes carried in snippets from scattered radios.

She turned at the end of the street and went the wrong way. She took the stairs to the third floor in an apartment building and knocked twice. Milne answered the door. Nat King Cole played softly behind him.

"I don't have long," she said.

9

The morning was bright. Milne stopped at a newsstand. He lifted the paper. On the front page was a photograph of a man lying facedown in an alleyway. The headline read: *Murdered Man Suspected To Be Spy.* He reached into his pocket and pulled out some change. He handed it to the man behind the counter.

He skimmed the first paragraph. A man had been shot in the back in an alleyway late in the night. He was found by a storekeeper. The next paragraph caught his eye: *Phillip Baron, 42, was found with incriminating documents in his possession.* Baron—the name was familiar. He read on: *While police have not issued a statement, sources allege that the victim is being treated as a potential foreign agent operating in London.*

Baron—he had heard Clifford use the name. Was it a coincidence? The paper said that he had been shot the previous night. He checked the date: *December 24th.* Today's paper. Were they wrong about when it happened? Had Clifford somehow known about it before the papers?

"Could be anyone," the newsman said.

"What's that?" Milne asked.

"The communists. They hide among us."

Milne nodded, distracted by his thoughts. Clifford could have been talking about any other Baron, of course ... Jacques Baron, the poet. He was active in Paris, a surrealist—a communist. It would not be unusual for Cliff to speak of him. He read the rest of the article, then folded the paper beneath his arm and continued on. The city was quiet. The snowfall was gentle.

On Christmas Day, he arrived at Marguerite's around noon. He brought wine, pudding, and trifle. They exchanged gifts. He brought her a silver teapot he had found in Camden. She gave him a beautiful copy of *Anna Karenina,* hand bound in leather.

They sat at the table together and lit a candle. They pulled crackers with their appetizers. Though Marguerite had only cooked for two, there was no shortage of food: turkey, roast potatoes, brussels sprouts, carrots, parsnips, cranberry sauce, and gravy.

They drank wine and laughed and talked. They tried to picture the Christmas dinners that other people were having. Then, they thought of home and sat and wondered how things were. The snow was gone and the rain returned, pattering softly against the windowsill. The candle slowly burned.

It fell quiet and Milne thought of Phillip Baron. He thought of Clifford and Colombia. He thought of their Russians. He watched Marguerite and wondered what she was thinking of. "Can you believe how successful we've been?" Milne asked, after a while, to break the melancholy spell.

"Is it ok to admit that I'm disappointed?"

"About what?" Milne asked, though he was sure that he knew.

She wondered if it was safe to expand. She didn't like feeling like she had to be on guard around Milne. "The direction we've taken," she said. "It is not what I had hoped."

214

Milne knew what she meant. "Soon we won't have to be anti-communist," he said. "Once people are won over, we just need to hold the line. That's when the magazine will really come to life."

"The magazine is alive, Milne. This is what it is."

Milne didn't reply. He wondered if she was right.

"When you wrote to me, you told me that this was about promoting artistic freedom. We don't even have freedom in our own magazine."

"At the moment, communism is the greatest threat to artistic freedom that there is. Cliff and Nicolas know what they're doing," he said.

"Don't be so foolish," Marguerite snapped. "You aren't as naïve as you play. The least you can do is acknowledge what you're fighting against. This isn't about freedom—it's about power. There isn't even any communism in Russia—not anymore. They have a centralized authoritarian state. There's nothing communal about that. An entire system based upon violence and compulsion!" Marguerite looked at him desperately. "At least acknowledge what it is you're fighting."

"What does it matter?"

"You don't even know who your enemy is," she said.

"Don't tell me what I do and do not know, Marguerite. I won't be condescended to."

"It's not condescension, Milne. You and Eric and Cliff keep talking about what communism is and does and I just don't see it. Yes, oppose the Soviets! The land, the factories—it's all nationalized, no different from the crown. Why say you're fighting communism?"

"Save your literature, Marguerite. Quoting books doesn't require thought."

"Pardon me?"

Milne saw tears welling in her eyes and realized that he had struck a blow. He felt that he had gone too far but his frustration was overbearing.

"I think," she said. "Probably a lot more than you do."

"What's that supposed to mean?"

"For god's sake, Milne! Look around! What has happened here? You're travelling the world! Berlin! Paris! First class tickets—first class meals. Look at this wine," she said, lifting the bottle. "Who can afford this? Not long ago we could barely afford to eat."

Milne stayed quiet.

"Did Colombia mean nothing to you?"

"What are you saying?"

"Who do you think is paying for all of this?" she asked. "Since when do artists have funding like this?"

"This is a different world than it was a year or two ago. There are a lot of people with a lot of money who realize how important this is. We're winning, Marguerite. Art is recognized."

"Look," she said. "You know that I have no sympathy for the Soviets. No love for that kind of regime. Yet, Clifford treats me like a sympathizer—Eric too, at times. Why is that? Because I won't play their games. I won't be a puppet. I question the consensus. I know what's worth fighting in this world but it isn't communism. There are things worth fighting right here."

"What we have here is nothing like what they have there."

"Maybe not," Marguerite said. "But Nicolas is in Paris right now, eating well and writing cheques. Do you know what else is happening in Paris? The French are arresting, torturing—even executing—radicals. Not just terrorists—students!"

"That's bullshit," Milne said.

"It isn't!" Marguerite cried. "I have friends in Paris too. This so-called export of culture—Asia, Latin America—it isn't benevolent. It's a subtle Sétif."

Milne stood up and threw his napkin on the table. "I've had enough, Marguerite! You've gone too far. You want to know why they treat you like a sympathizer? Listen to what you're saying! We've worked hard to build this magazine and I still think it's worth something! These years weren't wasted," he said, staring through Marguerite.

"Milne, please," she said. "I don't want to fight, really. It's Christmas."

He said nothing.

"You're my closest friend. I came here for you." She stood as well. "I just can't understand why you won't see."

Milne turned and walked away from the table. He grabbed his coat, threw the door open, and left. As he strode down the hallway, the sound of the slamming door reverberating in his mind, he tried to think about what she had said. His mind was too clouded with bitterness and anger—all that drew forth were thoughts of resentment. Who was Marguerite to criticize him? Who was Marguerite to say where there was and wasn't communism? He had been a fool to bring her over, he thought.

He tried to relax his tensed muscles. He took the stairs two at a time. The echo throbbed. He felt the fog gradually lift. By the time he reached the front door of her building, he wished that he hadn't stormed out. Why couldn't he remain calm? What had angered him so much? He stepped into the rain and felt it against his head—it streamed down the side and itched its way down his face against the stubble on his cheeks. He had forgotten his hat and umbrella upstairs. He glanced up at the light in her window and knew that he could not go back up. He turned away quickly in case she came to look out for him. The paper crown from the cracker was still on his head. He crumpled it in his fist and dropped it in a puddle. The darkness of the street surrounded him. He began to walk toward a streetlight on the corner.

Marguerite watched Milne's silhouette disappear into the rainfall. She drew her hand and let the curtain fall into place. Tears streamed down her cheeks. Coming to London was a mistake. This wasn't her fight at all. There was a struggle in Quebec that she should have been part of. She wondered about Maurice and Alexandra, and everyone else back home. It was probably time to go. Sensations of home ran through her—the streets, buildings and people. She thought of train rides out of Montreal. Vast, endless forests of pine and rising mountains—the lakes. She thought of the dirt roads behind Cap-Rouge. Her father's hard, wrinkled skin. If he got sick while she was here, would she even find out?

She lit a cigarette and looked at the patterns on the kitchen wallpaper. She ran her hand along the countertop—crumbs of bread trailed behind. A half-eaten meal wasted on the table; an open bottle of wine and two half-empty glasses. Milne's hat hung on the hook beside the door, his umbrella leaned against the corner beneath it. He would be soaked—good, she thought. Tears streamed steadily. She wiped them with the back of her hand. She stubbed out the cigarette.

She went to her desk and opened the top drawer—stacks of magazine articles. She closed it and opened the one beneath. She lifted a stack of paper and set it on the desk. She wiped her cheeks again. Her handwriting scrawled across the page. The words were familiar but distant. This was the work she should have been doing. Marguerite leaned back and pushed the curtain aside again. She looked out into the rain. After this issue was complete, she would return to Montreal.

10

When Milne woke in the morning, he was embarrassed. Another thought lingered in his mind, gnawing at the subconscious shield he had erected around it: what if she was right? The money was a puzzle, he could see that clearly. Never before had there been too much money. The correlation from there was not as clear. Money did not mean deceit or intrigue. It was just money, constantly changing hands. They were finally getting a piece.

He sat up and leaned against the headboard. He looked at the curtains dangling beside the window. Through the gap, he saw the identical façade of the building across the road. It was all the same, day in and day out. His clothes were strewn across the floor and chair. His wardrobe was open in the corner. He reached over to the bedside table and checked the little clock. It was just past 7:30. He got out of bed and dressed. He turned on two burners. He put the kettle on one. On the other, he placed a pan. Once it was hot, he cracked two eggs into it. He wondered how Carson was doing.

He could not remember the last time he had written. He'd written as an editor, of course—editorials and the occasional essay—but he couldn't remember the last time he had worked on something of his own. He put on toast and when the eggs

219

were cooked and the kettle was boiled, he sat down at the table and ate. He sat alone and listened to the radio. He read. He sat at his desk with a blank notebook. He watched the snow fall. He had nothing to write and went to bed early.

The next day, he went into the office after breakfast. He read articles and edited. The morning went quickly. The afternoon soon followed. Something that Marguerite said bothered him. It had reminded him of Carson, of Edna. He stood up and crossed to another desk in the room, unused by any of the editorial staff.

He flicked the switch—the lamp cast a dim glow. The room around him was dark and silent. A series of envelopes and folders were piled upon the desk. He ran his hands over the smooth manila cover of the first. He opened it: outgoing expenses. He flipped through the sheets and then closed the folder. He opened the one beneath it: funding details—income for 1950. Small foundations, arts boards, and anonymous donors made up most of the list. Income ranged from hundreds to thousands per donor.

He turned the page. His finger traced the list through the months. He was looking for a single name. 1950 passed—May, June, July. Small amounts trickled in piecemeal. Funding increased following the conference in Berlin and stayed steady for the rest of the year. The board in Paris was a blessing, he thought. So much time had been dedicated in the past to finding and applying for funding. Now, it was seamlessly taken care of for them. He reached the last sheet—December 1950. He scanned the list. It was more of the same.

He pushed the folder aside and opened the next. Immediately, a name jumped out: January 5, 1951—The Pearson Foundation. It wasn't just the name that stood out but the number attached to it. From the beginning of 1951, the anonymous and individual donors thinned out greatly. Once a month, every month, The

Pearson Foundation contributed generously. It was, by far, the largest donor they had. He thought, momentarily, about Phillip Baron, the murdered spy.

The door opened. Milne jumped. Light poured in. Eric stepped inside and turned on the light above.

"What are you doing sitting here in the dark?" he asked.

"I was working. I guess I didn't notice the change."

"What are you working on?" Eric asked. He paused and looked closely at Milne's face. "You didn't come in on Christmas, did you?"

Milne laughed. "No," he said. He paused and watched Eric search for something on his desk. "Have you ever heard of the Pearson Foundation?" he asked eventually.

"No," he said. "What's that?"

"Apparently it's our largest donor."

"Good for them."

"You don't know anything about it?" Milne asked.

"We've always let Paris worry about the money. Why are you asking?"

"No reason," said Milne. "I was just surprised that I hadn't heard of them before."

"Is that what you're doing here?" Eric asked. "Looking at the accounts?"

Milne shrugged. An expression of sadness passed briefly over Eric's face. "Ava's out with a friend," he said. "Want to go for a drink or something?"

Milne looked down at his watch. He wondered who Ava was with. "I'd better head home, actually."

"We could go down to the club and shoot pool," Eric said. "Just a game or two. For old time's sake."

Milne glanced down at his watch again. "Alright," he said. "A game or two."

They went down to the club and signed their names at the door. The snooker tables were full but Milne was glad because he was a lousy shot across the distance. They took a table in the corner and Eric racked. Milne broke but nothing sank.

Eric chalked his cue, lined up, and took a shot. The cue ball made contact with its target but the target ball cut in too soon and missed the pocket. "You need to get out more," he said to Milne. "Meet a girl. How long have we been in London? I haven't even heard you mention a woman."

Milne shrugged. "I've been busy."

"Marguerite must know some," Eric said. He watched Milne. "Carson certainly does. Meet an actress—have some fun."

Milne pocketed a ball. "You're reds," he said. He tried not to look at Eric directly. He chalked, re-positioned and lined up again. He sank a second ball. They finished out the game. Milne won with ease. They racked and played again. When they were done, they went down to a pub on the corner and sat near the window.

"What do you think of Edna?" Eric asked.

Milne set his pint down carefully. "What do you mean?"

"She's alright, isn't she?"

"I don't know."

"Come off it, she's stacked," Eric said.

"Come on, Eric."

"Why? Because she's married?" Eric sipped his whiskey, watching Milne. "What about Marguerite, then? Not bad either, eh?"

"Why are you talking like that?"

"What? You haven't gone off women, have you?"

"No," Milne said.

"Hard to keep track these days," Eric said.

Milne took a drink and looked around the pub. It was quiet.

"That's how you got out of service, wasn't it?"

"What?"

"Homosexuality," Eric said.

Milne looked at his friend. "I'm not a homosexual."

"But you pretended to be, didn't you?"

"No," Milne said. "I was still at the university," he added, though he was aware that Eric already knew.

"That's right," Eric said. "I remember now. A schoolboy."

Milne tilted the glass to his lips and then set it down on the table again. "I taught too."

"Why didn't you go?" Eric asked.

"I didn't have to."

"You were scared."

Milne looked down into his beer. Eric was being belligerent. He didn't know why. "Maybe I was."

Eric looked away. "I didn't mean it," he said. "I'm sorry. I'm a little tight."

"It's alright," Milne said. "You went and I didn't." He remembered the night in Paris, when Eric had spoken of his father. There was some kind of darkness in the man. Liquor let it out. He had been jealous of Eric. Now he felt pity.

Eric finished his whiskey and set the glass down. He stared at the bottom of it, then looked up. "You're in love with my wife," he said.

Milne looked into Eric's eyes. It was a question at heart, not a statement. Still, his hands began to tremble. He tried not to look uneasy. "What?"

"You heard me."

"Why do you say that?" He wondered what Eric knew. He was wrong either way.

"I've seen the way you look at her."

"You're drunk," Milne said.

"And you're a coward."

Milne finished his beer. "It's late," he said. "I'm going home."

"I'm sorry," Eric said. "Stay for another."

Milne stood up. "I'm going home."

"I'm having another."

"Alright," Milne said. "I'll see you later, then." He turned and walked away from the table, leaving his old friend alone. He pushed through the door and stepped out into the night. The cold air hit him hard.

Eight voices merged and clashed gently—a single wave of sound underwritten by cascading notes and bars from the radio, entrapped in the walls of the coffee shop. Overhanging lights beamed down, gradually blackening the wall-to-wall windows looking into the street which, itself, darkened as the evening passed.

Milne sat in the back in a low chair, letting the hot coffee warm his chest. At the table next to the door, shivering every time it opened to a cold wind, was the clean-cut owner of a local pub—he sat with a younger bearded man that Milne didn't recognize. At the table next to them, tucked into the corner beneath a hanging plant, was Caroline Saunders and her clueless husband, Elliot. At the most central table in the coffee shop, three women around his age sat talking—one of them was Emily Rutledge, a housewife; another was Sarah Brookner, a schoolteacher; and the third was a haughty blonde lady who he didn't know yet. The last customer was Samuel Bellow, a driver for a local cab company—he was reading in the opposite corner. The other tables were all empty.

Elliot pushed out his chair and stood up. He leaned over the table and kissed Caroline on the cheek. On the way to the door, he glanced back. The pub owner, whose name Milne couldn't think of, looked at Caroline and smiled.

To try to make it last, he thought. That's why we write. To make something temporary permanent. The passing moment. Was it the driver or the barman for Caroline? The driver was more interesting, wasn't he? Samuel. Maybe he wasn't reading but had just walked in and was ordering coffee as Elliot walked out. Yes, and then he sat with Caroline while Elliot went off to wherever he was headed next. Who was behind the counter? A new girl. A student of Sarah's—not a favourite.

Did he really write for all of that? What he wrote was entertainment, release—relief. But, it was more than that too, wasn't it? Wasn't it all? The lights were too bright looking up. Snow was falling outside—yes, it was winter not autumn. Thick coats hung over the backs of chairs and a wet floor—the new girl was mopping when she wasn't serving. Samuel's boots trailed slush from the door, he hadn't wiped them well. Caroline glanced up as he left the counter. His jaw was strong—he'd just shaved his beard and was self conscious still, he didn't know that it looked good. He had piercing eyes—another word, too hackneyed, but that was what they were.

He had wasted so much time. He didn't write enough. Samuel took the seat that Elliot left. Through the dark windows, the lights across the street dimly cast a glow on the falling snow. A plow rumbled past. Caroline laughed a little too much and the table of women talked quickly amongst themselves in low voices. Sarah glanced over her shoulder at her nearby student.

The table was smooth beneath his hands. His fingers ran across it. The mug was hot—the coffee probably too hot. The passing moment—that was a good one. *On Writing*—maybe one day. He would prefer *On Reading*. *The Passing Moment*—it could be a title.

The clash of voices had subsided. It was almost silent in the coffeeshop. Chairs, brown tables. Tile floor. What then? It was empty. Silent—how to fill it? Milne looked around the room, too aware of his own presence. He wished that he had a book with him. It was the rhythm of the words, the flow of the sentence, that was all he needed to get going. *Under the brown fog of a winter dawn, a crowd flowed over London Bridge* ... how did they do it?

Work methodically. Samuel. Samuel was divorced. He'd married late, out of desperation, and had watched it slip through his fingers one week at a time. Caroline married early, out of love or the idea of it. She would never leave him. The temperature inside was high because outside it was low. Sarah's sleeve drooped low on her shoulder—what she couldn't wear to work. Sarah was happy. The clean-cut pub owner was happy. Nobody else was, really. Maybe the faceless beard—it would remain undecided. Caroline spoke, the shaky words left her lips paler than before. Samuel flushed, she paled. The balance. Certain feelings unexplored, others broken open entirely. Was there hatred? No, not this one. He couldn't stand to write about hate.

Sarah's low voice carried through the coffee shop to Milne. She was thirty-five. She lived in a two-bedroom apartment above a shoe store. She had a little dog named Jasper. Emily's brown eyes swam with deep swirls of amber. The haughty blonde lady chattered, entirely oblivious to the world but so annoyed by every aspect of it. Caroline spoke softly; Samuel shifted and scratched at the unfamiliar stubble under his chin. Snow gusted beyond the glass.

He took a sip—he'd let it cool a little too long. It would be cold by the time he finished. It was the wide-bowl mugs, he thought, they cooled much too fast. He ran his finger around the rim. A gesture—that's what separates the story from the novel.

Caroline was talking quickly, quietly. Samuel listened with uneasy excitement. The table of women enclosed, stooping forwards, hushed words encircled the trio. The pub owner, the younger bearded man—what about them? The haughty blonde, Belinda, dreamed of tennis in backyard courts. Crisp white shirts. The girl behind the counter watched Sarah's hushed conversation. A lesson from the day before lingered in her mind. Eric, the clean-cut owner, shook hands with the younger bearded man and bade him goodbye. His presence had served no purpose. His absence might. Eric sat alone by the door.

Purpose? A series of observations, nothing more. The voices subsided, giving way to the dull drone of the inanimate. There was no conflict, only tension. The coffee shop emptied out. Milne took a sip. His coffee was cold. The floor felt solid beneath his feet. Caroline, Samuel, Eric. Belinda, Sarah. The girl. Elliot, of course. What else? An occurrence—an intersection.

A set of taillights through the window—the silhouette of a car in the snowfall. Hazy trails seeped from the back of the idling vehicle. Caroline and Samuel could not see it, they were too focused upon one another to look through the dim glass wall. Eric faced the wrong direction. The huddle was encapsulated. From where he sat, Milne could see it lurking. Steam expelled from the brewer behind the counter, bursting into the room. Conspiracy settled into aromatic atmosphere. It fit well. The wave of voices broke. Milne faded in his chair. The coffee shop shifted, working into its image. Whispers slipped, emerging from little cracks here and there. The doors opened, carrying a harsh wind with the rattle of the bell. The pen flowed.

The chill wore down the back of his neck. Marguerite was supposed to meet him thirty minutes ago. He was no longer angry. Two small children wearing oversized leather gloves boxed in an alleyway across the street. A group of children danced around them, laughing and taunting. He checked his watch: 2:45. He opened the door and entered the pub. He took a seat at the bar in view of the entrance and ordered a pint.

Marguerite wasn't generally late. She wasn't generally one to hold a grudge either. He was looking forward to seeing her—to righting things. A man knocked the bottom of an empty glass on the bar a little further down. He nearly slipped from his stool, then grinned widely and put his hand on the shoulder of the man next to him, who pulled his sleeve free and looked away. The man looked further along the bar, searching for a friendly face to share the self-deprecation with. The bartender tried not to glance his way—he made eye-contact with Milne and shook his head sadly. "Irish," he mouthed.

Milne tilted back his glass and felt the cold bitterness on his lips. He thought of the articles still to be edited and looked at his watch again. Things were more tense with Clifford in London. There were just a few days left before the deadline. It was stuffy. He got off the stool and walked through the pub to the toilet, past Guinness and Imperial advertisements between wooden and leather booths, tables, chairs, and narrow windows. The toilets were down a short set of stairs.

When he returned to his seat, he checked his watch again. It was after three. He finished his drink and ordered another. He took it to a table in the corner. He drummed his fingers on the table and looked around the pub. Could she already be inside? At some table hidden behind countless bodies of men? He scanned the tables but could not see her. The door opened and he leaned across the table to look—two older men walked

228

through slowly, greeting their fellows one by one. Didn't any of them work? Nobody was paying him any heed.

He thought about Ignazio. Why would he defect? He had been targeted by communists, threatened. Had he really been in danger in Paris? He remembered the fear—the excitement. He wasn't ready to give up yet. He sat for a while and finished his drink. Ignazio had been smart; why would he cross over? He thought of Stalin. What kind of a man was he? What twist of fate put you there? Not a conference in Paris.

The door opened and a woman walked in. It wasn't Marguerite. She was young and alone. The air in the pub became quickly stagnant. All attention shifted. She was singular—the focal point. The solitary object of interest. She approached the bar, leaned over, and asked something of the man behind it. The bartender responded. She thanked him, crossed the floor, and walked out, oblivious to the disruption she had caused. The door rocked on its hinges and the air began to circulate again. The scattering of men eyed one another.

Eventually, he left the pub. He looked up and down the street, then turned and walked to the intersection. He checked his watch and crossed to the opposite corner. Time passed, and he stepped onto a streetcar. A man huddled in the back of the car mumbled to himself. Milne saw a bottle on the seat beside him. He watched the city pass, row upon row. He thought about Hector. After more time passed, he stepped from the car back onto the street. He made his way to the next corner and turned.

He saw her building ahead. When he reached it, he took the stairs up to her floor. Would she be home? Or, was she delayed somewhere between here and the pub? He reached the floor she lived on and walked onto the landing. He knocked on the first door on the left. He waited for a while, looking down at the frayed carpet at his feet, but no one came to the door. He

229

heard nothing inside. He knocked again, harder, and waited. There was no reply. "Marguerite?" he called out. Still nothing. Something compelled him to go further. He tried the handle—it was unlocked.

Milne looked up and down the hallway, then opened the door. He called through. "Marguerite? Are you in there?" There was no response. He pushed the door in and stepped inside. The apartment seemed empty. Had she forgotten to lock it? He moved through the hallway into the kitchen. A half empty cup of tea sat on the countertop. He peered into the living room: there was nobody there. The bathroom door was slightly ajar and the light was on inside. "Marguerite?" he called out. "Are you there?" When there was no response, he knocked lightly on the door, then pushed it in with his fingers. It opened slowly.

Marguerite's body floated in the bathtub millimeters from the surface of the red water. Her head was tilted. Her pale face dipped slightly into the water. One half of her hair was matted and wet, the other was dry. Milne stood in the doorway. His strangled voice could not form words and was lost to involuntary shudders of shapeless sound. The groan that emitted from his chest and throat disgusted him. He felt his knees dip slightly and quickly—he grabbed onto the doorframe. He lurched forwards towards the bathtub and dropped to his knees on the cold tile beside it. His arms sank into the bloody water, which seeped into his sleeves until they clawed around his arms, clinging to his elbows and wrist. A revolver lay on the ground beside him.

He grasped desperately at the water, not wanting to touch her. He realized that his legs were soaked. He stood and tried to wipe the water from them with his dripping hands. Splatters of pink seeped into his white shirt. The wet stains grew further on his pant legs the more he wiped and he fell backwards against the wall.

Marguerite's face emerged—her gentle eyes welling with tears at the dinner table. This strange body in the tub was not her—he felt no connection to it. The yellow window stood out against the rain. He got to his feet, steadying himself on the toilet. His eyes fell to the gun again. His stomach turned. Wet strands of hair clung to her skin. He rushed the door and stumbled into the hallway.

He lifted the phone—the cord hung down limply. He tried to dial. The phone would not work. What number was he trying to reach? Who was he calling? He replaced the phone on the receiver. He lifted it and tried again. Eric answered. The voice rang hollow from the other end. The phone rested against the side of his face. He tried to speak. He couldn't say her name—his mouth wouldn't form the word. He didn't know what else to say.

"Eric," he said eventually. "I need help." His voice sounded strange. The voice on the other end asked something—there was concern. Milne said something else, he didn't know what it was. There was some miscommunication. What was Eric missing?

"She's been shot," he heard himself say. "Please come over."

He dropped the phone and fell back against the wall. He slid down it, clutching his arms to his chest, and began to cry. He clasped his eyes and shut out the world. It was quiet.

Then, there were voices in the hallway. The door opened. Eric's voice—Cliff's voice. Two others. He felt a hand on his shoulder. He opened his eyes. Eric's blue jacket beside him. Two police officers stood over him. Water trailed from the bathroom door. Milne closed his eyes again and tried to bury his weakness in front of them all. One of the police officers returned. He made a phone call from beside Milne. Eric pulled on his arm. Milne struggled to his feet.

"She's dead," he said.

III

The Wasteland

I

Marguerite was rapt; her focus with this woman alone—temporary, blissful isolation. Within her, between them. The sofa was plush and deep. They sank slowly towards the center, cradled. He could not fault her. He had not considered it—had not realized that this could happen. He saw that it was authentic, unashamed.

"Entirely revolting," somebody uttered.

The room stopped. Focus collected on the sofa. Marguerite's head lifted. Her eyes found him in the crowd. He saw fear. He stood along the wall. She dropped her eyes. He identified the speaker, between women draped in Desmarais, by the triumphant look on his face. Marguerite made for the door. Milne followed. He grabbed an open bottle of wine from the table on the way. She disappeared through the doorway and he called after her. She didn't slow.

She was already on the street when he caught up to her. She didn't look at him. He handed her the bottle. "I'm sorry," he said. Marguerite took it from him without speaking. She took a drink. She felt the bottle in her hands. She turned and continued to walk backwards slowly. She flipped the bottle quickly, smoothly. Wine splashed from the opening and covered the front of her dress. She caught the bottle by the neck. It leaked onto the pavement. She stopped walking, took a step back towards the house, swinging her arm as she did, casting the bottle through the air. Milne watched it fly and waited for it to collide with the brick and explode. Instead, it flew directly into a window beside the door and punched through. Marguerite's face paled. It was momentarily silent on the street but the ever-present hum of the evening. Then, simultaneously, they turned from the house and ran. The air was fresh and invigorating. The snow was sticky and translucent—the kind that marked the last spell of the season. Before the end of the block, Marguerite's laughter rang in his ears.

Now, she was gone. The funeral was in Montreal. He did not go home for it. Milne sat in the dark with the curtains drawn. Somebody was knocking at the door. He did not move to open it. He listened to the muffled voices on the other side. They went away eventually. He slept little—three or four hours a night. Every night, he dreamed of foxhounds.

He recalled arguments. *What is sentiment but the subconscious drawing upon learned and lived experience?* she had asked. *Emotion, not reason,* he had replied. Her writings would be valuable—intellectually, philosophically. He would gather them when ... the dawning recurred: she was gone. Suicide, they called it. She had been alone in London. He had brought her into an abyss—he should have known. He knew how she thought—what she thought. It was not compatible with the liberal milieu they sought. She had argued with him. No, he had argued with her. He couldn't believe that she'd done it. The thought didn't sit properly—he didn't believe it. If she had done it, it was his fault.

He had brought her to London because he had believed in the struggle for cultural freedom. For freedom from interference, from politics. Why had that fallen away? Why did he allow it?

236

She was right—the line they·ran was far too thin. They needed distance. She had known that nothing could be apolitical.

How had it happened? How had she come across a gun? He remembered: that damp, sticky, translucent snow. It was the same night, or may as well have been, that Marguerite was told of her brother's death. There was another knock at the door. A familiar voice carried through the wood, Eric: "Milne. Open up." He knocked harder. There was a pause, then a second voice, Ava: "Milne, please." A gentle murmur followed, discussion between the two. He harboured something inside. It was drawn forth, settling in somewhere beneath the grief. He had little power over it or the sensations it carried. It was deep-seated or thrust upon him from somewhere else—he could not determine which.

There was another knock. He lifted himself and moved to the door. He drew the bolt. After a moment, the handle turned and the door inched open. His head swam. He stepped back, away from the light. Eric stepped in and Ava followed. "How are you holding up?" Eric asked. Ava glared at him.

There was a distinction that existed within them, he thought, separating what happened in war and what happened outside of it; yet, there was no restoring that innocence towards life and death. They saw differently. He meant no harm. He had cared for her too, Milne reminded himself. Ava stepped towards him, reached out, and touched his shoulder. Milne flinched and stepped back.

"I'm fine," he said.

"That isn't true," Ava said. "But that's ok. We thought you might need company."

Milne shook his head. "I don't."

Eric crossed the room and pulled the curtains. Harsh light streamed in. Milne sat back down. Ava went into the kitchen and put on the kettle. They stayed and talked and filled space that he would rather have stayed empty. Ava tried to catch his eye but he avoided it persistently. She was better than him. More practiced, maybe. To have them both in his room at the same time would have been unbearable under other circumstances. Milne did not hear their words. He sat and thought of Marguerite. Of hermit thrush singing in the pine.

When they left, he sat until he remembered her writings. He stood and put on his hat and coat. He left the apartment for the first time in days and closed the door behind him. He drifted from his flat to hers through the empty London streets. His body must have taken him there of its own accord for his mind was elsewhere. It was only as he climbed the steps that he realized what he was doing. He began to feel and willed himself into a vacant haze.

He took the stairs quickly. The peeling wallpaper reached towards him, curling at the ripped seams. He turned down the hall. Marguerite's door hung open. He could see into her apartment from the hall. An empty armchair sat by a desolate fireplace. He stepped slowly towards the door. A chill ran across his shoulders. The floorboards creaked with every step.

He peered inside, and then stepped in. The police investigation lingered. Boot prints stained the carpet. Things moved out of place had not returned. The presence and absence of Marguerite clung to the room: it rolled towards him like a fog. He avoided looking directly at the bathroom door. Luckily, it was closed. He breathed slowly, deeply. Tried to force sentiment from his mind. He moved further in, swarmed by broken images.

Familiar objects carried emotion. He stepped around the table and entered the bedroom. He stayed focused—shifted his eyes directly to the desk. The surface was clear. He approached it and opened the drawers—they were empty. He frowned and glanced around the room. A single page lay on the floor beside the desk, hidden by the shadow of the wall. Milne stooped, resting his hand on the windowsill. He lifted the page. Two lines were written upon it:

> *That Love is all there is*
> *Is all we know of Love;*

Lines from a poem he didn't remember. It was Marguerite's hand. It wasn't her poem. He recognized that, at least. He folded the page in two and slipped it into his pocket. He stood and looked back at the desk. Where were her writings? Why had they been moved? He looked beneath the desk and then shifted focus to the bare bedside table. Somebody had taken them.

He couldn't bear it any longer. He left the bedroom quickly. Once again, bits of Marguerite's life scattered around him. Books once neatly stacked in the corner were rifled and strewn. A vase of flowers on the windowsill; an empty cup on the coffee table; an ashtray; a book on the countertop: *Anna Karenina*. He had forgotten it. She must have sat with it, unwanted, undesired. He left the front door open when he stepped into the hall. He took the stairs to the ground floor.

Nothing made sense. Fragments of an explanation were strewn across time. He could put none of it together.

2

Griefstricken faces poured slowly across the bridge. A sighing mass collected on the other side. The papers at the newsstand displayed variants of the same message: *The Nation Mourns: Death of King George VI in His Sleep; A Lifetime of Service to the Nation; Long Live the Queen.*

"I went to Marguerite's flat," Milne said.

Clifford looked up from his paper. He examined Milne's face. "I'm sure that was upsetting. Why did you do that?"

"I wanted to gather her papers—her work, her writing. It's all gone."

"It must be somewhere," Clifford said.

"Of course it must be. Wherever it is, it isn't there."

Clifford looked back to his paper. "Maybe the police took them for their investigation," he said.

"What would they need them for?"

Clifford shrugged. "To find an explanation—maybe she left a note."

"It doesn't make sense," Milne said.

Clifford folded his paper and tucked it beneath his arm. "I know," he said.

"No. I mean, I don't believe she did it herself."

Clifford looked Milne in the eye and spoke calmly. "She was unstable, Milne. Radical. Not to mention, away from home ..."

Milne looked at Carson. "She wouldn't have done it. It doesn't make sense."

Clifford placed a hand on Milne's shoulder. "I'm sorry," he said. "I know that this is difficult."

Milne leaned on the railing. "Where would she get a gun?"

"Milne don't work yourself up. We can't explain why people do these things. You'll drive yourself mad searching for an explanation. Trust me, I know."

Milne stood and felt the gentle mist against his face. There was loss and confusion, and little else. He watched the procession move across the bridge.

"My offer stands," Clifford said. "Take some time off—full salary. Go home or get away. Go somewhere warm. We can get you a ticket, write it up as a work expense. You need a break." He looked out over the dark water passing beneath them. "We could all use one."

He left Clifford at the newsstand and walked, searching for somewhere to be. Almost everything was closed because of the King. He passed locked doors and heard gasps slipping from open windows. He walked until he lost track of time and the day itself began to slip away. Then, along the waterfront, beneath a towering stone bridge, he came across a pub that kept its doors open. A tattered green flag bearing a golden harp hung in the window. The light above the shaking river was dimming. A stale aroma—beer and cigarettes—lifted from the cobblestones. He stepped inside.

The pub was half full. He bought a pint and a whiskey and brought them to a table in an alcove hidden at the back. Two old men played chess beside him. They did not speak. A conversation carried to him from the bar about the lightweight

242

champ, Jimmy Carter. He sat for a long time and thought of Marguerite. He finished his drink and bought another. He thought of Clifford and wondered what he knew. He did not realize how long he had stayed until the barkeep called out to him and he realized that it was not the first time. He stood and walked with false confidence. The door was locked behind him. The two playing chess stayed on.

The moonlight was faint above the black water. Milne moved towards it. From the shadows, he heard a call. He turned. A makeshift tent sat, crooked, in an alcove beneath the bridge. Candlelight spilled from it, shaking gently on the wet stone. A woman's voice called out from within. He could not hear her words.

Milne approached the tent and the world around him throbbed. He pushed the curtain aside. Candles burned on every surface. A ragged, Turkish carpet covered the wet ground. A woman sat, hunched, over a table in the center. Tarot cards lay scattered, disordered, before her. She tilted her head toward him. Strands of knotted grey hair hung loose over her face. Thin leather skin clung taut to jutting bone. "All I see is death," she said. Her voice seemed to emit from the fabric of the tent itself and filled the air. It was hot and damp and smelled of rotting flesh. He stepped backwards through the curtain and fell into the street. The sky was dark and heavy.

He stumbled to the edge of the river and stared into it. He thought of falling forward to embrace the swell. It seemed easy; to be dragged deeper and deeper and emerge later to be picked by gulls, or not at all. There was silence. Then, something disrupted him—a shimmer in the corner of his eye. He turned his head: bats fluttered beneath the bridge's arch. He carried on and wandered, listening to rats scuttle along the gutters and walls, until he reached the stairs to the street. He climbed them and emerged in the bluish light in front of a cathedral, stretching upward into the sky. He stopped in front of it. Marguerite did not believe in God—he wondered what that meant. He approached the wooden door and grasped the iron handle in his hand. He pulled. It was locked. The door did not so much as rattle on its hinges. He turned from it and continued to walk, his footsteps echoing from the stone. Marguerite came to him in fragments. The night sky darkened above.

3

Flies circled the ceiling lamp above them. Every ripple and fold of the sheets dug into his back. He was exhausted. He felt too much. He tried to shift position to comfort himself. He found new bumps wherever he lay. The sounds of the street beneath the window were harsh and loud: sirens somewhere in the distance; a truck rattling on cobblestone; something clattered; somebody yelled.

Milne watched the flies. Memory and desire stirred: a gentle fire, drifting snow through panes, the comfort of winter's blanket before the break.

"We can't do this," she said.

"I know," he replied.

"So, what do we do?" she asked.

"I don't know," he replied.

He turned his head. Ava's eyes were open. She, too, watched the flies. The skin on his chest felt thick and loose. He shifted the blanket over his bulging stomach. Ava sat up and lifted her cigarette case from the bedside table. She removed a cigarette and lit it. He sat up and rested his back against the headboard. Thick raindrops, in London fashion, began to slap the roof above them. A droplet in the corner trickled down the wall.

"If he wasn't gone so often," she said.

"I know," he replied.

"It's been so hard."

A dog began to bark somewhere in the building. A piece of ash fell from the end of Ava's cigarette and onto the duvet. He brushed it with his fingers, smearing black ash. He turned and let his legs fall over the edge of the bed. He felt his feet on the floor and stood. The blankets fell from his waist. He dressed quickly, conscious of the open window, then stepped into the bathroom. He looked in the mirror above the sink. He didn't look good. His hair was messy. His face was pale and thin. His skin seemed to sag where it once held firm to sharp lines of bone. Milne Lowell—the name felt foreign to him. A mouthful of soft sounds.

"You should go,"—a voice from the other room. She was right but it hurt to hear. He ran the water, soaked his hands, and ran them through his hair. He supressed the sickened feeling in his chest when he saw the bathtub behind him.

Ava was still in bed, smoking a new cigarette. She didn't look at him. He looked down at his watch—8:35. He picked up his coat and left. It was easier to be cold. He slid his arms into the coat and took the stairs to the bottom floor. On the staircase, the fear that he would run into someone took hold. There was no way out.

He reached the bottom safely and walked through the front door. The air was cold. As he stepped onto the street, a car door opened. A man stepped in front of him—a movement almost identical to one he had seen before. The man wore a small-brimmed hat and a well-tailored suit. His raincoat was long and grey. He walked towards Milne and did not take his eyes from him. "Mr. Lowell," he said, when he reached him. "We would like to speak with you." His voice was soft and calm, nearly lost in the rattle of the street.

Milne recognized him—they had met before. He searched the face and tried to place him. He looked over the man's shoulder at the outline of another in the car. "Are you police?" he asked.

The man smiled. "No," he said. "My name is Mr. Peters."

"I'm sorry," Milne said. "How do I know you?"

"We have met before."

Milne looked down at his watch. "I'm in a bit of a rush. What's this about?"

Mr. Peters stepped closer. "Please come with us. Let's speak somewhere more comfortable." He paused and glanced briefly upwards. "Your friend might come to the window or her husband might come home."

"Who are you?"

"There's a restaurant at the end of the street," Mr. Peters said. "The Golden Hen."

"I know it."

"Meet us there in ten minutes. We'll go on ahead."

Milne tried to think—to rationalize the situation. Mr. Peters walked back to his car, opened the door, and sat inside. Milne thought of calling after him but didn't know what to say. The engine started.

It had started with excitement—enjoying his company more than she should have. Neither of them had been fooled that complication could be left aside. When excitement inevitably unfolded and revealed desire, and then erupted into passion, it was clear that nothing would be simple. The fact was, initially, they simply did not care. It was not a question of deciding that the consequences were worth it—they needed to embrace what they felt so wholly and urgently, needed to feel with intensity

247

and power and instantaneous active fulfilment. And so, she felt, she had never thought it through and now was stuck.

The rain still pelted the windowpanes and roof and she listened to it as she lay in bed. Eric was another matter—her feelings for him were no less than they had been before. She had set them aside—may have allowed them to become misplaced for a time—but they were no less real, she told herself. His feelings for her would change, of course, if they had not already. If he already knew and just hadn't yet acknowledged it, it was already over. If he didn't yet know, it was still salvageable.

She lifted a book from the bedside table and opened it to the page where she had left off: *And now the silence put a spell upon them like solemn music. It was anguish—anguish for her to bear it and he would die—he'd die if it were broken ... And yet he longed to break it ...* She couldn't read further. Her attention was drifting. Where did she go from here?

The Golden Hen. He stopped in front of the door and stared at it. A rooster was painted in the center between two narrow stained-glass windows. He put his hand on the door and pushed it in. The restaurant was clean. Tables were neatly placed throughout the room. He spotted Mr. Peters at a booth against the back wall. He sat with a woman. Both were drinking tea.

Milne recognized her immediately—the context was right. It was the couple from Molly's inn. The couple who had left him a copy of his book. In the time that had passed, he'd nearly forgotten all about it. He stood near the doorway and watched them. He was unsure of what to do. If they noticed him, they made no indication of it. Peters wasn't the name they had used before—what was it?

He looked around the restaurant quickly and then made his way to the table. Mr. Peters looked up as Milne approached. The woman slid further into the booth to make room for him. An empty cup waited for him.

"Mr. Lowell," Mr. Peters said. "Thank you for coming. Sit down."

Milne stood beside the table and said nothing.

"You are perfectly safe," the woman said.

"Who are you?"

"I'm Mr. Peters, as I've already said. This is Miss Phillips."

"Your names were both Haydon the last time we met. Where did you come across that book?"

Mr. Peters smiled but said nothing. Milne hesitantly sat. "Are you with the Crown?" he asked. Mr. Peters shook his head. Miss Phillips filled his cup with tea from a steel pot—a thin line of steam rose, dancing, from it.

"We are ... friends of Moscow," Mr. Peters said. Milne tried to stand. Miss Phillips seized his arm.

"Sit," she said. "Do not draw attention."

Milne turned his attention to her. Her features were sharper than he remembered—her grey eyes hid behind subtle shadow. There was something intimidating within them.

"You're Russian?" Milne asked.

She shook her head. "English."

"Turncoats, then."

"No," Mr. Peters said. "That is incorrect."

"What do you want from me?" Milne asked.

"We only want to talk."

Milne looked around the restaurant again, trying to determine if others were with them. He couldn't tell. Couples, families, and single people scattered the room. "We have nothing to talk about," he said. "You're going to get me arrested."

"Please," Mr. Peters said calmly. "You'll want to hear what we have to say."

Milne was tired of the uncertainty and confusion. The clatter of saucers and silverware eased his nerves—it was a public place. "What do you know?" he asked.

"A lot. We have been watching you—all of you—for some time."

"It was you who broke into our office."

Mr. Peters shook his head. "No," he said. He hesitated.

"They were friends of ours," Miss Phillips interrupted. "They've since been compromised. They may be dead."

"The couple in Paris?" Milne asked. His voice was shakier than he expected it to be.

"No."

"Who were they?"

Mr. Peters shrugged. "Friends."

"Why? Why are you watching us? Why did you leave me that book?"

"It's a mental game," Miss Phillips said. "There are a lot of cards at play."

"You wanted to scare us."

"We wanted you to be aware—to be wary."

Another thought itched for release. It could not be contained any longer. "Marguerite ..." Milne began. His voice wavered.

"Yes, Mr. Lowell?"

His throat felt instantly hoarse. "Did you ..."

"We did not kill your friend," Miss Phillips said quietly.

Milne didn't look at her. He cleared his throat and looked over Mr. Peters shoulder. "Friends of yours?"

"No," Mr. Peters said. "We had no involvement in that."

"But you know who did?"

Neither responded. Miss Phillips slid an envelope down the table.

"What's this?" Milne asked.

"A letter."

"From who?"

"Open it," Mr. Peters said.

Milne examined the envelope in front of him, slightly bent at the edges. He lifted it and raised the unsealed flap. He took a letter from it—a single page, folded twice. He unfolded it. It was handwritten:

Frank,

It has come to my attention that certain activity related to the Labour Party may be jeopardizing to our program in London.

This is our greatest asset. Success depends entirely upon the appearance of complete independence—the result of strong convictions of like-minded citizens. We hang on a thread as it stands, it seems. Without Ward, we simply have no credibility.

I request a list of witting persons in London.

- C.B.

Milne set the letter back on the table. "C.B.?"

"Clifford Bernstein. We intercepted it on the way to New York."

Milne thought of the little strands leading to nowhere. "What's this about? Who's Frank?"

"Frank Moore," Mr. Peters said. "He works for the U.S. State Department."

"Why are you showing me this?"

"Because things aren't what they seem, Mr. Lowell," he said. Then, he smiled. "Or, maybe you'll find that they are exactly what they seem," he added.

"You're talking in riddles," Milne said. "I've had enough uncertainty. Tell me what you want."

Mr. Peters leaned across the table. "You work for the American government," he said. "I think you already know this. You're an asset—a supposedly unwitting agent."

"This hardly says that," Milne said, lifting the letter. He thought of Colombia. He thought of Marguerite. "What could they possibly use me for?"

"Don't play naïve," Miss Phillips said.

Milne examined the letter again. "What's this about the Labour Party?"

"Does it matter?" Mr. Peters asked.

"It does to somebody," Milne said. "You told me to listen—tell me something clearly."

"Fair enough," Mr. Peters said. "To be frank, we don't know exactly what he's referring to. The Labour Party is a constant battleground. It's probably just two Billy goats butting heads."

"How can I trust you about any of this?" Milne asked.

Miss Phillips sighed. "You don't have to," she said. "It's up to you to decide what to believe, but, I assure you, we are being forthright. Clifford Bernstein works for the American government. The Central Intelligence Agency. This is an open secret across the board."

Milne stared through her. He thought of gulags and purges.

"We have documents," Mr. Peters said. "Correspondence, records. In the end, you just need to follow the money. You're funded nearly entirely by one source. The foundation itself is not even as old as your magazine. It was set up immediately after your show-case in Berlin—that conference put you on the books. Some rich do-nothing has his name on the docket."

"Lewis," Miss Phillips said. "Corn money."

"Corn money?"

"Corn money."

"There's corn money on the docket. State money flows in, corn money flows out. Bernstein oversees everything on the ground. Your board in Paris is at his beck and call," Mr. Peters said. "He's the real thing—a big fixer, they say."

"If I'm to decide what to believe," Milne said, "why would I decide to trust a Soviet?"

Miss Phillips reached into a handbag beneath the table. She retrieved a folder and placed it in front of Milne. "Mr. Bernstein is meeting British contacts this afternoon," she said. "We don't know where or when."

Milne looked down at the folder. "What's this?"

"Proof."

"If I take this, I'll just be a pawn in your game."

Miss Phillips laughed. "You're already a pawn in the game," she said. "On one side of the board or the other. You're just blind to the second player. Your friend wasn't."

Milne's chest tightened. "Don't you dare speak of her. For all I know, you're responsible for what happened."

Mr. Peters stood and lifted his coat. He slipped his arms into it and placed his hat back on his head, then straightened his glasses on his nose. "Your friend was a problem for somebody," he said, "but it wasn't for us."

"Pardon me," Miss Phillips said, as she prepared to get up. Milne stood and she exited the booth.

"Mr. Lowell," the man said. "In the game that we're playing, it is best to accept a hand if it's extended, even if you don't much care for the other man."

Edna answered the phone after several rings. "Hello?" she said.

"Edna, it's Milne."

"Oh! Milne! How are you?"

"Fine," he said. "Is Carson there?"

"He just went out. The air does him good in the mornings. You know how it is. Can I pass on a message?"

Milne hesitated. He glanced up the street. A black car parked a little further up caught his eye. He tried to make out the driver through the window.

"Is everything alright?"

"Yes," Milne said. "Well ... I don't want to say much over the phone. I think ... there might have been something to your concerns." There was a pause on the other end. Edna began to speak and Milne quickly cut her off. "Can you tell Carson that I'll call him later?"

"Yes," Edna said. "Yes, of course."

"Thank you."

"Be safe, Milne."

"I will," he said. "We'll talk later, ok?"

"Yes, ok. Goodbye, Milne."

"Goodbye," he said. He hung the receiver back up. Then he stepped from the booth and crossed the road. He walked down the street to the end and took a right turn along the river. Birds stood in tight rows along the gutters above. He sensed their eyes upon him. He felt the beaks and talons surround him. The wind blew silently across the Thames, drawing wavers from its surface.

His mind raced. Milne looked at the folder in his hand. He did not want to open it. He did not know what it contained, and if its lies would poison his mind forever. These were Soviets— masters of deceit. Before he realized it, he was standing at the office door. He opened it and stepped into the entryway. He looked up and down the street before closing it. It was foolish—if they were on him, they already knew where he was headed.

A square of foggy light passed through the glazed window of the office above, letting a murky glow into the stairwell. He climbed the steps towards it. He stopped in front of the door and tried to make out the shapes behind the glass. He inhaled—deep and slow—he wrapped his fingers around the brass handle. He turned the handle: with the creak of hinges, he heard the distant sound of church bells ringing.

The door opened. He stepped in with it. Cassandra smiled. "Good morning, Mr. Lowell," she said.

"Is anyone in?"

"Just yourself," she said.

Milne looked down at his watch. "Isn't it time for lunch?"

Cassandra smiled politely. "It's only eleven o'clock."

"Go on," Milne said. "Take an early lunch."

"I always bring my own."

Milne reached into his pocket. He placed a shilling on the desk. "Treat yourself."

"I couldn't …"

"I insist," Milne said, forcefully.

Cassandra smiled. She stood and gathered her things. She stopped briefly at the door: "I'll be an hour."

Milne nodded. When he heard her footsteps click down the stairs, he opened the door to the offices and stepped inside. His eyes fell upon the desk in the far corner. A framed photograph of Clifford's wife sat upon it. On the surface, there was nothing else.

Milne looked down at the folder in his hands. He was hesitant to open it. He didn't want to know what was inside. He was scared of what he might find. He was unsure if he could trust it.

Instead, he walked over to Clifford's desk and ran his hand along the wood. He pulled on a handle: the drawer was locked.

He pulled harder—it held firm. He got to his knees and peered through the crack along the top of the drawer. He reached into his pocket and took the jackknife from it. He slid it into the crack and applied pressure. The handle bent slightly away from the blade at the joint. It felt like it would break under any more pressure.

He took it out and lay on the floor. He looked up into the belly of the desk. He reached into it and felt along the side of the drawers. His fingers ran over a thin metal beam. When he jiggled it, the drawer rattled. It was the kind of lock that might be on a schoolteacher's desk.

Milne stood and went back out to Cassandra's desk. He took a thick letter opener from it. He brought it back into the room with him, and then got back onto the floor and inserted it behind the metal beam connecting the lock to the desk. The small nails creaked under the pressure and then pulled away from the wood. The drawer opened a fraction. He grabbed the handle and pulled hard—it creaked but did not move any further.

Milne sat up and leaned against the side of the desk. He tried to think—to formulate a plan. Instead, he thought of the Soviets, of Clifford, of Marguerite.

He turned over onto his knees and pushed hard, turning the desk onto its side. He heard the picture frame slide first. It tipped from the table and shattered. Then, the desk crashed to the floor. The walls shook around him. He stood and felt the side of the desk. He took aim with his heel. Shocks ran to his knee as he kicked repeatedly. The wood creaked, cracked, and then split. He grabbed the leg and pulled it down, leveraging against the floor. The wall separated from the drawer. He kicked the leg hard. It pulled away, taking a piece of the desk with it. The metal locking mechanism fell. The drawer dangled loosely.

Milne looked down at the broken desk—the splintered wood across the floor. His foot was aching. He opened the drawer and sifted through the papers inside. Most meant little. Then, he came across an envelope, the same size and shape as the one he had in his pocket. He flipped it over and lifted the flap. He pulled a single sheet of paper from it, folded in the middle. He reached into his pocket and pulled out the letter that was given to him. He compared the writing on the two—the penmanship was identical. The message seemed insignificant. The letter was addressed to Frank.

A door opened and shut somewhere. Milne straightened. Footsteps. Somebody was climbing the stairs. Milne ran to the window and looked out. He could tell nothing from it. He heard the footsteps cross the room outside—they were too heavy to be Cassandra's, he thought. He turned and waited. A shadow passed behind the glazed window, blocking out the yellow light. Milne froze—he watched the handle turn. The door opened.

Milne breathed a sigh of relief. "Carson," he said. "Thank God."

Carson stood in the doorway. He wore a brown blazer. His eyes fell to the broken desk. He stepped inside and closed the door. "What happened? Edna told me that you rang the house. She's worried."

"You were right," Milne said. He took a step towards Carson and held out the letters. Carson took them from him and read them slowly.

"I didn't know who else to talk to," Milne said. He lowered his voice: "Two So–" he paused. A thought crossed his mind. "Do you think it's safe to talk here?"

Carson motioned to Milne and opened the door. He stepped into the lobby and then crossed to the stairs. Milne followed. They took the stairs to the bottom floor, then Carson stopped.

"I don't know if it's safe or not," he said, "but it's probably safer here."

"The Soviets came to me this morning," Milne said. His words echoed in the stairwell.

Carson stepped back from Milne. "Russians?"

"English, I think. I don't know. Soviets."

Carson glanced over his shoulder at the entryway. He lowered his voice to a whisper. "What did they want?"

"They showed me that letter—they said it was from Cliff."

"Frank Moore," Carson said. "I've met him. At a dinner in Paris. I was told that he was helping to arrange funding."

"They said that Cliff's meeting British contacts today—that he's an agent of some kind for the Central Intelligence Agency ... that we all work for them, essentially."

Carson nodded. He re-read the letter in his hands. "I think they're right," he said. "I've been doing some digging of my own."

"They gave me a folder," Milne said. "I haven't looked at it."

"Where is it?"

"Upstairs on my desk."

"And they told you that they were Soviets?"

"More or less."

"Jesus. Can they be trusted?"

"They said they were friends of Moscow."

"Jesus," Carson said. "Why haven't you opened the folder?"

"It could be full of lies. I didn't want to ... they implied that Marguerite ..." he felt his voice tremble and trailed off.

Carson put his hand on Milne's shoulder. "She couldn't have been working for them, Milne."

Milne shook his head. "No, not that." He paused to steady himself. "They implied that the Americans did it," he said. Tears streamed silently down his cheeks.

"What do you think?" Carson asked.

Milne shrugged. "I don't know."

Carson nodded then glanced up the stairs. "Milne, you won't be able to explain what happened to that desk."

Milne leaned against the bannister. "I know."

"What are you going to do?"

Milne crinkled the letter in his hand. He ran his thumb over the fold. "I want to be sure."

"What do you mean by that?"

"I'll follow him. I'll see if he really meets with anyone."

"You can't do that, Milne."

"I owe it to her. Then I'm getting out of London."

"If he sees you ..."

"I know."

Carson looked at Milne. He saw pain and confusion. He saw that it was something that he needed to do. "What time are they meeting?" he asked.

"I don't know. This afternoon."

"I'll ring his house," Carson said. "If he's home, I'll keep him on the line. Get over there as quickly as you can. I'll stay here and attend to that desk, or at least keep everyone out of the office."

Milne looked down at his watch. "It's almost twelve. We'd better get moving."

It was a damp, February day and the lunch crowd was slim. A pea-soup fog clung to the streets. At half past twelve, Milne reached the apartment building where Clifford was staying. He leaned against a lamppost and waited, watching the entryway of the building. His only hope was that Clifford was still at home.

He could barely see the distance through the yellow-black haze. He turned away from the wind to light a cigarette, then turned up the collar of his greatcoat and pulled his hat low to stave off the blowing mist of droplets in the air.

An elderly woman passed him, coughing into a handkerchief. The minutes were slow. He watched the vehicles that passed along the road carefully. A truck slowed just ahead. A thought struck him: what if he was still being followed? He saw nothing abnormal on the street. The longer he stood, the more nervous he became. A slight tremble began in his legs and worked its way through his arms and into his hands. He wondered what would happen if he was seen. He thought of Marguerite.

He felt conspicuous standing against the lamppost. He stepped between two parked cars and crossed the road. When he reached the other side, he stepped into a doorway and turned to watch the entryway again. The wind picked up and blew into the doorway, dragging slush and grime with it. He hadn't thought this through at all, he realized. What would witnessing this meeting accomplish? What more would he really know? It would confirm that there was conspiracy, secrecy. That they had been pawns in somebody else's game. What did that matter? If he had known, he wondered, if he had been asked, would he have played along anyway? A crowd of men walked past him, momentarily blocking his view. He fumbled with his cigarettes, lit another, and left it dangling from his lip. If not for Marguerite, he would have. He would have thought that they were right to. That was why he needed to see.

It was beginning to warm up. The wind died down. Then, he saw Clifford—he was walking down the street towards the entryway to his apartment building, gradually taking shape as he got closer. Milne felt his legs weaken and leaned against the wall. He had missed him. Why did he return? Had he been tipped off? Milne was shaking again. Clifford reached the building and went inside. Milne dropped his cigarette butt and stepped on it. He looked down at his watch—it was one o'clock.

After two minutes, the door opened and Clifford stepped back out. He saw Clifford's face clearly across the street. He felt hatred. Clifford began to walk and he followed. A fruit truck was parked along the curb. He hurried to it and leaned against it, letting the cool air fill his chest. He shook less.

He looked around the back of the truck: Clifford turned the corner. Milne waited until he was out of sight and then hurried across the street. He rushed to the corner and peered around the side of the building. He could make Clifford out in the crowd by his walk. He turned the corner and followed.

The back door to a butcher shop opened, letting the pungent odour of slaughtered pigs into the air. The butcher's assistant poured some steaming pink liquid down the drain. Steam rose from it, sifting into the cloud above. Milne followed Clifford for three blocks. He hung back as far as he could without losing him. At every corner, he shook with the fear that Clifford would turn around and spot him. He checked constantly for a tail of his own but saw nothing unusual.

People passed him by. He caught glimpses of their faces. Most walked with their heads down. Some held handkerchiefs to their mouths. Before Clifford reached the end of the block, he stopped and entered a small restaurant. Milne waited for a gap in traffic and then crossed the street. He realized that this must be where the meeting was taking place. What now? He saw Clifford through the front window of the restaurant. He was sitting in the corner alone. There was no way that he could get inside without being seen.

A streetcar stopped a little further down the street. A bell rang. Milne waited until it left and then moved to the stop. He leaned against a post and watched the window. He could barely see through it from here—he saw the shape of a waitress pouring coffee, so he watched the door to see who entered.

The dewy-sweet smell of damp petals drifted from a flower shop, hanging out of place in the February air. A woman in a long brown coat lingered at the door of the restaurant. After a moment, a man rounded the corner and approached her. Milne leaned back and tried to look inconspicuous. They spoke and then walked away from the door together. The minutes passed slowly and the fog thickened on the streets, trapped between buildings.

An elderly man with a cane hobbled into the restaurant alone, bent at the spine. He wore a tight cap and a checkered blazer. Milne shifted position—he moved closer so that he could see through the window. He hoped that Clifford would not look out. The old man was sitting somewhere out of sight. Clifford was still alone. He sipped his coffee, then smoothly folded the newspaper and set it on the table. Milne stepped backwards, out of sight again. He couldn't risk being seen. He embraced the shroud. He checked his watch: two o'clock.

After a few minutes, the door to the restaurant opened and Clifford stepped out. He turned his collar up and glanced to the sky for rain. He placed his hat on his head and buttoned his coat. Milne quickly turned and looked through the window of the flower shop. Was that it? Had the message been passed? He glanced over his shoulder. Clifford was gone. It must have been the old man, he thought: a tremendous disguise. He scanned the street until he found Clifford—he was walking quickly.

Milne waited for a break in traffic and ran. His left foot sank into a puddle and slushy meltwater seeped into his pant leg. It soaked his sock and filled his shoe. Somebody slammed the brakes and yelled from the window of a van. He reached the other side of the street and hopped onto the curb. He walked quickly after Clifford. He couldn't give up now—even if he had missed the meeting, he needed something. He needed to see something.

At a distance, he followed. Clifford slowed. He walked the streets, looking through store fronts and occasionally entering. He appeared to be shopping for shirts but made no purchases. A group of three women ahead of him burst into laughter beneath smog masks. He wondered what had been said. One of them wore their hair like Marguerite. Like Marguerite had. The city did not miss her, he thought. It carried on. It did not realize.

Clifford entered a tailor's shop. Milne slowed again. Clifford could be meeting people in any one of these stores. The storekeepers, the tailor, any one of them could be his contact. Milne sank back against the wall of a jeweler and felt tears welling in his eyes. He was in over his head. These were professionals—this was their life. Marguerite was dead, and there was nothing he could do about it. Even if he saw a meeting first-hand, what did he plan to do? He would know, that was it.

He was grasping blindly. Trying to do something in a world where he had no power. Marguerite had known how to work in this world. He breathed deeply, inhaling a mass of yellow-black particles: they caught in his throat and lungs and burned—he coughed violently. He pulled a handkerchief from his inner pocket and held it to his nose. Bodies streamed, slipping, coughing, in and out of thick pockets. Coal burned and thick smoke rose from millions of little chimneys. Factories pumped plumes into the air from the corners of the city. If it got much worse, they wouldn't be able to go on.

The clock tower struck. Milne looked at his watch. Three o'clock. He would go home, he decided. Flee the city. The door opened and Clifford left the tailor's shop. He quickly glanced up and down the street and then crossed it. Milne ducked into the doorway, dropping the handkerchief onto the stone. He looked after Clifford: he was entering a pub directly across from the tailor's. A wooden sign hung over the street: *The Vesper*. A purple star was painted on it. It swayed gently on its hinges.

Milne felt adrenaline surge. His fingers trembled. This was it, he thought. This was the meeting. Clifford was sure to be watching the door carefully from inside. He wouldn't be able to enter from the front. He walked towards the pub. Before he reached it, he turned down a narrow alleyway leading away from the main street. The walls loomed over him on either side. He moved quickly. The ground was slick. A vent poured hot steam into the air above him. He followed the alley to the right. He walked down as far as the pub—the smell of frying chips leaked from it. There was a heavy door on the back of the building for the kitchen or delivery.

Milne wrapped his fingers around the handle and tried the door. It opened. The busy sounds of a kitchen. He stepped inside. He tried to quickly formulate an excuse—a reason for entering—but the kitchen workers were off to the side, and nobody paid him any heed. They did not even notice him enter. He quietly closed the door. He walked steadily past the kitchen and pushed through a swinging door. He was in a narrow hallway beside the bar. The pub was large—at least two levels.

It did not take long to find what he was looking for: Clifford sat with two men in a corner booth near the front door. Milne couldn't make out the faces of the men from where he stood. When he moved, he recognized one immediately. Phillip Muggeridge, Harry Pankhurst Jr.'s guest on the fox hunt. He was drinking a pint and laughing. The other man was very thin with a sallow face. He wore horn rimmed glasses. Milne recognized him too. He tried to place him. The man reached

264

down and fiddled with a small homburg that sat on the table in front of him. That was it, Milne realized, he had been at the conference in Paris. He had seen him twice in the streets.

Milne stepped into a stairway leading down to the toilets. His heart raced. As far as he was concerned, it was confirmed. Cliff had been playing them, using them. They had been little more than a mouthpiece to him. He needed to think quickly, act quickly. He breathed deeply and tried to calm himself. He just needed to make use of the opportunities that presented themselves, he thought. He needed to be careful. They were sitting along the right-side wall in a booth. If he moved along that wall, they would not be able to see him.

Milne breathed and gathered himself. He had come this far and owed it to Marguerite to learn what he could. He took one more look around the corner to be sure that they weren't watching, and then went over to the bar. He ordered a pint and the barman poured it for him. He tried to move casually. He stepped around a table and saw Phillip's shoulder at the end of the booth. He slipped quickly into the booth directly behind them. He collapsed into the seat, heart pumping and head throbbing.

Clifford spoke. "You know that isn't possible, Lenny," he said. Milne felt a chill run down his spine. The tone was low and steady and cut through him.

Phillip said something in response but Milne couldn't make it out. The third man, who must have been Lenny, spoke next. His voice was calm, soothing. Again, it was difficult to make out the words. Milne pressed his head against the back of the booth and listened as intently as he could. Before he could catch what Lenny said, Clifford was speaking again: "If they go ahead … obvious … if we lose Ward, this whole thing collapses. Half of Europe thinks … propaganda already … the only thing giving us an ounce of respectability."

"Have you brought it up with …?" Muggeridge asked.

"You know how these things are."

Lenny said something and then Phillip replied. All three laughed. They spoke more quietly. Milne could hear little at all. "No," Clifford said. "I have this dinner tonight. I need to break it to him that I'll be back in Paris by Wednesday."

The voices were quiet again. The words were no longer audible. His nerves began to take hold and he could not handle the pressure much longer. He looked quickly over his shoulder and slipped from the booth, stooping low and keeping tight to the table. He stepped around the other side and walked quickly down the back wall. The barman was looking the other way. He slipped past him and moved past the kitchen as well. He threw the back door open and left the building.

Cold air swept his body. It was getting dark. He hurried down the alleyway, back the way he had come. Cars passed on the streets, their headlights solidified in the sulphurous air. He tried to retrace his steps—he had no idea where he was but he knew what he needed to do. Marguerite believed that they could live better—be better. She had devoted her life to publishing—printing anything she thought the world needed to see, casting light on crimes of power. People were good, she thought, inherently. With freedom, that blossomed. That was what he had told her they were doing here. Then he had betrayed her, failed her. He would not fail her again.

He hurried through the streets, moving towards anything that he recognized. He could see only metres ahead, and after that even well-lit places were blurred. He began to figure out where he was. He knew where he needed to go, at least. He heard somebody cough behind him—was he being followed? He turned the corner at the end of the block and began to run. He took side streets and crossed a small bridge. He saw a park

266

ahead and made his way towards it. It was getting darker. He glanced over his shoulder again. He needed to calm down. He was paranoid, scared.

He ran through the park as the evening dimmed. He hoped that he would not lose all of the light before he reached Carson's house. He knew that it was childish to fear the dark but the possibility of a knife in the back seemed much more real at night. If he had been spotted, they could be lurking ahead, waiting for him to pass through the shadow of a fountain or hedge. On the other side of the park, he saw streetlights and cobblestones. The glow was warm.

He ran harder, listening to the sounds of his footsteps as they fell. They were the only ones he heard. He made it through the park and ran onto the street. As soon as he stood beneath the yellow glow of the streetlight, he stopped running. His lungs burned. He doubled over at the waist and sucked air. He looked behind him—he was alone. He looked up and down the empty street. He didn't see a soul.

He stood and walked the rest of the way to Carson's home. It did not take long to reach. The house was large and narrow. It was brick and stood between two others that looked nearly identical. It had a neatly manicured garden and a set of trimmed hedges leading to the front steps. Light leaked from the curtained windows.

He took the stairs slowly, remembering the first time that he and Marguerite had arrived there together—the fire, the dinner, the wine. He pressed the doorbell. Within seconds, Carson opened it. "Did you find him?" he asked.

"Yes," Milne said. "He's going back to Paris in a few days. This is our only chance."

"To do what?"

"Anything. We were right."

Carson looked up and down the foggy street and waved Milne in. "I know," he said. He led Milne into the front room. The brown folder sat on the table. "Do you want to see what's inside?"

Milne stared at it. The adrenaline that carried him began to fade. He felt fear, deep and overwhelming. "No," he said. "Not yet."

Carson studied his face. Inside lay the answers Milne sought. Still, he would not open it. "What did you learn?" he asked.

"Nothing," Milne said. "He met with them—Phillip Muggeridge was there."

"Harry's friend?"

"Yes."

"You think he's an agent?"

"He must be. Where's Edna?"

"At her parents. It's safer. We should think this through," Carson said. "Plan this out."

"We don't have time. Did you do anything with the desk?"

Carson shook his head. "What could I do? We could say there was another break in."

"For all we know, they have people watching. They might have seen me tonight—I'm not taking the chance."

"What happened at the meeting?"

"It's something to do with this Labour situation. They think it'll get back to you. I think Cliff's worried about scaring you off. He said they need you to keep face."

"One moment," Carson said. He stepped into the hall. He came back in holding a thin leather briefcase. He held it out to Milne. "It has everything I've managed to piece together since Colombia."

Milne took the case. He opened it. His eyes instinctively skimmed the first words on the top sheet inside: ... *support the spread of a social and cultural environment conducive to American political and economic expansion ...* It was Carson's hand. Marguerite's face flitted before him. Another hand took form in his mind—his own: *I am writing to invite you to join me in London.* He felt something deep inside—bitterness, resentment, shame. Quickly, he took the unopened folder from the table and slipped it inside. Then, he closed the briefcase. When he looked up, Carson's eyes were on him.

"What's your plan?" Carson asked.

"I don't know," Milne replied. He ran his fingers over the briefcase's brass clasps. He thought of the meeting he'd witnessed. "Cliff should be out for the night. He mentioned a dinner," he said. He wondered what Clifford knew. He thought of Baron, the name he'd overheard Clifford use before a man was shot in the back. "I think we should try to get into his apartment," Milne said.

"And do what?"

"Take whatever we can. Anything that will help. Letters, notes, documents, names ... whatever is in there. I want to know what he knows," he said. "If I can get to Bournemouth tonight, I'll fly to Newfoundland in the morning. If I can't get there, I can take the ferry and fly through Shannon. I don't know how much time we have before someone comes for us. Either way, I'll figure this out. Once I'm out of London I'll be a lot safer."

"These are dangerous people, Milne."

"I know."

"Look at the folder. This runs deep."

Milne thought of Marguerite in the bathtub. Of the wet gun on the cold tile. Of Phillip Baron face down in the snow. He thought of Clifford's face beneath the lights of the Chelsea Bridge. He wondered if Ignazio was still alive. "I will," he said, "after."

"And once you reach home?"

"I'll figure this thing out. I have a friend at the *Toronto Star*. I think he'll do the right thing."

Carson nodded.

"You realize," Milne said, "that, if we do this, you won't be able to stay in London either. You might have to leave England entirely."

"Edna and I have been looking for a change," Carson said. Momentarily, the fear and pain on his face faltered. He smiled. "Don't you worry about us. Just take care of yourself."

Milne nodded. Carson poured two scotches and set them on the table.

"Can I use your phone?"

"Of course," Carson said. He led him to the phone and Milne placed a call. He said only what he needed to. They sat in the front room for a while and then went outside. The case was heavy in his hands.

It was calm and quiet on the street. The fog was lifting. They sat on the front steps together and listened to the evening air. Milne thought of the speech that Carson had given in Paris, the first time they met—his passion and intensity as he spoke of America. It felt like a different era. Glowing lights cut into the darkness along the street. A Morris Minor pulled up to the curb.

Milne stooped to peer through the window. He saw Ava's silhouette behind the wheel. He opened the passenger door. Ava looked at him but did not speak. If she had questions, she did not ask.

"Hold on," Carson said. "There's something I need in the house."

Milne got into the car. Carson disappeared into the house and then reappeared moments later, holding something long and thin in the crook of his arm. Milne couldn't make out what

270

it was until he passed beneath the streetlight on the way to the car. He opened the back door and put the shotgun onto the seat first, then climbed in after it.

They rolled away from the curb. Ava steered the car—she didn't look at him. Carson rode in the backseat with the Holland & Holland. Milne tried to speak—he ran through the possibilities as they revealed themselves—but there was nothing right to say. His eyes lingered on Ava for a while, her hands carefully guided the wheel. He looked back through the windshield.

The journey to Clifford's apartment seemed far too quick. Ava parked along the curb. Milne opened the door. He stepped onto the street and entered the building. He took the stairs slowly. With each step, they creaked. When he reached the third floor, he stopped. He looked up and down the hallway, reading the numbers on the door. He saw Clifford's at the end of the hall next to a narrow window.

The hall was empty. The door was locked. He pushed against it with his shoulder but the door didn't budge. He stepped back, looked up and down the hallway, and then kicked the door as hard as he could right next to the handle. It cracked and flew open—splinters of wood scattered across the floor.

He stepped inside. Though he'd kicked in the door, he didn't want to turn on the light in case it was visible from the street. He moved slowly into the apartment, which was small and sparse. His eyes adjusted. A drying rack stood next to the furnace—socks and underwear draped its beams. A small television set was in the corner. A brand new sofa sat in front of it.

As Milne was inside, Carson and Ava sat in silence on the street out front. The sky darkened. Clouds slowly drifted in from the west and brought rain with them. The minutes stretched on. Sounds, imagined or otherwise, emerged from the darkness around them. Carson lowered the window and held the shotgun beneath it. If Clifford returned, he would take no chances. He wondered if it would feel the same to pull the trigger.

Though every moment longer filled them with dread, not a single person passed through the street before Milne reappeared in the doorway. Carson reached into his pocket and retrieved his cigarette case. He took one out: it bent and broke in his shaking fingers. He dropped it onto the floor of the car and left the case open on the seat beside him. Raindrops on the window caught some stream of light—his head turned toward it. The front door opened and Milne got back into the car.

"Did you get anything?" he asked.

"I think so," said Milne.

Ava shifted and pulled out onto the street. She drove in silence. The familiar streets revealed themselves to Milne for what was probably the last time. They felt different tonight. There was no traffic. Parked cars sat along the edges, glistening with rainwater. A lady with an umbrella stepped through the fog. A vague memory of a Paris street flitted through his mind. Leaves rustled against the edge of a balcony; swans drifted aimlessly on a still lake. The jukebox played its tune; Marguerite danced alone in the center of the floor.

A wave broke: he ascended a twisting staircase in the Novak, moonlight cut in and spread across the floor; Ignazio peered through a dusty window—*Les Liaisons dangereuses*; French women stormed the stage, waving banners; Freddie Mills lay slumped and battered on the canvas; a puddle of deep red spread across the hardwood; muffled voices wore through the wall, reverberations pulsed in the palm of his hand; a slight breeze entered the courtyard, trees vibrated; a man stood, sheltered, in a darkened doorway; footsteps echoed; concrete crumbled; vines stretched across embossed cream; foxtail swayed in the morning mist; neon flickered; blackbirds perched on a windowsill; green mountains faded into cloud; pillars of black smoke rose from the city.

He watched the street behind them through the rear-view mirror. Though he saw nothing, something began to stir in his stomach. Dark alleyways and roads stretched away from them on all sides, concealing. Stairs descended to the Underground. A row of black cabs lined the street in front of the train station. Milne eyed them uneasily. Ava slowed. He clutched the briefcase tightly. It was the only thing he had. He opened the car door. The air was cool—the drops fresh against his skin. He looked across at Ava. For the first time tonight, she was looking directly at him. He leaned toward her without a word. Her lips were warm—they softened into his own. Rain rattled the windshield. Carson looked out into the darkness, averting his eyes. All he saw through the window were shadows. He felt the weight of the shotgun in his lap—his hands ran over the smooth wooden stock and the cold steel barrel. Milne stepped out and closed the door. A whistle blew in the station behind him. Rain fell upon his shoulders and head. Church bells rang out over the city of London, twelve tolls long.

UNCORRECTED GALLEYS

Books Quoted

Page 87: Bowen, Elizabeth. *The Heat of the Day*. New York, Knopf, 1948.

Page 105: Voynich, Ethel. *The Gadfly*. New York, H. Holt, 1897.

Page 161: Stevens, Wallace. "Thirteen Ways of Looking at a Blackbird," *Harmonium*. New York, Knopf, 1923.

Page 226: Eliot, T.S. *The Waste Land*. London, Hogarth Press, 1923.

Page 239: Dickinson, Emily. "That Love is all there is," *The Single Hound: Poems of a Lifetime*. Boston, Little, Brown, and Company, 1914.

Page 248: Mansfield, Katherine. "Psychology," *Bliss and Other Stories*. New York, Knopf, 1920.